Advance Praise for *The Holiday Honeymoon Switch*

"Not just one, but two gorgeously romantic and heartwarming
love stories set in two of the most idyllic locations
you could imagine. The perfect book."
—Paige Toon, international bestselling author of
Only Love Can Hurt Like This

"A pure escapist delight that wholly captures the spirit of
the season! Whether you're sipping mai tais on the beach
or cozied up under a chunky knit blanket by a crackling
fire, this book will make your heart sing."
—Amy Lea, international bestselling author of *Exes and O's*

"Full of sugar and spice, and comfort and joy, *The Holiday Honeymoon
Switch* is everything I love about holiday movies in book form. Savor
this one in front of a cozy fire with a warm drink. Delightful."
—Laura Taylor Namey, *New York Times* bestselling author of
A Cuban Girl's Guide to Tea and Tomorrow

"This book sucked me in immediately and never let go of my heart.
Twice the swoon! Twice the romance! Prepare to be swept away on
holiday by this funny and charming gem of a novel!"
—Kate Robb, author of *This Spells Love*

"A story of enduring love—of the BFF variety. Holly and Ivy were
meant to be! How fun to then watch them stumble their way into
romantic love, too."
—Jenny Holiday, *USA Today* bestselling author of *Canadian Boyfriend*

"A bighearted story filled with ride-or-die friendship and swoony
romance, times two . . . best enjoyed with a cup of cocoa!"
—Uzma Jalaluddin, bestselling coauthor of *Three Holidays and a Wedding*

"Holiday romance? Beach read? Both! *The Holiday* meets *The
Unhoneymooners* in this fun, friends-swapping-places romance
that has it all. Mistletoe and make-out seshes, plus sun, sand, and
swoony sex scenes that'll make you want to read this book at the
holidays and over and over all year long!"
—Chantel Guertin, bestselling author of *It Happened One Christmas*

T0190827

ALSO BY JULIA McKAY

Writing as Marissa Stapley

Three Holidays and a Wedding (with Uzma Jalaluddin)

The Lightning Bottles

Lucky

The Last Resort

Things to Do When It's Raining

Mating for Life

Writing as Maggie Knox

All I Want for Christmas

The Holiday Swap

The Holiday Honeymoon Switch

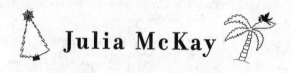

Julia McKay

G. P. Putnam's Sons
New York

PUTNAM
— EST. 1838 —

G. P. PUTNAM'S SONS
Publishers Since 1838
An imprint of Penguin Random House LLC
penguinrandomhouse.com

LIBRARY OF CONGRESS CATALOGING-IN-PUBLICATION DATA
has been applied for.

ISBN 9780593716281 (trade paperback)
ISBN 9780593716298 (ebook)

Printed in the United States of America

1st Printing

Book design by Lorie Pagnozzi

For Sophie

The Holiday Honeymoon Switch

PROLOGUE
December 16, 2016
New York City

Some things are meant to be together, especially at Christmastime—like popcorn and cranberries threaded through the boughs of a Douglas fir, or clementines studded with fragrant cloves. Stockings and fireplaces, angels and treetops, hot cocoa and marshmallows, ice skating and Rockefeller Center, mistletoe and stolen kisses, chestnuts and an open fire. The holly and the ivy.

Or, Holly and Ivy.

As in Holly Beech and Ivy Casey. The kind of best friends who finish each other's sentences *and* each other's experimental multicourse dinner party dishes. (Even the cassoulet pan.) The ones for whom those necklaces that say "best" on one side and "friends" on the other were created. Friends who have their own karaoke song (the Spice Girls' "Wannabe," naturally), a lexicon of inside jokes (that only get more humorous the less other people find them funny), and always say yes to randomly themed movie-marathon dates (for example, Every Movie Brad Pitt Has Ever Been In, Including and Perhaps Especially *The Favor*). Taylor and Selena, Oprah and Gayle, Cameron and Drew, Bette and 50 Cent, Marissa and Summer . . . all of these friend duos have nothing on Holly and Ivy—who are about to meet for the first time.

Christmas break is almost here, and to mark the occasion, Phi Delta Epsilon is hosting its annual Columbia-U Christmas Kegger. Holly is already eyeing the door, though she knows her boyfriend, Matt, will, as usual, want to be Last Man Standing. (He has the T-shirt. He's wearing it.) "Hey, sweetheart," he slurs, pressing a red plastic Solo cup into her hand. "You gotta try the rum and eggnog."

Holly tries to arrange her grimace into a smile as she looks into his flushed, handsome face. She accepts the cup and says, "Maybe you should stick with beer, though, Matty. Remember what happened at the Purple Jesus party." He grins and gives her a sloppy kiss that smears across her cheek. "You're always right. That's why I love you, Holly McBollyface."

He heads off in search of the beer, and she goes searching for somewhere to dump the noxious nog. She finds a windowsill and sets the cup down, longing for something slightly more palatable, knowing she won't find it here. When she brought a nice bottle of wine to one of Matt's fraternity-sorority mixers, she overheard two girls in the bathroom—people she had believed were, if not exactly her friends, at least friend-*ly* acquaintances—whispering about her. "I mean, what, is she forty?" A giggle. "Like, is she my *mom*? Who brings *Chablis* to a toga/foam party?" Holly had tucked her feet up in the bathroom stall so she wouldn't be spotted.

She is used to this. She has been called an "old soul" since she was five, when she begged her parents to let her stay up late and watch the Barbara Walters interview with Monica Lewinsky. Or when her nana got her a subscription to *Highlights* magazine when she was seven, and she asked if she could exchange it for the *New Yorker*. Still, she resolved never to bring wine to Matt's frat parties thereafter unless it was in a box. She tries to fit in.

Lost in her thoughts, she stumbles over a group of partiers engaged in a bottle-flipping competition. "I did it! I landed it!" A girl with a high ponytail jumps up and down, her sleek hair bobbing along with her. Holly touches her own dark hair, which she flat-ironed for the party. The frat house is as humid as an August afternoon at the monkey hut in the Bronx Zoo, and she can feel the strands around her face and neck frizzing already.

Holly turns in another direction—and is nearly hit in the head by two people attempting to take selfies while high-fiving themselves. "2016, you are *crazy*," she whispers, backing away. But the reminder that a new year is approaching in two weeks brings a smile to her face. Despite having a festive first name, Holly has never connected with Christmas as she has with New Year's Eve. Even thinking about the approaching blank slate of a new year causes a twang of anticipation to thrum through her body. New day planner, new set of notebooks, new goals, new dreams. On New Year's Day, anything feels possible—and Holly has never understood why so many people end up spending such a sacred, possibility-filled twenty-four hours curled under duvets like hungover shrimp.

Matt has joined the bottle-flippers, and waves joyfully at Holly from across the room. She waves back and checks her watch: only 11:15. Too early to duck out, and besides, Matt needs someone to steer him away from the nog should he lose his way again.

Holly and Matt have been together since they were freshmen and locked eyes over a mud pit during a frosh week tug-of-war her new roommates dragged her to as a "team-building" exercise. Holly would likely have spent most of her college years at the library studying. Or in her room binge-watching nature documentaries—which she used to refer to as her "guilty pleasure" until her older brother, Ted, explained that watching documentaries about climate change and endangered species did not meet the definition of a guilty pleasure. The important thing is, Matt brings her out of her shell. Their dads went to Yale together, and their moms know each other from Vassar. Everyone is thrilled with the match, and they have their life together all planned out: graduate from Columbia, get accepted to Yale Law, move in together, article, secure jobs at A-list firms, get married, have kids.

Next week, Holly will see Matt's parents at the annual Beech Family Christmas Eve Carol Sing, and she'll be reminded of what a smart choice she's made in her boyfriend. It will almost be enough to get her to enjoy the Christmas Eve Carol Sing—which is the opposite of the warm, welcoming gathering its name suggests. It's a catered affair at Holly's parents' Brooklyn Heights town house. Musicians are hired to sing the carols; last year it was the Lumineers. Holly's mother will stress about the caterer serving East Coast Canadian oysters when she requested West Coast. Holly's brother—who works out of Belgium now as a chief scientist for the Environmental Defense Fund and only comes home at Christmas—will get in an argument about politics with their father, and Holly fears the 2016 political argument will be the worst one of all. Holly will find herself biting her nails to the quick, counting down the days until Christmas, with all its never-quite-met expectations, is behind her and she can start fresh in the new year, and spend at least one day feeling like she could be anyone and do anything.

She has plucked a bottle of water from a stack meant for flipping and is making a beeline for an empty couch she has just spotted in a dim corner when Matt calls out her name. "Holly! Come over here! There's someone you have *got* to meet!"

Ivy Casey hates keg parties. But her current boyfriend, D'Arcy, is Phi Delta Epsilon. Ivy met him at a pub night she accidentally walked into after a life-drawing seminar. She has never dated a frat guy before and is pretty sure she isn't going to be dating one for much longer—but she said yes to the keg party to give her roommate at Cooper Union and her visiting out-of-town boyfriend privacy. Plus, she figured if she didn't have fun, it would be easy enough to duck out unnoticed and tell D'Arcy the next day that she was there all along; he just doesn't remember.

She contemplates him from across the room. D'Arcy is tall, muscular, and Theo James–level handsome, complete with square jaw and cocky grin. He flips a plastic water bottle, lands it, and hugs the dark-blond, equally handsome guy beside him like he's just scored a winning Hail Mary touchdown in the final quarter-second of the Super Bowl, complete with butt pats and Jesus-thanking hand gestures. As Ivy watches, she wonders if her latest relationship is going to make it through the night, let alone the holidays. Then she tosses her long, dark braid over one shoulder as she moves through the party, searching for somewhere to sit.

The song changes from "Work" by Rihanna to "Last Christmas" by Wham!, and half the room starts singing along. Ivy glances at her watch. 11:15. If the Christmas music lasts until midnight, she's turning into a pumpkin and Cinderella-ing out of here. Her family doesn't really do Christmas, and she's never grown that attached to it. Her father sees the season as a capitalist plot designed to boost materialism, stupefy the masses with sugar and fat, and drown the planet in excess plastic packaging. Fair points. Last year, when Ivy went home to spend the holidays on her parents' maple syrup farm in Quebec, she discovered her parents had left for Brazil to take a shaman-led ayahuasca journey in the Amazon rainforest, which was paid for by swapping farm equipment with an offbeat travel agent since her parents lead an entirely cash-free existence. Ivy wasn't hurt—her parents have always marched to the beat of their own drum, and so has she. It just reminded her of why she doesn't love the season. Too many expectations.

She spots an empty couch and starts toward it. She hears D'Arcy's voice. "There you are!" He grabs her from behind and kisses her ear, then her neck. Ivy feels a small shiver of the attraction that made her notice D'Arcy in the first place. Maybe he's just as tired of this party as she is and is about to suggest they go back to his room and do the one thing she is definitely sure she likes about him: he's inventively great in bed and surprisingly generous for a total bro.

But no such luck.

"Isn't this the sickest party?" he says. "And there's someone I need you to meet. My best buddy, Matt—remember, I've told you all about him?" Ivy nods vaguely. "You've got to meet his girlfriend! Trust me, it's a Christmas miracle! Come on, come on." Pressing his body against hers from behind, he shuttles her through the room. The dark-blond guy D'Arcy was celebrating his bottle-flip with earlier is waving at them.

"This is Matt!" D'Arcy says with a flourish. Matt then pulls a pretty brunette with wide-set dark eyes, a heart-shaped face, gently frizzing hair, and a shy smile into their little semicircle. Matt and D'Arcy look like kids on Christmas morning. What is going on here?

"Ta-da!" Matt exclaims.

"Umm. Hi?" Ivy extends a hand to the young woman, who looks just as confused as she does.

"I'm Holly," she says.

Realization dawns.

She winces. "I'm Ivy."

"Oh, great," Holly says, just as Matt and D'Arcy break into an intoxicated version of the carol "The Holly and the Ivy"— except they don't know the words because no one does, so they mostly just shout-sing "The holly and the ivy! The holly and the ivy! *Dadadadadadaaaaa!*"

"And!" D'Arcy says. "Look at you two. You're like . . ." He searches for the right word and finally finds it. Sort of. "Doppelbangers."

"I think you mean doppel-*gängers*," Holly murmurs.

"You both look just like Summer on *The O.C.*," Matt chimes in. "You two are like . . . twins! Twins who are *also* triplets with Rachel Bilson!"

"It's a freaking Christmas miracle," D'Arcy says, and the two bump chests before Matt stares into his empty cup and says, "Think we've earned a refill," then pulls D'Arcy with him toward the back of the keg line. "We'll leave you two to get acquainted!" Matt calls out over his shoulder.

Holly and Ivy stand staring at each other like two shy girls on a playdate their moms set up for them. Ivy isn't usually socially awkward, but feels suddenly nervous. She studies Holly and has to admit there is a similarity between them. Same thick eyebrows, wide mouths, and pointed chins. Same carob-brown shade of hair.

"I *really* hate keg parties," she says—at the exact moment Holly says the same thing. They both laugh. The ice is broken.

"You wouldn't, by any chance, care for an ice-cold glass of sauv blanc, would you?" Ivy asks, shaking the vacuum-sealed metal water bottle she's carrying.

Holly's eyes widen. "Are you kidding me? That is precisely, *exactly* what I would care for."

They head for the empty couch, grabbing Solo cups along

the way. When they're settled, Ivy fills Holly's cup, then her own. Holly takes a sip and closes her eyes.

"This is *so good*. Thank you."

"My dad's friend owns a winery in the Loire Valley, and my dad trades him a case of maple syrup for a case of this every year. My parents' preferred libations are cannabis cocktails and hard kombucha, so he gives it to me. I usually save it for special occasions, but the new year is almost here." Ivy can't help it; she grins at the thought. "And I still had one bottle left, so . . ." She taps her cup against Holly's. "*Santé.*"

"Trading for maple syrup, I don't think I've ever heard that technique for getting good wine. Most people I know just buy it."

"My parents live completely cash-free, and after the Great Maple Syrup Heist of 2011, my dad realized maple syrup is like liquid gold. So he and my mom traded their yoga-and-meditation chalet in the Laurentian Mountains of Quebec, where I mostly grew up, for a large maple tree acreage nearby, and now that's what they do."

"Great Maple Syrup Heist?"

"Maybe you have to be Canadian to have heard of that one." Ivy shrugs. "Although I'm a dual citizen, actually. I was born unexpectedly in a yurt at a New Mexico silence retreat. But here I am, talking too much about myself and not asking about you. Tell me about yourself, Holly. I want to know everything."

"Oh, I'm not nearly as interesting. Born in New York City, live in New York City, probably will forever."

"Not a bad thing, New York City is the *best*. Which part?"

"Brooklyn Heights. But seriously, enough about me. I can see why D'Arcy's so crazy about you. You're fascinating! Tell me more about growing up at a yoga retreat, then a tree farm."

Ivy bites her lip and decides to be honest. "Listen, I don't think I'm really . . . very well matched with D'Arcy. I know he's your boyfriend's best friend, but I already like you and I can't lie to you about this. I'm pretty sure I'm leaving this party tonight without him and may not see him again." She tilts her head. "I'm sorry, that sounds cold. I'm not really a romantic. I try—but I haven't met the right guy yet, maybe. Is it too mean to break up with someone at this time of year?"

Holly looks stunned for a moment, and Ivy wonders if her honesty has been too much. But then she says, "Wow, that was refreshingly truthful," and Ivy is so relieved she hasn't scared Holly off that she grasps her new friend's arm.

"I mean, don't get me wrong," Holly says. "D'Arcy is . . . well, he's a good friend to Matt. They're like brothers. But I personally could not imagine dating him. Plus, he has the attention span of a fruit fly. As much as he likes you, I'm sure he'll be fine."

Ivy decides not to go overboard on the honesty and blurt out that she thinks Holly is dating an alternate version of

D'Arcy and that she couldn't imagine dating Matt, either—and instead says, "Matt seems great. How long have you two been together?" She refills their cups as Holly briefly details their two-year relationship, which sounds to Ivy like it ticks a lot of boxes.

"Do you love him?"

Holly seems surprised at the question, but then smiles and looks down at her lap. "I do. We were meant to be. We have our life all planned out. I feel lucky I found him because I'm not exactly a social butterfly, but he gets me out of my comfort zone." The song has switched to "My Only Wish (This Year)" by Britney Spears, and half the people at the party start singing along again. Ivy and Holly both roll their eyes at the same time.

"Even Britney doing Christmas isn't enough to get me in the spirit tonight," Ivy says.

"Me neither! I could seriously skip right over Christmas and straight to New Year's Eve." Holly's eyes are wide. "I don't think I've ever told anyone that."

"You've come to the right place. My parents don't celebrate Christmas because they say it's an empty, materialistic holiday designed for the sole purpose of fueling the economy and bolstering capitalism—"

"*Whoa.*"

"Yeah. Sharon and Ron are a lot, but I love and accept them for who they are. Anyway, when I was a kid, I just sort of glommed on to New Year's. Shouldn't that be the big event of the holidays? The moment when everything resets and we all get to start fresh? How exciting is that?"

"*So* exciting. It's like you're reading my mind. My parents make it seem like if we don't have a perfect Christmas every single year, our lives are ruined, but the result has always been the same. Something inevitably goes wrong. It's always a letdown. But I am *never* disappointed by New Year's Eve because no matter what, you get to wake up the next day with something brand-new and all your own. A whole new year. And, if you've thought ahead, a new day planner, too."

Ivy is grinning. "I'm so glad I didn't sneak out of this party early."

"I'm glad you didn't, too. If you had left and never seen D'Arcy again, I never would have had the chance to meet you."

Ivy sighs. "I do feel bad, okay? I'm not totally heartless. He's a sweet guy. I want to feel a spark, I really do. I've just never . . . been swept away by anyone, you know? I mean, aside from my high school boyfriend, who I was madly in love with. But that was seventy-five percent hormones and twenty-five percent proximity, and everyone has to have their heart smashed to smithereens at least once, so I'm just glad I got it out of the way early."

Holly is nodding. "I get it. Swept away. Like in that Brad Pitt movie, the one where he's the grim reaper."

"Yes! *Meet Joe Black*! The scene where Anthony Hopkins tells Claire Forlani she and her boyfriend have as much passion for each other as . . ."

"A pair of titmice!"

"Yes! And then he says he wants her to get *swept away*."

"*Levitate*."

Ivy raises her hands in the air. "*Sing with rapture and dance like a dervish*. Anyway, I'm happy you have that with Matt."

Just then, Matt jumps up on a chair and starts gyrating his hips, Elvis-style, along to Britney Spears's voice. Holly gazes at him, an inscrutable expression on her face.

"Do you think it's fair to titmice to say they lack passion?" she finally says, looking away from Matt. "Maybe titmice are quite passionate."

"Entirely possible. I mean, they have the word 'tit' in their name."

Holly laughs, but then grows serious again. "I'm not sure Matt has ever made me levitate or dance like a dervish—and I'm pretty sure the only thing that makes *him* feel that way are keg parties. But we're still good together. I don't think movies always provide the most accurate depiction of true love."

"You mean I should not be taking dating advice from a movie where Brad Pitt plays the grim reaper?"

Holly smiles. "Definitely not. But maybe 2017 will be the year you find rapturous, passionate love. Who knows?"

"Or titmouse love. Either one. Meanwhile, I'm ready to say goodbye to 2016 and see what's next."

For the next hour, they sit on the couch, drinking Ivy's wine and making a list of all the things they're looking forward to saying goodbye to once 2016 draws to a close.

"Bottle-flipping," Ivy says.

"Dabbing," Holly adds.

"The rainbow-food trend. I do not want a rainbow burger!"

Ivy groans. "Or a rainbow bagel!"

"No more rainbow food, full stop!"

"Avocado on everything. Please, no more avocado on *everything*."

"The 'is it a puppy or is it a bagel' meme trend."

Ivy nearly spits out her wine laughing. "And the 'is it a baby or is it a bread roll' one!"

They keep volleying back and forth, giggling—or sometimes getting serious, and still agreeing on everything—until the wine is almost gone and their cheeks and sides hurt from laughing.

"Okay, but there must have been something good about 2016, right?" Ivy pours the last of the wine into Holly's cup and folds her legs underneath herself.

Holly thinks for a moment. "Beyonce's *Lemonade*?"

"*Yes.* And I think I read somewhere there are more tigers now."

"And more solar power."

"Jackie Chan won an Oscar."

"Meghan Markle started dating Prince Harry this year."

Ivy sighs. "Yeah, but that means he's no longer available for *me* to date."

"You'd want to date Prince Harry?" Holly asks.

"Sure, for a couple of weeks. I'd date anyone for a couple of weeks. Especially a prince."

"I have no idea what that's like, serial dating. Is it so fun?"

"You're a serial monogamist. Correct read?"

Holly ducks her head. "Correct. I dated the same guy all through high school, and Matt and I met during frosh week. So . . . yeah. You've got me pegged."

"Well, *chacun à son goût*," Ivy says. "I promise. I'll never judge you."

"I promise I'll never judge you, either." They lock eyes for a moment and the promise is sealed.

"And we'll always be honest, the way you were with me about D'Arcy."

Ivy rustles around in her woven bag. She takes out a hair elastic and hands it to her new friend. "Your hair," she says. "It's getting a little . . ."

"*Thank you.*" Holly grabs the elastic. "Bad night to choose to straighten my hair. It's so humid in here! I'm a frizzball."

"That's why I went with a braid."

"Same curly, wavy, doesn't-really-know-what-it-is hair?"

"The very same."

"Want to know one good thing about 2016, Ivy? Us meeting." Holly smiles as she ties back her hair, and Ivy smiles back—and they both agree for years to come that the night they met was the most fun they've ever had at a Christmas party.

1

IVY
December 16, 2024
New York City

A nd *that's* when I knew we were going to be friends for-ever," Holly says, holding up a glass of Sancerre to toast Ivy, her maid of honor. Ivy thinks her friend looks so happy and gorgeous, standing there at the head of the table in the holly-leaf-green dress they found on sale at Saks. The same shopping trip where Ivy had discovered the perfect cranberry-hued jumpsuit on a clearance rack. They had laughed at the absurdity of it: two people who were am-bivalent about Christmas dressing in coordinating holiday outfits.

Ivy feels emotion gathering like a glowing ball of star-dust in her sternum. Holly looks so hopeful and expectant, standing there with her glass raised. Ivy feels the urge to make the biggest wish possible with all that stardust inside her, a wish that her friend will have the charmed life she deserves, the one she's always wanted, the one she's been planning for the past decade.

"I already had my soulmate in Matt," Holly continues—and now Ivy has to fight to keep the supportive, well-wishing smile on her face. To her, Holly has no flaws—at least none that are deal-breaking and friendship-ending; Ivy knows no one is *actually* perfect—but she has never been able to grasp what Holly sees in Matt. This is the one secret she has kept from her best friend since deciding the first night they met that radical honesty was going to be their policy. It's kind of a big one, though. Considering the ways in which disliking your best friend's partner might cause more and more complications over the years makes the ball of starry joy in Ivy's chest morph and twist as it slinks its way down to the pit of her stomach. "And after the night I met you," Holly is saying, "I had a soulmate best friend, too. How lucky can one person be? Thank you for always being there for me, Ivy, through the planning of this wedding, and literally everything else for the past eight years. I can't imagine my life withou—"

"To Matt and Holly!" Holly's mother, Barbara, cries, jumping from her seat and cutting her daughter short. "Cheers, cheers, *santé*—or should I say San-*ta*! To the happy couple and their Christmas wedding!" There's a shocked beat of silence as the guests process the fact that the mother of the bride has interrupted her daughter's rehearsal dinner speech like she's orchestra music and Holly is Matthew Mc-Conaughey at the 2014 Oscars. Ivy keeps a big smile pasted on her face, but the nerves in her stomach start doing a wild dance. She has always felt protective of Holly, but at moments like this she feels helpless to protect her. Then Holly's brother, Ted, seated to Ivy's left, nudges her gently. "Typical Barbara power move," he says out of the corner of his mouth. "You know she's just jealous that you've always been there for Holly in a way she's never allowed herself to." Ted's wife, Mingzhu, shoots Ivy a sympathetic, knowing smile, and Ivy is reminded that Holly does, in fact, have some excellent people in her corner. She manages to lift her glass and toast along with everyone else at the table, while forcing herself to believe that a happy ending for Holly really is possible.

Except Holly is now banging a knife on her wineglass and looking a little mad. The dissonant sound quiets the guests around the large harvest table at Cote. "No, no, *wait*," she says determinedly. "I'm not finished. I'm the bride, everyone has to do what I say for the next twenty-four hours, *at least*."

"Cheers to *that*!" Ivy calls out.

"Ivy," Holly says firmly, "planning the most festive, most Christmassy wedding possible with you at my side has been a dream come true and *so much fun*." She holds her friend's gaze for a moment, her eyes dancing. Ivy knows what she's really saying. It should have been torture, but eventually the shock wore off that Holly had agreed to get married at Christmas. Her reasoning had been that if she went along with the December date Matt and her mother were pushing, she'd be able to have a holiday season honeymoon and spend Christmas in Hawaii with her new husband, thus managing to forgo all the Beech family Christmas parties and events she always finds so disappointing. Plus, she would get home from the honeymoon in time for New Year's Eve with her bestie, meaning this wedding date offered the best of all worlds. After that, Ivy threw herself into helping to plan a festive wedding with joyful, somewhat ironic abandon. A mini mince pie and mulled wine cocktail hour while a gospel choir sang Christmas carols? Check. Secret Santa wedding favors that guests could fight over? *Yes.* Hiring an actor to make a surprise Santa visit at midnight? Happening. Filling the venue—Lotte New York Palace—with bauble-strung Christmas trees? You know it. Hiring two acrobats to perform in a giant thirteen-foot snow globe, glitter falling constantly over the pair as they put on a showstopping routine? Okay, so Holly and Ivy couldn't make that one happen, but all Holly had to do was whisper the words "giant snow globe" and they'd both start laughing uncontrollably.

"I'm so grateful for you, Ivy," Holly says. "And I know that you, like Matt, are going to be in my life forever." Now her eyes shine with tears. "I couldn't imagine my life without you, Ivy. Thanks for everything." Once this round of glass clinking is over, Holly turns to Matt, who is sitting to her right. But he's fidgeting with his dessert fork and there's a sheen of sweat on his forehead. Ivy wonders if he's still hungover from his bachelor party a few nights earlier, when, she happens to know, he ended up naked at the top of the Empire State Building. *He's such a schmuck*, Ivy can't help but think. Except Holly is staring down at her sweaty, uncomfortable-looking fiancé like he's the *Mona Lisa* and she's just arrived in Paris for the first time and rushed straight to the Louvre. "Matt, tomorrow is the day we've dreamed about practically since the moment we met—when we just . . ." She places a hand on her heart, and her berry-red nails shine in the candlelight. "We knew. We gazed at each other over that mud pit and we *knew*. I'm so excited to become Mrs. Carter. Well, I'm not going to take your name, but I'll be Mrs. Carter in my heart, okay? I'm so excited to spend the rest of our lives together, starting tomorrow. I love you." She looks down at him expectantly, clearly waiting for him to stand and join her, lift his own glass, make his own speech—but Matt just keeps flipping his fork over on top of the tablecloth like it's a competitive sport. As the awkward silence stretches, he finally looks up at Holly. He looks startled, as if he just noticed her there.

"*Oh*. Thanks. That was really nice. Um, I . . ." He clears his throat, loosens his tie as if it's suddenly choking him. "Right. Yeah. Shit. I'm supposed to make a speech tonight, too." He stands and grips the back of his seat. Ivy can't help but notice his knuckles have gone white. Across the table, D'Arcy, still his best friend, looks sweaty and uncomfortable, too. But when he sees Ivy looking at him, he shoots her a suggestive eyebrow waggle. Although they only dated for a few weeks eight years ago, and the best thing about their relationship was that it led Ivy to Holly, D'Arcy still goes around telling anyone who will listen that Ivy is his ex. After a few drinks, he also says she's "the one who got away" and "an absolute minx in the sack." Ivy looks away from him, fights hard to get back that sense of happy hopefulness for her friend. Meanwhile, Matt is still clearing his throat and fiddling with his tie.

"Mom, Dad, thank you for planning this dinner." His parents beam at him proudly. "It was great. Eight courses, all meat or meat-adjacent. My dream meal." Ivy, meanwhile, being the only vegetarian in attendance, got six courses of green salad and one very sad stuffed pepper. Even the dessert contained gelatin, and she'd had to leave it untouched. "And Ed and Barb, thank you for . . . well, you know, everything. You've been so great." His voice wobbles, and Ivy is surprised by the sudden show of emotion. He's acting weird, even for Matt. He dashes at a tear with a clenched fist, holds up his glass, says "Cheers, I love you all!" in a wobbling voice. The table clinks glasses again, and no one seems to notice that Matt's glass is empty—and that he didn't even address his bride-to-be. No one except Ivy. She sees it all and feels sick to her stomach.

"Uh-oh, I'm a bit tipsy," Holly says as they get in the back of the town car that will take them to Ivy's apartment. "My face will be all puffy tomorrow for my wedding."

"Please—you could drink all night and walk down the aisle in flannel pajamas, and you'd still be the most beautiful bride in the world."

"Aw, Ivy." Holly leans her head against her friend's shoulder and Ivy pats her hair. "I don't know what I'd do without you."

"Back at ya," Ivy says.

"We're going to be friends for life."

"I know we are." And Ivy does. She knows married life is going to change things, but also that they can survive it. When Holly went to Yale for law school and Ivy stayed in New York City to start a grueling internship at the ad firm where she's now a senior graphic designer, they sometimes went weeks without seeing each other—but never let it go longer than a month before one of them would take the train either into the city or to New Haven for a girls' weekend.

Holly leans forward and looks at the clock on the dash of

the town car. "Forty-five more minutes until midnight, and then the day will be here. My wedding day."

"The countdown is on. Less than sixteen more single-girl hours for you."

"What's the plan for the rest of the evening?"

"Sheet masks and a movie."

"Perfect. Which movie?"

"It's a surprise. And I agonized. I mean, just *one* movie and not an entire marathon? Tough to pick just one. But I did it. I found the most romantic, but also the weirdest, but also one of our most favorite movies of all time—"

"*Meet Joe Black*!"

Ivy laughs. "You guessed it. For movie snacks, I have collagen water, this Aztec chocolate that's supposed to make your skin look like a newborn baby's, *and* maybe the smallest, tiniest bit of top-shelf tequila—because everyone knows you don't get a hangover with the good stuff. And a bubble bath for you, and then . . . one last sleep before you're officially a married lady!"

"Married lady," Holly repeats. Then she sighs. "I'm not going to turn into my mother, am I?"

"Holly, I promise, there is zero chance of that."

"I'm sorry she was so rude tonight. It's not that she doesn't like you . . ."

"It's just that she hates me," Ivy finishes. "And that's fine. Really, Hol. You know I'm not sensitive about it. She wishes you two had the relationship we do—"

"And we can't because she's such an asshole all the time."

Ivy snort-laughs. "That is exactly why."

"One day, it will be you getting married," Holly says. "And I can only hope I'm half the maid of honor you are."

"Maybe," Ivy says.

"Maybe I'll be half the maid of honor you are?"

"Oh, God, no, you'll totally nail it the way you nail everything. You'll leave me in your dust. Just, you might never get the chance."

"It's going to happen. One day, you'll find love that makes you levitate . . . dance like a dervish . . ."

"Screw like a horny titmouse?"

"The full package. Horny titmice and everything."

The car arrives at Ivy's Greenwich Village apartment building. "I'm so glad I can be myself with you," Holly says as they tumble out of the car and link arms.

"I'm glad I can, too, and that you love me for it." Ivy is generally herself with everyone, and sometimes not everyone's cup of tea. But with Holly, she doesn't have to worry about being considered abrupt, or offbeat, or too honest, or too frank about sex. Holly likes her just the way she is. And, Ivy can't help but think, shouldn't that be the case in Holly's life, too? Weren't you supposed to be yourself with the person you were marrying?

"Hey, you okay?" Holly asks as they stand, waiting for the elevator.

"I'm great."

"It'll happen," Holly says, misinterpreting her friend's morose expression. "He's out there somewhere right now, just waiting to meet you. I wonder where he is."

Ivy unlocks the door to her apartment, and they step inside as Holly keeps talking, her voice dreamy. "He could be any-where. In this city or . . . maybe a dude ranch in Montana . . ."

"Now there's an idea. I've never slept with a cowboy, maybe I need to?"

"Not sleep with, *marry*," Holly corrects, following Ivy into her tiny galley kitchen, where Ivy pours pints of water from the tap, and tequila from a blue-and-white ceramic bottle. They head into the living room, where she's set up the coffee table with makeup remover, cotton pads, sheet masks, and snacks. She cues up the movie as Holly starts removing her eye makeup.

Once she's done, she sips her tequila. "*So* good," she says.

"Only the best for the bride-to-be."

"I love that we both drink good booze. I've never seen the point of drinking just to get drunk."

"Al-*though*, every once in a while, getting lightly buttered—"

"Gently toasted."

"One and a half sheets to the wind."

"—is really a lot of fun. And as you said, this chocolate is going to reverse-age me—"

"Plus, you're already perfect—"

"These sheet masks are going to restore and rejuvenate me, and despite the drinking, I'll look fine tomorrow."

"Better than fine, Holly. You're going to be the most beautiful bride in the world. With the best heart. Also, the smartest."

"Thanks, friend. Movie time?"

Ivy hits play, and the moment Brad Pitt gets randomly walloped by a car while crossing the street, Holly dissolves into laughter and they rewind and replay it, the way they always do. "I'm so sorry," she says, trying to catch her breath. "I know it's not supposed to be funny, but . . ." Pitt flies through the air again, and she buries her face in a throw pillow that comes away damp from her tears of mirth.

Then they reach the moment when Pitt's character tries peanut butter for the first time. As usual, Holly says, "This part *always* makes me crave a peanut butter sandwich," and Ivy goes into the kitchen to make her one—just as Ivy's door buzzer goes off.

Holly raises an eyebrow. "Is this one of your booty calls?"

"God, I hope not," Ivy says. "The guy I've been sort of seeing is an emergency room doctor, though, so he does keep odd hours. Maybe if I ignore him, he'll go away."

But the buzzing continues until Ivy stands, exasperated. "Hello?" she says into the intercom.

"It's Matt. I need to see Holly."

"Matt? Awww," Holly says. "This is so sweet! So un-Matt-like!" She stands—but then her eyes widen with alarm. "This is *so* un-Matt-like, to just show up, all spontaneous and romantic. Do you think something is wrong?"

Ivy was wondering the same thing. But she smiles and says, "Of course not. Your groom is so madly in love with you, he needs to see his bride-to-be the night before the wedding. For a passionate good-night kiss."

But when Holly is gone, Ivy slumps against her front door, her sense of forboding intensifying. Matt seemed so off tonight. Something isn't right, and Ivy knows it. She distracts herself by going into the living room and picking up her cell phone. There's some work stuff she ignores given that she is now officially on vacation, and a new email from Aiden Coleman, the host of the eco-cabin in the Hudson Valley she has rented for the two weeks following Holly's wedding. This is her annual art honeymoon, which she takes every Christmas season. Ivy studied visual art in college, and even got a partial scholarship at Cooper Union because of her talents. Her professors encouraged her to pursue making a living with the lush oil pastel landscapes that were her art school signature. But while her unconventional, bohemian upbringing is one she looks back upon fondly, Ivy has always craved more stability for herself. Making a living trading landscape art, the way her father had insisted she surely could, held zero appeal. So, in her last year of college, she took some graphic design courses and found she was good at it. She graduated, and the final art show of the year was the last she ever did. She left her art behind, surprising everyone except herself by taking an internship at Imagenue, one of New York's most prestigious branding studios. Now she uses her artistic skills and visual-storytelling abilities to help build brands. She doesn't love her job, but she likes it. It pays the bills, which is important given that living in New York City as a single woman is not nearly as effortless as Carrie Bradshaw made it look in the '90s. Ivy had student loans to pay off, and after that was done, paying rent in her favorite neighborhood—Greenwich Village, which she fell in love with during college—was expensive. She needs her job.

Except that during her first two years in the corporate world, Ivy found herself falling into a mental, spiritual malaise that veered far too close to full-blown depression for her comfort. So, she decided to take her first ever "art honeymoon" during her third year working at Imagenue. She booked a cabin in the Catskills, and spent fourteen glorious days eating instant ramen and sketching the landscape, which was at once pastoral and rugged, stark and luscious. Eventually, all the oil pastels she brought had been reduced to colorful stubs, her fingertips tattooed rainbows. She gave the pieces to friends and family, hung some in her apartment, and felt better. It was enough. It got her through the year. So she did it again, and kept on doing it. In fact, this year was going to be her fifth art honeymoon.

She taps out a quick reply to Aiden, telling him her estimated arrival time in two days, and allows herself a moment of anticipatory excitement about two weeks spent solely focused on creativity before she goes back to worrying about Holly, and why Matt's here.

When she hears her friend's key in the door a mere seven minutes later, her body floods with relief. No one breaks off an engagement the night before the wedding in *seven* minutes. He really did just want to kiss his bride-to-be good night. Maybe Husband Matt will be more palatable to Ivy than Boyfriend Matt has been.

Except, when Holly enters the living room, the laughing, silly, slightly tipsy friend Ivy saw seven minutes ago is gone.

"Holly!" Ivy jumps up from the couch "What happened? Are you okay?"

"I . . ." Holly stands still in the middle of the room. ". . . don't know."

"What happened?" she repeats.

Holly opens her mouth and closes it.

"You're scaring me. What's going on?"

"He ended it." Holly's voice is the sound wave equivalent of a marble statue. "There's someone else."

Ivy pulls Holly toward the couch, pouring her a shot of tequila, knowing this is going to call for a lot more than one and a half sheets to the wind. All three sheets are going to be hanging on the line tonight, if only to get Holly to unleash the torrent of emotion she's clearly holding in, making her eyes look like she's one of the zombies in *The Walking Dead*.

"What did he say?"

Holly shakes her head. "Something like . . . something that sounded an awful *fucking* lot like he was quoting Anthony Hopkins in *Meet Joe Black*." Holly shakes her head, her eyes dazed. "How falling in love feels different than what we have. He said the sparks you're supposed to feel . . . never really happened with us. He said . . . that maybe we got together because we felt like we were ticking boxes on a list our families had made for us."

Ivy hates that she agrees with Matt. She holds her best friend's hands and hopes her expression is not betraying her, but Holly sees nothing as she stares straight ahead like an automaton. "I don't think he actually came out and said he never loved me, but he didn't have to. It was unspoken. He doesn't love me, he doesn't want to marry me. And I *do* love him, Ivy. I do." She pauses and rakes her hand through her hair, which is flowing in shiny waves down her back, the result of a recent pre-wedding keratin treatment. "Don't I? I can't have been planning to marry a person just because we fit. And besides, isn't fitting a good thing? Aren't you supposed to find your missing puzzle piece and marry that person?"

"Yes," Ivy says. "Yes, you are." She does not say that she refuses and has always refused to believe Matt is Holly's missing puzzle piece. Now is not the time. She just keeps squeezing her friend's hand.

"I mean yes, we work well together as a concept, and our families get along." Holly stops talking and stares down at her glass, then slugs it back and holds it out. This is a drastic scenario, so Ivy pours more tequila and gets her friend a glass of water, too.

"What else did he say?"

"He met someone at work and he doesn't know where it's going to go, but he has to . . . explore it."

"And you? What did you say?"

"'Okay.' That's all I said. '*Okay.*' I just stood there thinking I should be screaming, crying, begging. But I didn't feel anything, and I still don't. I just . . . feel empty."

"I'm so sorry."

"When I turned around and started walking back into your building, he called out to me. And I thought, 'Oh, he didn't mean it.'"

"What did he want?"

"He asked me if I still wanted to go on our honeymoon. He said the trip was nonrefundable and nontransferable, and my parents had spent so much money on it, and it would be such a waste not to use it. He said, given the shock of everything, I should really go and just spend two weeks . . . I forget the word he used. 'Decompressing'? 'Processing'?"

"What did you say to that?" Ivy manages.

"I said no, of course. That would be way too painful. Then I came back up here." She puts her face in her hands, but when she looks up again, she's still dry-eyed. "I mean, it really *is* such a waste. He's not wrong. Not just the honeymoon, but all of it."

"Oh, honey." Ivy keeps rubbing her friend's back gently, trying to channel her own mother. "I'm here, okay? Whatever you need me to do, I will."

"I don't even know what I need to do, though! Do I have to tell everyone?" She looks panicked at this.

"Of course not. You don't have to do anything, okay? I'll call your parents and let them know what has happened. And then I'll call a few of our friends who we can trust to get the message out."

"Okay. Thank you. I just can't."

"Of course. Are you sure you want me to call them now? We could wait until morning. Maybe Matt will come to his senses."

"I can't marry someone who is so unsure this is the right thing to do. He said what he said. There's no going back. Just call them. Please."

Ivy leans forward and hugs her friend, then stands. "I'm going to call them from my room. I'll be back in a few minutes."

"I'm good," Holly says, with a smile that doesn't reach her eyes. She lifts the bottle. "I have Don Julio to keep me company."

As Ivy enters her room, she fights the urge to call Matt

and tear a strip off of him for hurting her friend. Instead, she closes the door and takes a deep, shaky breath—which snags when she sees Holly's wedding dress hanging on her closet door. It's snowy white, with a square neckline and wide straps that frame her collarbones perfectly, a plunging back and a ball-style skirt with deep pockets that are the best part of the dress—all made of the softest silk. Holly looks like a literal Disney princess in this dress, and somehow not in a bad way. Ivy quickly pushes it inside her closet and slams the door on the train. No one needs to see that dress right now.

Barbara doesn't answer, so Holly tries again. It goes straight to voicemail. "Mrs. Beech, this is Ivy. I'm calling to let you know that Matt has just informed Holly that he no longer wants to go through with the wedding. It's off. Holly is understandably devastated. I can email the caterer and text the hairdressers and makeup artists. Could you call the venue in the morning to let them know what has happened, and perhaps send out an email as soon as you get this message? I'm working on trying to let as many guests know as possible in our friend circle, and I'm counting on you to let your family know. Could you also please get in touch with Matt's family, if he hasn't done so already, to make sure they spread the word, too? Call me when you get this. Please. I'll be up all night. We can get our girl through this. Thanks."

She hangs up and goes back out into the living room just in time to hear Holly's phone ring. Holly holds it up. "Barb."

Ivy grabs the phone. "Hello?"

"Holly, is that you? What does Ivy mean, the wedding is off? Is she drunk? Is she high? That *can't* be true. It would be such an embarrassment, I don't know if we'd ever live it down. We've spent so much money, we'll never get any of the deposits back, plus the honeymoon, plus the—"

For a woman from a family who often talks about how their ancestors arrived on the *Mayflower* with actual chests of gold—and whose husband inherited a healthy chunk of a shipyard fortune—Holly's mother is surprisingly opposed to "wasting" cash. Sure, she once spent almost six figures on the abalone for her father-in-law's retirement party, but Barb had made certain she got the *best possible deal* on that rarest of shellfish.

"Mrs. Beech? This is Ivy. Holly can't talk right now."

"Put my daughter on the phone!"

"Did you listen to my entire message? Will you call the venue in the morning? And notify the guests you have contact information for—"

"This is not happening!"

Ivy is angry, and she is sad for her friend, and she will probably never understand how someone as lovely as Holly—and her brother, Ted, for that matter—could have been raised by a mother like Barbara, and her father, Ed, who is about as emotionally supportive as an empty lobster tank at Grand Central Oyster Bar. She is also determined not to let her emotions get in the way of doing what she promised she would do for Holly: Take care of everything. Shield her from these details. "I'm afraid it is happening. And we need to be here for Holly. I'll work on getting the word out to our friends. You will contact your family members and friends. We'll divide up the vendors and we'll talk tomorrow."

"But—"

"*We will talk again tomorrow.*" Ivy ends the call.

"You know," Holly says, her laugh shaky, "sometimes, you scare me. For someone raised by the most peace-loving hippies I've ever met—I mean, aside from when your dad starts on one of his rants about corporate America—you do one hell of an impression of Margaret Thatcher."

Ivy laughs, too, equally shaky. "I will be the Iron Lady for you if I need to be."

Holly smiles another one of those sad smiles. She picks up the tequila bottle, then puts it down. "This isn't helping."

"I'll make some tea," Ivy says. "We're going to get through this, okay? I won't leave your side until you're okay again."

Holly looks thoughtful. "No," she finally says. "That's not true. You need to leave for your art retreat, day after tomorrow. You *can't* stay by my side. You *love* those trips. You *need* your art honeymoon."

Ivy shakes her head. "I'm not going anywhere without you. That's final."

"But—"

Ivy holds up a hand. "I would do anything for you. You

know this. But leaving you on your own right now is where I draw the line."

"Agree to disagree," Holly says, which is what they always say instead of arguing. "We can talk about it tomorrow. For now, some tea would be great."

As Ivy walks into the kitchen to turn on the kettle, she feels her eyes fill with tears, but she tamps them down. If Holly hasn't cried yet, she isn't going to, either. She will be as strong as her friend—and when Holly inevitably breaks, Ivy will be by her side to hold her up.

2

HOLLY
December 17
New York City

Holly bolts upright. "Ahh! We overslept! It's my wedding day." Then her brain catches up and she realizes that, *no*, it's not her wedding day. It *was* her wedding day. Now it's . . . just a day.

She's on Ivy's couch—and Ivy has jumped up from the chair she fell asleep in, dazed and panicked at once. "Are you okay?! Are you hurt?!"

Holly squeezes her eyes shut and flops back down on the couch, which is extra wide and comfortable precisely because she stays over so often. She has the same super-comfy couch at her Upper East Side condo; she and Ivy got a discount when they bought two of the same at a furniture store that was going out of business.

"I'm so sorry," Holly says. "I woke you. And there's absolutely no reason for us to be up at . . ." She sits up again and rummages on the coffee table for her phone to check the time, but comes up empty.

"It's in my room," Ivy says. "I turned it off. Is that okay?"

Holly nods. "Well, whatever time it is, we don't need to be up. Since there's nowhere we need to be today." The half-empty tequila bottle is still on the coffee table, but she feels perfectly hydrated and physically fine. Except for her chest. Something is wrong with it. She lifts her hand to her heart, holds it there for a moment.

"You look like you're checking to see if your heart is still in there."

"That's exactly what I'm doing," Holly says. "I can feel it beating, so objectively, I know it's there. But it's like . . . there's a big empty space where my heart is supposed to be. Is that normal?"

"I'm so sorry. This is not fair. I hate that this is happening to you."

"It *did* happen, right? I didn't dream it?"

Ivy shakes her head sadly. "This is real. Do you want to try to go back to sleep, or do you want coffee?"

Holly sighs. "I want both. To be able to sleep if I need to, but also to have the warm comfort of a cup of your coffee with a splash of your dad's maple syrup."

Ivy stands. "I think we've finally found the only situation decaf coffee is good for, then."

"A silver lining." Holly manages a weak smile.

As Ivy leaves the room, Holly pulls the duvet around her shoulders and turns toward the large, east-facing windows that are her favorite feature of her best friend's cozy, boho-chic Greenwich Village walk-up. The city is still dark, the dawn bejeweled with lights, but a glow is starting to shimmy over the skyline like a teenager sneaking back in the window after a night out. This day will officially begin soon—and it will not be the one Holly has been imagining for a decade. She touches her chest again, feels her still-beating but sensationless heart. Everyone talks about the pain of a broken heart, but no one has ever mentioned the yawning chasm. The nothingness of it all. Holly supposes that's because it wouldn't make for a very good love song: *My heart is a terrifying pit of loneliness.* Definitely wouldn't make the top forty. She hugs her knees and keeps staring out the window. Shouldn't she be angry? Is she doing this right? Why is she so numb?

Ivy is back, holding two steaming mugs. Holly accepts hers—she always uses the one that says "I hope your day is as nice as your butt," a gift from one of Ivy's old boyfriends; Ivy always uses the mug with Bigfoot on it that says "I believe," which they bought on a California road trip—and inhales the fragrant steam. It smells like home, friendship, comfort. "You always make the best coffee," she says.

"But you're staring into the mug like you're channeling Carly Simon."

"Clouds in my coffee, yeah." Holly peers deeper into the cup. "I wish there were some answers in here."

"You know you don't have to have all the answers right now, don't you? It's okay to just wallow."

Holly looks up. "Matt said there was someone else." She hates the way this becomes more real when she says it aloud. "I told you that last night, right? It's a bit hazy."

Ivy nods. "You did."

She closes her eyes and presses her lips together. This is hard to say, but she knows she can admit it to Ivy. "I think I knew." She puts her mug down beside the unused sheet masks from the night before. "As soon as he said it last night, that he was having an emotional affair, I *knew* who it was. We were at a work thing a few months ago, and there was a new lawyer on his team named Abby. There was a vibe between them. They finished each other's sentences. They were both Blink-182 fans. Then, a few weeks ago, he texted me, 'I can't wait to see you tonight, Abby.' A minute later, he wrote, 'Oops, my phone autocorrected from "baby"! LOL.' But he's never called me 'baby.' Not once. It was right there in front of me."

"Crushes happen, though. Even when people are in a committed relationship, they just do. It's human nature. So the fact that you chose not to freak out and throw a jealous fit because he had chemistry with a coworker, and sent a text with a typo—that's just a testament to what a levelheaded, reasonable, excellent partner you are. It was not *your* responsibility to stay on top of whether Matt was having an affair, emotional or not. But it *was* on Matt to sort this out and decide if it was something you needed to know, a long time before the eve of your wedding. This is not your fault. Don't do this to yourself."

"I know you're right. It's just . . . I have no idea how to do this!"

"Do what? Be sad? There's no right way to deal with heartache, Hol. You just have to let it happen."

"Can you come sit beside me?"

"Of course." Ivy joins Holly on the couch, puts her arm around her friend. Holly feels grateful for the comforting proximity, but it doesn't help. "You're not alone, okay?" Ivy says.

"Remember that night in the summer when we went out with Oscar, after he got dumped by Kyle?" Oscar is one of Ivy's friends from her college years, and now a good friend of Holly's, too.

"I think so . . ."

"I remember you told him that everyone has their heart broken at least once, and that it builds character. You said all that stuff about being stronger in your broken places, and I'm pretty sure you also talked about kintsugi—"

"Oh, dear. I'm sorry," Ivy says.

"No, no, you helped him. But the truth is it scared me a bit. It's like I had a premonition that night. I've always played it safe. My high school boyfriend and I broke up mutually and respectfully—"

"Like you were a teenage Gywneth and Chris. I've always marveled at the yearly Christmas card he sends—"

"Yes, exactly. Of course I was nostalgic for a while, but I wouldn't say I was heartbroken in the technical sense. Then there was that guy who slid the anonymous Christmas card in my locker—"

"Which you have kept for all these years, because you are adorable."

"It was a really sweet card! The things he wrote, whoever he was, made me feel so *seen*."

"Right. And you always regretted never finding out who he was."

"Always. What if he, whoever he is, was the one? I mean, doesn't that seem like a romance plot straight out of a movie? But then I went to college and met Matt. I thought I had it in the bag, my life completely in order. This wasn't supposed to happen. It doesn't feel like my life. There's so much uncertainty. This wasn't the plan."

Ivy squeezes her close, and Holly puts her head on her friend's shoulder. "I'm not going to lie and say this is going to be easy. But I will be with you. You won't be alone."

Holly falls asleep again. When she wakes up, Ivy is watching her with a concerned expression on her face. "Are you hungry yet?"

"Starving, actually."

"Murray's bagels with Nova cream cheese for breakfast, *and* egg-and-cheese rolls from the bodega, too?"

"And yogurt parfaits from Culture. I'm ready to try to eat my feelings."

"John's pies for lunch—Margherita *and* piccante. Zucchini sticks. Cokes. An entire cheesecake from Mah-Ze-Dahr for dinner."

"But you have to pack for your trip, not deal with indigestion."

"I told you, I'm staying right here. We can have a movie marathon every day. If you feel up to leaving the apartment, we can walk over to Greenwich Letterpress so you can get your 2025 day planner. We can—"

They're interrupted by Ivy's phone ringing, and Holly is grateful because she hates hearing Ivy talk about doing everything except the one thing she's been looking forward to all year: her solo two-week art retreat.

"That better not be your mom," Ivy says, retrieving her phone from the easy chair. "Nope, actually, it's *my* mom. She's leaving for Peru tonight and will be officially off the grid until January."

Ivy answers and walks into the kitchen again with her empty coffee mug.

Left alone, Holly is suddenly gripped by the urge to check her own phone. There are probably things she needs to be doing to make sure her wedding is called off according to whatever protocols exist in situations like this.

In Ivy's room, she retrieves her phone and turns it back on, and it immediately rings in her hand. Answering it without checking who it is is a reflex she immediately regrets.

"Holly, is that you? Have you gotten any of my messages? I can't leave you any more, your mailbox is full."

"Mom, I—"

"I've spoken to Matt's parents. They're on their way over here to the town house. Kitty feels sure she can get Matt to come with them. We can work this out together. We'll have it sorted by the time the wedding is supposed to start. No one even has to know."

"Mom, the wedding is off—"

"What exactly did he say to you last night, Holly? What if you're overreacting? You can be a little sensitive sometimes."

All at once, Holly can hear Matt's voice, and every single word he said to her the night before—as if his words have been permanently burned into her brain.

"I'm so sorry," he had said, his eyes full of torment. "I just can't."

"You . . . can't?"

"*We* can't. We can't get married, Holly. Admit it, we've both been on autopilot for years. The past few especially. We've been on this train, just going along the track, not even looking at the scenery, not even realizing..." He had trailed off, searching for the right words; Matt had never really been one for metaphors. "Without realizing that during the trip, we've changed. We've grown apart. We want different things. Maybe we want to get off at different stops now."

"We . . . do?" Holly had felt like a person in a dream who wanted to move but was frozen in place.

"Okay, well, *I* want something else, then. And I want it for you, too." At this point, he'd taken her in his arms and said, "I'm in love with someone else."

Holly had pulled away from him and said, "Please don't touch me when you say something like that to me."

"We're like roommates, and if this is what it feels like now, imagine how it's going to feel in another ten years, twenty, for the rest of our lives."

The thing was, Holly *had* imagined how it was going to feel. And she knew he wasn't wrong—she just thought this was what marriage was. You found someone you either loved or liked enough to marry, someone who ticked all the boxes and made your family happy—which was important, wasn't it, a route to less conflict, more harmony, an easier, happier life?—and you married that person. You braided your lives together. Maybe it wasn't as dramatic as they made it look in the movies or as sexy and exciting as it was in romance novels, but that wasn't real life. Desperately passionate, kissing in the rain, needing the person as much as you needed oxygen . . . that wasn't real, and if it was, it wasn't sustainable.

And no, Holly had never felt that way with anyone. Not even Matt. But standing in front of Matt the night before as he broke things off, while festive flakes of snow fell between them, all those thoughts had simply piled themselves up on top of one another in her head and she had been unable to articulate any of them.

"Do you really want to go your entire life never feeling passion? I don't. We can't do this, Holly. We have to call off the wedding." He held out his empty hands, as if this proved something to her. "Can you say something? Please?"

"Okay," she'd said, morphing into the emotionless automaton she was when she woke up this morning.

"Holly? Are you still there?"

"Mom, he said he doesn't want to marry me. He said there's someone else he's in love with."

"What?! His parents are going to be livid. They are not going to stand for this—"

"He's not a toddler who's been bad. We're not kids. We're adults."

"You're not acting like adults! You can't just cancel a wedding on a whim, without even making an attempt at reconciliation!"

"Let me get this straight. You want me to attempt to reconcile with a person who said he's having an emotional affair with someone he met at work, he thinks he loves her, and he doesn't want to marry me."

"Oh, please. Workplace romances are a fact of life. At least he's being honest. And it's not just the wedding, it's the honeymoon! That beautiful trip to Kauai your dad and I bought you two as your wedding gift—I never imagined you'd be canceling, so I didn't get insurance." This was very typical Barbara, to spend tens of thousands of dollars on a trip but then balk at the cancellation insurance.

"I'm sorry that money got wasted. I'm sorry it's *all* such a waste. Ivy is making calls, and she said you would, too. People need to be notified. That's all we can do right now. I have to go."

Despite her mother's protests, Holly hangs up. She turns her phone off again and walks back into the living room. Ivy is standing by the window now, still talking to her own mom. She hasn't heard Holly come in.

"She seems okay. But . . . she hasn't cried yet. I'm worried. It's like she *can't*. Like it's all bottled up inside. She's flat out refusing to come with me to the Hudson Valley, but she doesn't want me to stay here with her, either. No matter what she says, there's no way I'm going anywhere. I'll tell her. I know. You love her, too."

Ivy is standing in front of one of Holly's favorites of all the art pieces Ivy has made. She sketched it their senior year, during a spring break trip to Aruba. It's of Eagle Beach and is the perfect depiction of the calm, clear water, in varying shades of turquoise and blue, and the shell-pale sand Holly remembers well. The beach is dotted with palapas and sunbathing tourists on towels; the water is studded with windsurfers, paddleboards, Jet Skis. It has the vibe of a Gray Malin photograph. Holly has one from the same trip, a gift from Ivy that hangs in pride of place over her couch. Guests always ask about the artist who created it, and Holly proudly tells them it's her best friend, who is so talented she can blend her pastels into the exact color of the ocean. It's her best work. Ocean- and beachscapes always have been.

"I can still get a refund, yes, tell Dad not to worry. Maybe I'll rebook for later in the winter—honestly, it's the least of my concerns, though. Yes, Hudson Valley. You're right, spring could be better. More color in the water."

Holly has an idea. As she continues to listen to her friend talk, it takes shape in her mind. A tiny town in the Hudson Valley, a remote cabin beside a frozen river . . . suddenly, Holly can think of nowhere that would better reflect her current mood. She's grateful for everything Ivy wants to do for her, but right now, all she feels is numb. She needs to thaw, by herself. She needs to be alone. She can pack cozy clothes and extra blankets, books, fill her laptop with downloads of all the shows she's missed out on binge-watching during this busy year of wedding planning. She can make a list of movies that are sure to make her bawl her eyes out, and she can do so in private. Perhaps it's not healthy to want to nurse a broken heart in solitude, but it's what she feels she needs—and she should follow her instincts, shouldn't she? Ivy always tells her this. Holly will go to the eco-cabin in the Hudson Valley—and Ivy can go on her honeymoon and spend two weeks getting the color of the Hawaiian ocean just right.

Ivy ends her phone call and turns. "Hey! My mom says hi and sends the biggest hug."

"Your mom gives the best hugs. Listen, I just had an idea."

They face each other on the couch, and Holly does her very best to explain her logic about the trip swap, but Ivy is still resistant. "Having me enjoying what was supposed to be your honeymoon will just make everything worse, I *know* it."

"I don't agree. Knowing something good is coming out of this, that you're there in Hawaii, making your beautiful oceanscapes—which you're amazing at—would help me feel a little better, I think."

"But I can't leave you."

"What if I want you to? What if I *need* you to? Getting away for two weeks to just hide and process and figure out what's next, it's what I feel I need. We've been best friends for years—and we always trust each other, right? So *you* need to trust *me* to know what I need."

"Wow. Sometimes I forget what a great lawyer you are."

Holly shrugs. "It's easy to argue something you believe

in." She's getting somewhere, she can tell. Ivy still looks hesitant, but her expression is softening.

"I just can't help but think you need a friend with you right now."

"You're not going to disappear on me. If I need you, I'll text, or I'll call. I promise."

"The trip isn't transferable, though. How can I go in your place?"

Holly has thought of this, too. "We look so much alike. You can use my ID."

"I'm pretty sure that's a felony."

"I'm a lawyer, and a good one, you just said so yourself. Plus, it's not a felony, just a misdemeanor."

"You're a corporate contract lawyer, though . . ."

"We won't get caught, okay? It's a domestic flight. They'll just glance at your ID and ticket, then off you go. I bet they barely look at your ID at the hotel, too."

"They'll want to know where your new husband is."

"Tell them he died."

"Holly!"

"Honestly, tell them anything. Tell them the wedding got called off and you want to be left alone. Tell them he has a fungus and can't leave the room. Admit it will be the perfect trip for you—you'll get to do nothing but stare at gorgeous scenery and make art for *two whole weeks*. Please, Ivy." She grabs her friend's hands. "Trade my Hawaii honeymoon for your Hudson Valley escape."

"Well—"

"When have I ever asked you for anything, aside from being there for me for every errand and decision to do with a wedding that didn't end up happening? *Please.*"

"Okay, fine. If it makes you happy, I'll do it. But the very second you need me, I'm getting on a plane and coming back. You have to promise you'll send out an SOS if you need to. That has to be part of the deal here."

"I promise. If I need you, I'll tell you."

"Immediately. Not the next day, not an hour later—in the moment."

"Promise."

"And we'll be together on New Year's Eve."

"Yes. New Year's Eve, we reunite and keep our dinner reservation at our favorite place, with all our friends."

Holly gets ready to go to her apartment and pack for a wintry two weeks in the Hudson Valley. She'll return to Ivy's in a few hours and spend what was supposed to be her wedding night with her best friend, a movie marathon, and *Gilmore Girls* gluttony levels of takeout. Ivy is already planning the food and the viewing schedule as Holly pulls her parka over her pajamas.

"Maybe the funniest movies of all time, to make you laugh—*A Fish Called Wanda* and Grinch rolls from Kotobuki, *Anchorman*, *There's Something About Mary*, and falafel from Mamoun's. *Or* movies to make you believe in love again.

Brokeback Mountain. The Umbrellas of Cherbourg. Magic Mike XXL. Every kind of ice cream you can think of."

"*Magic Mike XXL*?" Holly can't help but laugh, even in her emotionally deadened state.

"Just trust me. See you soon?"

"An hour, tops."

Holly catches a glimpse of herself in the wavy elevator mirror and looks away. Her eyes have dark circles under them, and she's the opposite of a glowing bride. Yet as this harsh reality sinks in, she still feels nothing but numb.

Outside, she raises her hand and hails a taxi. As the car glides across town toward her Upper East Side condo, where she will replace the bikinis and sandals in her suitcase with sweaters and thermal socks, she focuses on what's ahead, not what's behind her. The future stretches before her like an endless, frozen river—one she never believed she was going to have to skate alone. "Miss?"

The car has pulled up in front of her building. The entrance is decorated with swags of cedar garland, and a light snow has started to fall. She tries not to think about what a perfect day it would have been for a Christmas wedding, pays the taxi driver, gets out of the car, and puts one foot in front of the other—because she knows that's all she can do until her heart unfreezes again.

3

IVY
December 18
Kauai, Hawaii

Ivy is on a propellor plane from Honolulu, circling the island of Kauai—the fourth-largest Hawaiian island, called
the Garden Island because of its lush greenery, which she
can see from above. The plane descends, lands with a
screech, and speeds down the runway. For a moment it feels
like the plane might plow straight into a pair of green-
covered mountains in the near distance—but then it slows
and stops. The pilot makes his announcement, and Ivy
breathes a sigh of relief.

The temperature in sunny Kauai, the pilot says, is currently seventy-nine degrees and rising, with no rain in the
forecast for days—unusual for this time of year. He signs off

with a jaunty "Mele Kalikimaka," and soon Ivy is descending the roll-up stairs onto the tarmac. She fumbles in her purse for sunglasses, then pauses and raises her face to the brilliant blue sky, soaking in the feel of the sun on her face. It's the perfect antidote to the stretch of bone-chillingly cold December days that had swept through New York City for weeks. She pulls her phone from her canvas carryall, turns off airplane mode, and texts Holly to see how she's doing. The reply comes in immediately.

Almost at cabin, just stopped for gas. I'm as fine as I can be. Don't worry about me! Have fun!! xo

Ivy soon emerges from the long and low one-story building back out into the warmth of the late afternoon, expecting to see a uniformed driver standing beside a white sedan, holding two leis and a sign that says "Mr. & Mrs. Carter, Newlyweds"—this is what Holly warned her had been arranged. Matt was always making comments about how she wasn't taking his name, how it would just be so much easier if she did. "Yeah," Ivy remembers grumbling to Holly. "Because you should definitely give up your entire identity just so airport transfers can be more straightforward."

Ivy's plan had been to tell the driver that unfortunately Mr. Carter had come down with a terrible disease resulting in scales all over his body and was convalescing at home while she took their honeymoon on her own—but none of the waiting drivers in front of the airport are holding a sign that says "Carter" at all. She drags her luggage to the taxi stand, where, thankfully, one car is still waiting. She gives the name of the hotel, and she's off.

The highway is bordered with lush fields, spread out like mossy blankets stretching to the horizon. Ivy can see why the "Garden Island" moniker has stuck. Everything is so gorgeously green, like a dream. She opens the window and feels the breeze in her hair. It smells like vegetation, but with a salty tang; she can smell the ocean, even if she can't see it yet. She snaps a photo with her phone of a particularly arresting mountain range, then reflexively attaches it to a text to Holly—but stops herself. Holly wants to be alone, nursing her broken heart. She doesn't want to be tormented with photos of what would have been her honeymoon. Ivy puts her phone away and focuses on staying in the moment, watching the scenery speed by, feeling the breeze on her face.

The car climbs a hill, then swings around a corner. The coast comes into view, and Ivy is dazzled again. The vivid, verdant green of the tree-covered mountains melts into the ocean. She takes in the yellow-white color of the sand on the beaches, the milky froth of the waves as they churn like butter against the shore, and, best of all, the kaleidoscope of blue, turquoise, green, aqua, cobalt, and indigo that makes up the ocean.

She feels a familiar surge of excitement; her fingers start to tingle from it. She imagines using her oiliest pastels to paint these scenes, their soft, oozing colors melting onto the paper the way the mountain ranges and cliffs seem to be melting into the sea. She already knows which colors she'd use for this afternoon's views: English blue for the sky, Prussian blue for the distant depths of the ocean, and cerulean, turquoise, and celestial blue closer to shore—with maybe a touch of emerald, olive, and cinnabar to catch the way the water lightens and glimmers as it touches the land. The sand will be tricky to get just right. She can already tell it isn't like the sand in Aruba, for which she used a mix of white and rose ocher. As the car climbs higher and the view stretches out in every direction—an intoxicating jumble of trees and cliffs, mountains and ocean and beach—she searches her mental color palette until she has it, the perfect color from the many pastels she has carried to Hawaii with her: Naples yellow washed over with transparent medium. She can't wait to get to the hotel and get started, and feels a wave of gratitude for Holly, for being so generous, for knowing, even in the midst of catastrophe, how much Ivy was going to love this island.

The car turns down a winding driveway that looks like a long gray ribbon leading up to the imposing main building of the Hoaloha Ocean Club Resort & Spa. It shines like a jewel in the lowering sun, all peaked roofs and gilded details. There are low-rise buildings and villas scattered about, dotting the resort grounds like pearls from a broken necklace. At first Ivy is awestruck—she gets to stay *here?*—but then, almost immediately, she feels a wave of guilt. *Holly* should be here.

Now the taxi is passing through a grove of palm trees, all hung with Christmas ornaments, their trunks wrapped in red, green, and gold ribbon, and wound with fairy lights. Ivy texts her friend. **I'm here**, she types. **It's beautiful. Thank you. It's a good thing pastels only take a few hours to dry, because I'll be working until they have to drag me out of here and put me on my flight in two weeks. Love you.** She puts her phone away as the driver says, "We've arrived."

Ivy thanks the driver, pays and tips him, and drags her luggage toward the wide entrance leading to the airy lobby. She had expected hotel staff to be there to greet the supposed newlyweds, but no one is around. There's a long, live-edge wood counter that serves as a check-in desk for the luxurious boutique hotel. It's been varnished until it gleams like polished gold in the light of the rattan chandeliers hung throughout the lobby. Enormous matching rattan ceiling fans shaped like palm fronds spin lazily above. Wall sconces give off a soft and doubtless flattering light, and she can smell eucalyptus and honey, hear the distant sizzle of a grill, smell broiling seafood and caramelizing garlic. The sounds in the distance are clinking glasses, murmurs and laughs, live ukulele music and a singer with a gentle voice. Outside, Ivy can see various glittering, round blue-topaz pools and one infinity pool that stops at the beach.

Ivy approaches the counter and waits, but no one comes. She sees a small brass bell, and depresses it as gently as she can. The sound is still jarring in the sleek, soothing atmosphere. Immediately, a dark-haired, bespectacled man in a navy suit emerges from a door behind the counter. His name tag says "Gerald."

"Welcome to Hoaloha Ocean Club Resort & Spa," he says warmly. "So sorry for the delay. I didn't expect any more check-ins today." Ivy slides her ID across the counter and hopes she doesn't seem nervous.

"I'm Holly Beech," she says firmly. "Honeymoon suite. I was supposed to check in with my husband, but he . . ." *Is a dickbag.* ". . . isn't here. So it's just me."

Gerald is looking down at her ID—and Ivy feels her heart thump guiltily under her light sundress. "Mr. and Mrs. Carter have already checked in," he says with concern. "They arrived one day early, but we were able to accommodate them."

"That's impossible. *I* am Mrs. Carter."

"I thought you said you were Holly Beech."

"Yes. Exactly. She wasn't taking his name—I mean, *I* wasn't taking his name. We were booked under 'Mr. and Mrs. Carter.'"

"Except Mr. and Mrs. Carter are already here," he says, bemused. Then his expression brightens. "In fact, there they are now! Perhaps we can clear up this confusion."

A startlingly familiar male voice: "Abby, baby, want me to grab us some mai tais on our way down to the beach?"

An unfamiliar female voice in response: "Sounds perfect, baby."

What. The. Actual. Fuck.

Ivy grabs Gerald's wrist and leans her head forward so her hair covers as much of her face as possible.

"Please," she hisses. He looks alarmed; she can't blame him. "Don't say anything. Don't call them over here. *Please.*"

"Of course," he says, eyes wide and slightly terrified.

"Are they gone?"

He nods that they are, and Ivy releases his wrist. "I'm sorry about that," she says. "Please don't call security. I'm just . . ." She's trying hard to process what she has just witnessed: Matt is here. With Abby. *The* Abby. And they call each other "baby." She squeezes her eyes shut. He and Abby arrived a day early. On what was supposed to be Matt and Holly's wedding day! He wasn't having an emotional affair; he was clearly having an *affair*-affair—and it's such a monstrously awful thing to do that Ivy has to fight the urge not to chase after Matt and Abby and confront him head-on. Except she can't see Matt right now. She can't trust herself not to murder him.

"Miss, you seem very upset. Is there anything I can do to assist you?"

"I'm sorry. I'm fine. No. I'm not at all fine." Ivy decides to be honest. Well, *half* honest. "Gerald, that's my ex-fiancé. He broke off our wedding, and I decided to come on our honeymoon by myself, but now it turns out he's here, too. With another woman. The woman he was cheating on me with."

Gerald's mouth drops open. "Why, that's terrible."

"It's the most horrible thing that has ever happened to me." She wipes at her eyes and hopes Gerald thinks that she's shaking from sadness, not rage. "I have no idea what to do. I have nowhere to stay." Now her voice does wobble, and Gerald shakes his head, eyes full of empathy. He types something into the computer, then nods his head and looks up again.

"You're in luck. We had a cancellation, and so I have a garden-view room left just for you."

"Oh, thank you." She sags into the counter with relief. At least she has somewhere to stay. But can she really stay at the same resort as Matt and Abby?

"At our superior-value rate: four thousand dollars a night."

"A . . . night?" There's no chance she can afford to stay here—not even for a single night. Her heart sinks all the way to the toe straps of her gladiator sandals.

"Miss—I'm so sorry. You look a little ill. What an ordeal this is. Would you like some refreshing cucumber water?"

Gerald is being so nice, and his kind brown eyes are still wide with care and concern, and she *loves* cucumber water, but she sighs with despondence. "What I need is to get a taxi back to the airport and a flight out of here," Ivy says, sadly taking in the gorgeous surroundings. But Gerald shakes his head.

"There are no more flights from this island until tomorrow."

"Okay . . . then any good spots you can recommend to sleep on the beach? Or perhaps you have an empty broom closet I can curl up in?"

He laughs and shakes his head. "There are a lot of beach villas and houses for rent around here that are in a lower price range than this hotel. Why don't you go down to the beach bar, enjoy something stronger than cucumber water if you like, get something to eat—all on the house, please— and use the hotel Wi-Fi to find somewhere nearby to stay."

She feels almost overwhelmed by his kindness, and says so.

"I'm heartbroken for you," he says. "And besides, 'tis the season," he concludes.

"I have a feeling you're nice all year round, Gerald."

"Oliver at the beach bar makes a killer mai tai. It's just beyond the pool—look for the beautiful kiawe tree that offers the perfect shade while having a drink." He comes around the desk and wheels her suitcase away, saying over his shoulder, "I'll keep your luggage in my office, you just let me know when you need it. Good luck to you, Holly."

Keeping her hat pulled low and her head bowed, just in case she runs into Matt and Abby, Ivy hustles through the pool area toward the beach. The sun is close to setting now, the western sky warming to a golden pink—rose ocher mixed with geranium lake light, to be precise, but knowing the exact colors of the spectacular scenery just makes her heart ache. She reaches a charming tiki-style bar sheltered behind the sprawling branches of what is indeed a very beautiful kiawe tree. Its many branches point skyward in what looks like a celebratory dance. Ivy takes off her sandals and stands in the sand in front of the tree for a long moment, trying to memorize it. Then she turns and walks toward the tiki bar.

A bartender is serving an older couple. He catches her eye as he flips a martini shaker in the air and catches it, like he's Tom Cruise in *Cocktail*. Despite the bleakness of her situation, Ivy finds herself momentarily mesmerized. Of course the bartender at this ravishing resort, on this exquisite beach, beside this majestic tree, is gorgeous, right down to the shirt unbuttoned just that little bit extra, revealing a smooth, toned chest. He shoots her a smile, revealing a dimple on his left cheek—just one, because of course he has a dimple on one cheek only, turning his sexy smile crooked and disarming. He mouths *One sec*, and Ivy sits down, dragging her gaze away from him and sighing at the unfairness of it all. This place is absolutely lovely in every way. And she can't stay.

As she waits to be served, she tries to breathe in a sense of calm along with the fragrant sea air. But instead, she feels indignation rising inside her again. How dare Matt do this to Holly? How *could* he? Ivy's parents raised her to believe violence is never the answer, but right now she's imagining finding Matt, tackling him, and holding his head under an ocean wave *just long enough* to scare the shit out of him but not do any permanent damage. She shakes her head from side to side, trying to dispel these dark, dark thoughts. She has never been so angry with someone in her entire life.

"Hey." It's Hot Bartender, and the dimple is gone. "You look like you're having some dark, dark thoughts."

"Oh." Ivy is startled. She looks away from the ocean, and her distracted gaze collides with turquoise-blue eyes framed by the faintest of feathery smile lines. The bartender's dimple keeps disappearing and reappearing. His eyes are an immersive experience. "I'm fine," she manages.

"I can tell that's not true."

"I heard you make a good mai tai," she says, trying to smile convincingly, wishing she, too, had an endearing dimple to distract him with.

He tilts his head. "Hmm," he says.

"Hmm, *what?*"

He looks at her for a long moment, and Ivy feels her cheeks grow warm.

He rolls up his shirtsleeves now, revealing tanned, muscled forearms covered in a mist of golden hair. She tries not to look at his muscles, but lands back on his sea green eyes. No help. Lime, turquoise, and light blue blended gently with the tip of her finger would get them just right, if she were to draw him. Which, of course, she will not be doing.

He's still sizing her up.

"I've got it." He holds up a finger, turns, bends down—*I will not look at his ass, I will not look at his ass*—and rummages in a cupboard before bringing out a bottle with no paper label, and the words "Grand Rhum Hawaii" embossed on the glass. "This rum," he says, lowering his voice, which she feels rumble all the way down to the base of her pelvis, "was bottled in 1925. Almost a hundred years ago. It has seen earthquakes and floods. Forest fires." He sighs. "And it has survived. Which means *you* can survive the bad day you're having." He lifts a hand and taps a cocktail glass down from a row of them hanging over his head, catching it just before it smashes on the bar top. She tries to keep her expression impassive. "Come on, that was impressive."

She shrugs. "I've seen better." She definitely has not. "How do you know I'm having a bad day?"

"Trick of the trade," he says, filling the glass with ice, pouring in a generous shot of the rare dark rum, mixing it with white rum and fresh lime juice, pouring orange curaçao as the top layer. "Bartenders know things." He puts the cocktail on a mat and slides it toward her. "Try that out. It just might heal your broken heart."

Before she can reply, he moves off down the bar to serve two couples. Ivy takes a sip of the cocktail; it's delicious. She puts it down and calls up the VRBO app on her phone. But every villa apartment she clicks on is booked. "Damn it," she mutters. It's the Christmas holidays. She's never going to find a place to stay. She sips the drink again and puts down her phone to stare out to sea, feeling her heart sinking as low as the sun. The clouds on the horizon turn purple and orange as she watches, the sky around them darkening to dusky blue as the sun hits the water. "*Fuck*, it's gorgeous here."

"Isn't it?"

Hot Bartender is back. She lets out a morose sigh. At this point, not even that one dimple of his can raise her spirits. "So, you said this drink could help mend a broken heart. What makes you think I have a broken heart?"

"Again, trick of the trade. Bartenders know things. And you look like . . ." He bites his lip, narrows his eyes, sizes her up. "Someone who has just been left at the altar." She nearly spits out her drink.

"Come on, what is going on here? You can't just *know* that."

He laughs. "Okay, fine, Gerald called me from the front desk to tell me your situation and make sure I treated you well. Your ex-fiancé is here with another woman when he's supposed to be here with you? That's dark, Holly. That's terrible. It definitely requires the hundred-year-old rum."

"I actually don't deserve the expensive rum," Ivy says, sliding the drink back across the bar. She can't do this anymore. "It's my friend who does. I can't lie to you."

"What?"

"Since I'm leaving here anyway, you might as well know, I'm not really Holly Beech. She's my best friend. *She* got left at the altar, then gave me her honeymoon because she is the kindest person in the world and wanted me to spend two weeks here making art. But now her philandering fiancé and his new girlfriend are here. Staying in what was supposed to be *my* room. How could he do something so low?" She flops her head down on the bar top.

The bartender's dimple has not gone anywhere. If anything, it's just deeper now. "If it's not Holly, what is your name?"

"Ivy."

"Yeah, right. Holly and Ivy."

She lifts her head from the bar. "That's really my name, and my best friend is named Holly, and *yeah*, *yeah*, we have heard *all* the jokes about the stupid Christmas carol. You know who loves to make jokes about our names? Matt does. And then he sings the carol, and it gets stuck in my head, and I hate him even more."

"So you've always hated your best friend's fiancé, even before he turned into the philandering ex?"

"Okay, maybe I didn't hate him. But I always knew he wasn't good enough for Holly. She's the best person. Her one flaw was blindness when it came to Matt's true character. I kept thinking she knew something about him I didn't. But now . . ." She trails off. In the silence, there it is again, almost as if she's conjured him: Matt's voice.

"Hey, bartender!"

"*Shit.*"

Hot Bartender clocks her horrified expression and quickly pushes open the swinging half door leading behind the bar, whispering "Down there" out of the corner of his adorable mouth. Ivy ducks down and clambers behind the bar, pressing herself against a surfboard leaning there. Because of *course* Hot Bartender surfs. She can just picture him hanging ten, his washboard abs encased in a tight wetsuit, nothing about his perfect butt left to the imagination. And then, all at once, the backside she has just been picturing is directly at eye level, and even through slightly baggy khaki shorts, she can tell it's perfect. She can hear him speaking, above the bar top: "Sorry, man, we're out of fresh lime juice. Oh, that? No, that's gone off. Nah, we're out of white rum, too. Mai tais are off the menu for today. Sorry. Maybe try the pool bar?"

His upper leg brushes against her shoulder, his calf against her arm. She feels her hairs stand on end and moves away a few inches, shifts her focus. Through the small space between the little swinging door she's crouched behind and the bar, Ivy can see another kiawe tree down by the ocean. It's not as large and gnarled as the one that shelters the tiki bar, but from this angle she can see the way it's leaning toward the ocean like it wants to dip its arms in. She would so love to draw that. Suddenly, Ivy feels frustrated tears rising to her eyes.

"Ivy? They're gone." She straightens up as he points in the opposite direction of the beautiful tree. "They went that way." Then his voice grows soft. "Hey—are you okay?"

She blinks her eyes, fast. "I'm totally fine," she says, even though she isn't, at all.

"No, you're not. You have the look on your face people get when it's their last day here. And you've barely been here an hour." He runs a hand through his hair, messing it up endearingly. "It's just not fair."

She manages a wobbly smile. "At least I got to see Hawaii at all, right? And I'll come back. Someday. Plus, I got to hear you pretend to Matt that you didn't have any rum or lime juice left. That was pretty good."

"I'm not serving that jerk again if I can help it. Excuse me a sec." Another couple has approached the bar, quickly followed by a group of men in golf clothes. Ivy takes her seat and finishes her drink as she searches for flights on her phone. With any luck, there will be one that leaves first thing in the morning; she can sleep in a chair at the airport.

Hot Bartender returns and leans his forearms against the bar.

"I'm just looking for flights," she murmurs.

"This is not right," he says. "It's the holiday season, which to me means nice things are supposed to happen. That the good guys are supposed to win—not the shitty guys like Matt."

"Yeah, well, it's nice that there are guys out there like you, but sometimes shitty guys like Matt *do* win."

"No way." He shakes his head. "Not on my watch, Ivy. I think I have a solution to your problem."

4

HOLLY
December 18
Hudson Valley, New York

It's late afternoon by the time Holly arrives in Krimbo, a tiny town in New York State's Hudson Valley, after an hour and thirty-nine minutes of listening to Joni Mitchell's "River" on repeat and somehow *still* not shedding a single tear, even when she switched to "A Long December" by the Counting Crows.

It's a cloudless day, and the trees she drives past are covered in icing-thick layers of snow, the reflected light glittering off of them like sun pennies, but she barely notices the scenery. She turns off the stereo of the baby blue BMW E3 that used to belong to her nana and makes a left onto a snowy side road. For a moment, the wheels slip and slide, but she slows down and avoids the ditch as her GPS's chirpy, British-accented voice—she and Ivy have nicknamed her Chrysanthemum—directs her to the eco-cabin. Soon she's pulling up the driveway, navigating the car into a parking spot that has been cleared of snow in anticipation of her arrival—or, rather, Ivy's. A path toward the cabin has also been shoveled.

She turns off the car and takes it all in. The cabin is made of cedar, shaped like a sideways pizza wedge set on a snowy embankment. Each side is made of glass, and there are solar panels on the sloping roof. She gets out of the car and stands looking at it, her solitary retreat for two weeks. Behind the cabin, she can see rolling, snowy hills for miles, acres of trees covered in cottony-looking snow, the river a frozen, undulating line in the distance. She snaps a photo, and sends it to Ivy along with a message that sounds lighter than her heart feels: **Here safe! It's so cute—and the scenery! Gorgeous. xo.** She takes another photo of a snow-dressed evergreen and sends that to Ivy, too, before she pops the trunk of the BMW and lifts out her duffel and laptop bags. These, some winter gear, and enough food for a basic dinner are all she has brought with her. She'll drive into town for supplies in the morning.

She unlocks the door with the key code Ivy sent her and enters the cabin. Every square inch of the tiny space has purpose: the walls are lined with cushioned seating and bookcases, a compact woodstove is tucked into one corner, and pots and pans hang from the ceiling above a small kitchen island with cabinet storage. The cabin is constructed of rough wooden pillars and planks, with white walls. It smells pleasantly of cedar, and there's a faint whiff of an ambery musk in the air, like a really good-smelling candle, although she doesn't see any around.

At the back of the living area, there's a ladder, which Holly climbs. She pokes her head above the loft floor to find a rough-hewn wood-framed double bed with a thick ecru duvet piled high with pillows. Another ladder leaning against the wall beside the window has folded plaid blankets on the bottom two rungs, and fresh white towels and facecloths on the top two. Holly fully climbs up and walks into the room. Out the window beside the decorative ladder she can see evergreens iced with thick layers of snow. Beyond that are rolling hills, a frozen river, and clouds turning pink as the sun climbs down the sky.

She descends the ladder with fingers that are now numbing with cold. The cabin has a warm, cozy design—but the temperature is freezing. She stands in the middle of the living room, blowing on her hands, looking for a heat panel. She finds one, but nothing happens when she turns it on. She approaches the woodstove, firewood lined up on a shelf beside it, and a bucket of what looks like large wine corks on the floor in front, but no instructions anywhere.

She finds the cabin manual—the cover appears to be made of birch bark—on the log coffee table and flips it open:

"Welcome to your eco-friendly haven in the Hudson Valley! I'm your host, Aiden—and if you need anything at all, you can reach me here by phone or text."

She flips past pages about things to do in the area and reads that there's a solar generator that needs to be turned on outside, and that the woodstove is a hybrid that burns either firewood or wood pellets. The instructions for the woodstove are complex; maybe she can find some simpler instructions for this model on the internet. But when she flips through the book looking for a Wi-Fi password, she can't find one. And inside the cabin, her cell signal is too weak to pull up the website instructions for the woodstove.

It's starting to grow dim in the cabin, so Holly turns her attention to getting the solar generator running. She goes outside and uses her phone as a light, but although she follows Aiden's instructions, she still can't get the generator to start when she pulls the cord. She feels helpless frustration welling up inside her.

She thinks for a moment, then takes out her phone again. "Taking you up on that 'if you need anything at all, you can call or text me' offer, Aiden the eco-host," she says as she types, wondering if this new talking-to-herself thing is going to stick, now that she's alone.

Hi, it's Holly.

She deletes that and retypes her name as **Ivy**.

**Just arrived at your place on the North Service Road
but can't seem to figure out the generator or
woodstove. Any tips? Sorry to bother you!!**

Immediately, response dots appear on Holly's phone
screen.

**I thought when we emailed about the reservation you
said you were an old hand at going off-grid?**

Holly feels a tingle of irritation. Isn't she—or, rather, Ivy—
paying to stay here? Shouldn't Aiden the eco-host be more
polite to his guests? But the dots continue and a smiley face
emoji appears on the screen.

**Kidding. The system is a little complex. Just out in my
truck and five minutes away—probably easier if I stop
by and show you. Sound good?**

That would be great, thanks. Sorry to bother you.

Not bothered at all. See you in a few mins.

It's so cold in the cabin, Holly decides to wait outside and
at least be cold with good scenery. The cabin property is
perched high, and the tiny village she assumes is the nearby
Krimbo is visible below, its lights sprinkled in the valley

like scraps of glittering Christmas tree tinsel. The air is crisp and clear, and everywhere there is silence—so different from the hustle of the city, so peaceful.

So *lonely*. How does Ivy do this every year? Holly tries not to think about how much easier it would be, how much warmer, how much less it would involve a woodstove and a generator, if she were in Hawaii right now with Matt. Except Matt doesn't love her, she reminds herself—daring her insensate heart to finally feel this truth. The dull ache intensifies, but nothing really changes. That's probably a good thing, because in the tranquil silence, she hears the rumble of tires on the driveway. It would be beyond embarassing to have dissolved into long-awaited sobs just as the property manager arrived.

She walks down the embankment to meet a white pickup. The truck stops, but the lights stay on. A tall guy wearing a red Canada Goose parka, his dark hair peeking out from beneath his black toque, hops out of the cab. "Ivy?"

"Yes! That's me!" Holly says, trying to sound as convincing about her name as possible. It's hard to see him, backlit by his truck's headlights, but she can tell he's eyeing her BMW.

"That's your car?" he asks.

"No, it was here when I arrived."

He frowns as he approaches her.

"I was joking—*yes*, that's my car."

"I thought I mentioned it's better to have four-wheel drive on these roads."

In fact, Ivy had mentioned that, too, but when she was getting ready to leave the city, all Holly had wanted to do was get out of town, and to do it in the comfort of her nana's old car, one she was used to driving.

"It's fine," she says, trying to keep her voice confident and insouciant, the way she imagines Ivy's would be when meeting what she now sees is a handsome stranger. His eyes are an icy blue, and his jaw looks like it was chiseled with a set of tools. Ivy would probably be flirting already, trying to melt this guy down. But how to flirt? Holly can't remember the last time she did. Did she ever flirt with Matt, or did they just fall into the routine of their relationship?

"My car can handle anything," she says, and hopes that sounds at least somewhat lighthearted and fun. He steps closer, looking down at her, still frowning, obviously impervious to her clumsy attempt at being blithe. "Okay," he finally says, shaking his head slightly. "Let's see about the generator and stove." He gets a lantern out of the truck bed, turns it on, then leans into the cab and shuts off the truck's headlights. "Follow me?"

She tails him around the back of the cabin and holds the lantern for him. "Okay, so you just have to flip this switch and turn this dial and . . ." In about ten seconds, the generator rumbles to life.

"I guess I didn't read the instructions very closely."

"That's okay, it happens." Aiden checks his watch. Obviously, this tall, handsome version of Paul Bunyan has other places to be. "You also wanted help with the woodstove?"

"If you could, thanks. Sorry to be such a bother."

"No bother, this is why my number's in the book."

They step inside the cabin together, and he removes his snow boots, sets them on the thick mat. Even with his bulky footwear off, he's well over six feet tall, and broad-shouldered. He crosses the room, and she follows again, noticing how nice he smells. Like botanical soap, and cedarwood shavings, and ambery musk. *He* must be the reason it smells so pleasant in here. He's like a walking natural air freshener. "Okay, so as it says in the manual, this is what's called a hybrid stove. You can burn regular wood." He points at the split logs stacked on the built-in shelf taking up most of the wall by the stove. "You just do that in the usual way." He turns to her, and in the now well-lit cabin, she feels a jolt. Has she met him somewhere before? "There are some newspapers and kindling in this bin here." He taps a galvanized steel bin filled with the aforementioned items as the déjà vu fades somewhat. "But with the wood pellets, you feed them in here." He opens a little drawer at the back of the stove. "And then you ignite them with this lighter—it's rechargeable, electric, with a little switch right there—close the drawer and wait. They'll start up in just a few seconds, and as long as you're careful not to let it smolder too much, it's the cleanest burn you can get."

"That sounds simple enough." She follows his instructions, and the hybrid side of the stove lights easily.

"Did you have any other questions, Ivy?" He's looking down at her again, and the sense of familiarity is back.

"Um, I didn't see a shower?"

He turns away again, pointing to the back of the cabin. "There's a solar shower right around back, and it will work if you get an hour or two of sunlight during the day, but not otherwise. It's pretty . . . refreshing, I guess, is the best way to put it, this time of year. Is there anything else I can help you with?"

"Before you go, can you recommend the best place nearby for me to get groceries tomorrow? Food, bottled water, basics like that?"

Now he grimaces as if she's said a distasteful word. "You don't need to use bottled water here. There's a mountain spring that flows all year, and it's the best water you can drink. Sorry, I thought we'd messaged about this last week."

Holly feels chastened, embarassed. She's tired of him saying, *I thought we'd messaged about this.*

No, we did not, Aiden. We have never messaged about anything. "Of course," she says, trying to keep the confident smile on her face. "No bottled water. Promise. So . . . where's the spring?"

"First, this filter"—he points to a contraption on the counter that looks like a miniature industrial coffee maker—"is for the water. It's pure, but just to be on the safe side, I recommend my guests filter it. Or you can filter melted snow in that, too."

"Right. Of course. Melted snow."

It's as if he can read her mind, see that she is picturing going into town and buying a case of Aquafina so she doesn't have to melt snow or find the mountain spring out in the dark cold night. "Come on, I'll show you where the spring is," he says. The seriousness of his tone and the somber expression in his iceberg-blue eyes surprise her. And all at once, she knows who he reminds her of: Henry Cavill as Superman. Except this guy is *Eco* Superman.

She puts her snow boots back on and follows him outside again. He hands her his lantern, and his blue eyes catch hers for a moment. She feels that flash of recognition—*Henry Cavill, here to save the world, remember*—then lifts a large stainless steel bucket off the front deck of the cabin and heads off through the deep snow. Soon, she can hear the burbling sound of a spring, light and joyful—so at odds with the sad heaviness she's been carrying inside. Above them, stars are coming to life in the navy blue sky, twinkling like distant Christmas tree lights.

"There we go," he says after the bucket is filled. "That should do it." He carries the water bucket back to the cabin as if it weighs nothing. He didn't put his parka back on, and she can't help but admire the muscles she can see rippling, even underneath his thick flannel shirt. Inside again, he pours the bucket of mountain spring water into the filter, then turns to her and finally smiles. "This is the best water you'll ever taste in your life, I swear," he says, his blue eyes now bright with excitement, all guardedness gone. She finds his enthusiasm somewhat contagious, even if the amount of work required to get water is daunting.

"I can't wait for my first sip," she finds herself saying, stepping closer to him, breathing in his appealing, amber-musk scent.

"You won't ever want to drink anything else."

As he turns to check something on the filter unit, Holly takes out her phone and sends a quick text to Ivy. **Hey, you didn't mention you rented a cabin from Eco Superman. He looks EXACTLY like Henry Cavill.** If she didn't know that Ivy made it a practice never to have any romantic dalliances during her art vacations, she would have thought her friend planned this. **AND he smells really good.** Holly finds herself stepping closer and inhaling deeply again.

"You okay?"

"*Oh.*" Her eyes snap open. Aiden has stopped fiddling with the filter and has turned back in her direction, catching her mid-inhale, eyes closed. "Yes. I'm just . . . so excited about the water. And all this fresh . . . air." The duck-quacking sound Ivy set her contact card to is going off repeatedly in her hand now, and Ivy's name appears, with the line **Well, you know what they say about getting over one man, right?**—then an eggplant emoji. Holly puts her phone face down on the counter with a clatter. "I think I'm just hungry," she says.

"Okay then. Any other questions?"

"No, I think that's it. Thanks for coming out here, Aiden."

"Sure thing, Ivy. Just text if you need anything more." He gives her a long, searching look before turning toward the door—but then he turns around again. "Can I ask you something? I'm sorry if this sounds weird—"

"I *promise*, no bottled water. Girl Scout's honor," she says, even though she was never a Girl Scout and has no idea where that came from.

"You really look familiar. I know the contract says your name is Ivy Casey, but you look so much like someone I used to go to school with. I wonder if you're related or something. You don't know someone named Holly Beech, do you?"

Holly thinks about just shrugging it off as a coincidence and continuing to pretend to be Ivy, but as she looks into his earnest blue eyes, she finds herself thinking there must be a special place in hell for someone who lies to Eco Superman.

"Aiden, I have to tell you something. I'm not really Ivy. She's my best friend, and we swapped holiday trips this year because . . ." Holly now experiences a heartache so sharp she puts her hand to her chest for a moment, wondering if she might need medical attention. But it passes, leaving behind the dull, empty ache that is becoming a familiar companion.

"Because?" Aiden prompts, looking concerned.

Holly's heart lurches into action again. She thinks fast. "This was a Christmas gift," she manages. "A surprise from my best friend. I'm . . . super into . . . eco-cabining, and Ivy knew that, so she booked this for me but then forgot to make the switch of our names after she gave me the gift. Sorry about that." She is so bad at lying and tries to rein in the details. "Work has been really hectic for me, and I needed to go off-grid and decompress. But yes, to answer your question properly, yes. I am Holly Beech."

As he steps closer, she searches her memory for an Aiden she might have known once—and, under his still-intense gaze, feels as warm as if a fire had already been burning in the cabin's stove for hours.

"Holly," he repeats, stepping closer. All at once, she feels the empty cavern of her heart spring to life again. "Dalton School, class of '13."

She watches, mesmerized, as he removes a pair of glasses from the pocket of his flannel shirt. When he puts them on, he's made the transition from Eco Superman to Eco Clark Kent—and, just like in the movies, she recognizes him immediately.

"Aiden! Aiden *Coleman*! It's been . . . forever. You've *changed*." *You got disconcertingly hot.* The Aiden she remembers from high school was tall, but scrawny and bespectacled. This version of Aiden is anything but, even with the glasses back on. His shoulders are football-linebacker broad, his jaw sexy and square. He looks like a model in a catalog for winter camping gear.

"Just reading glasses now," he says. "I got laser eye surgery a while ago. And you . . ." She wonders what he's thinking as he continues to stare at her, his expression a mix of surprise and something else she can't parse. "I can't believe it's you" is all he says.

"I can't believe it's you, either." Now that the shock is wearing off, she feels something else: curiosity. Back in high school, Aiden was her academic rival. He disappeared, didn't come to grad, and she never saw him again. But she had always wondered what became of him.

"I can tell what you're thinking," he says, biting his lip and grinning. "And no way, I am *not* telling you my SAT score."

"Come *on*! I heard someone got higher than me, and I figured it was you!"

He crosses his arms over his firm, broad chest. "My SAT scores are my business and my business alone." But he smiles when he says this, and then adds, his voice full of shy pride, "I did get a full scholarship to MIT, though."

She laughs at his humblebrag. "I'm not surprised." They hadn't traveled in the same social circles, but the Aiden Coleman she remembered had been brainy and driven. If she won the academic medal for highest average in the school, he would get it the next year. She got the Outstanding Student Award, but he got the Principal's Award. Back then, she'd half expected she would see his name as the CEO of some high-tech start-up someday, but he vanished from her view, and her thoughts. Until today.

"I've tamped down the competitiveness over the years, so it's fine, you don't have to tell me your score."

"Really?" he teases.

"Was I that bad?"

But she knows she was. Which is why she had to put a stop to it. When Holly reached college, she was tired of constantly comparing herself to others, exhausted from the pressure she was putting on herself to excel. When she met Matt, she was happy to simply keep up with him—which was certainly easier than keeping up with someone as smart as Aiden Coleman had been, for example. But now she admits something uncomfortable to herself: Perhaps she stopped trying so hard so *Matt* could shine. Maybe she was trying to turn him into the man she wanted him to be by shining a little less brightly. The aching pain in her chest is returning; she pushes the thoughts of Matt away—but Aiden is now regarding her with concern.

"You weren't bad at all, Holly," he says, his expression turning earnest. "You were amazing. Smart, kind, interesting..." He trails off, as if there's more he wants to add, but doesn't. "I really admired you." There's something familiar in his words, but the sensation is fleeting and then slips away from her.

"Thanks," she says, with a grateful smile that belies the ache still pressing against her chest. "So . . . what have you been up to all these years, Aiden? With a full scholarship to MIT, surely you must have done some amazing things."

He looks away. "A little of this and that," he says, his tone evasive now. "How about you?"

"I'm in corporate law. Mostly patents. Budgell, Hall, Jansen and Jones."

"Right. The job you're here trying to decompress from."

"It's intense," Holly says—and her junior lawyer job *is* busy and at times all-consuming, but that's not what she's here to get away from. She feels a small spasm of guilt from all the lies she's told Aiden so far. In the awkward silence that follows, she misses the sense of comfort she just felt with him—and the memory of the person she once was.

He glances at his watch, and his expression now fills with regret. "I have to run. There's a dinner I need to get to in town." He takes off his glasses and slips them back into his pocket, and she finds herself struck again by the clear blueness of his eyes. "Do you mind if I bring a new contract for you to sign tomorrow? I think technically there might be an insurance issue if there's someone else staying in the cabin other than the person who booked it and signed the original contract."

"Oh. Right. Of *course*. I'm so sorry. I'm a lawyer, I should have thought of that," she says, slightly embarrassed.

"It's no big deal, truly." He walks to the door and pulls on his winter boots. "Around nine o'clock tomorrow morning okay for me to stop by?"

"Perfect. Great to see you," she says.

"You, too, Holly."

She stands at the window and watches his taillights retreat down the snow-banked driveway, then disappear into the starlit winter night, still trying to reconcile the handsome, broad-shouldered, *great*-smelling adult male with the gangly, bespectacled teenage boy she went to high school with. He has changed so much. And so has she. But she knows they both contain shadows of the people they were, that those high school kids were the seeds for the adults they now are. She feels a surge of nostalgia. It felt nice, for a few minutes, to forget about the present and get lost in the past.

She retreats from the window into the kitchen, where she opens up the bagged salad she brought along for dinner and pours the salad dressing directly inside—feeling a flash of guilt at what Aiden would say about the single-use plastic bag. She pushes the guilt aside and sits down on the couch, wrapping herself in a soft, cozy blanket as the cabin fills with warmth from the stove. She'll get some proper food tomorrow—no single-use plastic, she promises herself, as if Aiden were still there in the room.

Her phone quacks again.

Hey! You okay? Still getting friendly with Eco Superman?

Turns out he's Eco Clark Kent! We know each other from high school, but I didn't realize that until he put his glasses on.

Uh-oh, does that mean the rental swap jig is up?

Yes. It's fine, he's coming by with a new contract for me to sign tomorrow.

What are the odds? Ivy texts.

It really is a crazy coincidence.

Sort of a romantic one?

Ha ha ha, but I have anything but romance on my mind right now.

So, you're doing okay?

As okay as I can be. Please don't worry about me. What's it like there?

Dots disappear, then reappear. Finally, Ivy types: **It's great!**

Enjoy yourself, make beautiful art, and let ME text if I need you, okay?

There's a long pause. Dots reappear and dissapear, and then Ivy finally texts, **Okay. Love you.**

Love you. Going to watch a movie and then bed.

How about "Can't Buy Me Love" in honor of the now-hot Aiden?

Holly smiles. **I only downloaded sad Christmas movies. I'm trying to make myself finally cry. Going to start with "Meet Me In St. Louis."**

Ivy responds with a row of weeping emojis. **Text me for moral support when you get to the part where Judy Garland sings "Have Yourself A Merry Little Christmas" in the SADDEST WAY POSSIBLE. Night.**

Holly puts down her phone and starts the movie on her laptop—but even when Judy Garland mournfully labors over every syllable of an already emotion-filled Christmas song, she remains dry-eyed. When the movie is over, she brushes her teeth, turns out the lights, and climbs up the loft to bed. Tidal waves of stars are visible through the skylight. She counts them slowly, one by one, before finally falling asleep.

5

IVY
December 18
Kauai, Hawaii

Ivy gazes into the resort bartender's arresting ocean-hued eyes as he repeats that he's found the perfect solution to her problem of having no place to stay in Hawaii.

"There's a beach house just around the corner from here, a ten-minute walk that way. I rent there when I'm here in Kauai, and I happen to know one of the rentals fell through just this morning. Meaning there's a vacan reasonably priced apartment right on the beach, and I'm sure Larry, who owns it, would be thrilled for you to use it." He sends a text, and his phone *bings* a response straightaway. He sends one more, then looks up at Ivy. "Two hundred a night sound okay?"

"But . . ." Ivy shakes her head. "I can't just go stay at some random beach house with two guys. I don't even know your name."

"It's Oliver." The one-dimple smile is back. "And Larry's a woman," he says with a laugh. "It's short for Larisa."

She tilts her head. "Why are you being so nice to me?"

"Because I'm *nice*. And you seem nice. And because, like I said, Matt seems like the ultimate dickbag." He holds up his phone. "You can chat with Larry yourself, see how you feel after that?"

She accepts his phone and chats for a few minutes with Larry, who has a warm voice, lightly laced with a Mexican accent, and insists she'd be delighted to have Ivy rent the now vacant apartment in her villa. Ivy hangs up and hands the phone back to Oliver.

"So, it's sorted?"

She hesitates, but only for a second. "I'm really grateful," she says.

"Honestly, it's what anyone would do. My shift is over in half an hour, and then I'll walk you down the beach and show you your new accomodations, okay?"

He serves a pair of women as she turns to watch the final glimmers of her first Hawaiian sunset disappear over the lip of the horizon. The constellations begin to wink on, one by one, above the bar and the kiawe trees—like Christmas stars that have lost their way and found themselves suspended above a tiny island in the middle of the Pacific. Ivy takes out her phone and snaps a few pictures, and feels her heart filling with joy. She doesn't have to go home. She gets to stay here and draw this gorgeous scenery. At least one thing feels right in her world.

"Oliver, this *place*," Ivy says. Even at night, she can see how charming her surroundings are: There are steps leading down from the villa's deck into a grassy little garden bordered by palm trees, then a solar-light-lined path to a beach with sand lit up by moonlight, showing itself to be the color of fresh-cut straw. The beach house is tucked into a bay at the foot of gently hulking mountains, which are clad head to toe in green velvet, like they're getting ready to go to a Christmas party. There's a hammock on one side of the deck, a small wooden table and chairs on the other. The deck is the perfect size for her to sit and draw.

"And you haven't even seen inside yet, come on," Oliver says, beckoning her forward.

The apartment is airy and open-concept. Ivy spins slowly to take it all in: There's a small kitchen at the back with a view of another tree-filled garden, and a trail that leads out to the road; the board-and-batten walls are painted seaglass green; a slatted wooden bed covered in white linen sits invitingly beside the biggest window; there are a few simple rattan rugs on the floor; a small gallery of framed photographs, all striking water and ocean-wave close-ups, decorate one wall; a coral-patterned fan quilt hangs on another. Salty, tangy air flows in through the windows at the front, and a floral-scented breeze drifts in from the back. "This place is like a dream. This is really kind of you, Oliver. And Larry."

"I'm glad you like it. But I feel bad—it's Christmastime, and there are no decorations in here."

Ivy shrugs. "Christmas is just okay," she says. "No need to find me any decorations."

He does a double take. "Just *okay*?"

"I'm kind of ambivalent about Christmas." She shrugs, and he looks amused.

"What exactly is it you think is 'just okay' about Christmastime?" he asks, then starts listing items off on his fingers. "The heartwarming music? The atmosphere of giving? The great food? The surprise gifts? The look of wonder on children's faces?"

"I think it's pretty clear where *you* stand on Christmas," she says with a laugh. "My parents are very anti-capitalist, to say the least. And say what you want about Christmas—it *is* a capitalist's dream."

"Well, bah, humbug, Ivy," Oliver says, but he's still smiling as if nothing can dampen his festive joy. Then he snaps his fingers. "I've got something that will get you into the spirit, guaranteed." He tilts his head and his sea green eyes twinkle even more. "Hey, Alexa, please play 'Mele Kaliki-maka.'" The speaker at the side of the kitchen counter lights up, and the upbeat Bing Crosby and Andrews Sisters carol starts playing.

"Who doesn't love this song? Come on!" He sings along, even hitting all the Andrews Sisters' high notes as he dances, joyful and completely unselfconscious. His shirt lifts, and she catches a glimpse of his flat stomach, the golden trail of hair on his firm abdomen. There's no question about it: Oliver is very hot. But she's not here for a fling, she reminds herself. Her art trips are *never* about flings—and she especially cannot squander this one, which has been given to her by her heartbroken best friend.

She grits her teeth as he continues his silly dance, willing her attraction away.

"Okay, okay, I can tell by the expression on your face it's not working for you. What music *do* you like, then?"

"Hey, Alexa," Ivy says. "Play . . . Leon Bridges." As the funky opening beat of the song "Steam" flows from the speakers, Oliver nods along.

"Not exactly festive, not as *stone-cold hip* as Bing, and certainly not as hype as the Andrews Sisters, but pretty good background music for the rest of the tour of the apartment."

"'Hype'?" she says with a laugh. "Do people actually call things 'hype' anymore? 'Stone-cold *hip*'?"

"*I* do." Their gazes snag and she feels caught for a moment, but then he turns to tell her about the cooling unit.

"Hello?" a female voice trills. "Knock, knock!" A tall, beautiful woman with long, honey-highlighted brown hair is standing by the sliding door.

"Larry!" Oliver calls out as she slides it open.

"Hi, honey." She enters the space on a cloud of tantalizing floral musk, kisses his cheek, then turns to Ivy, beaming. "And you must be Ivy, our new tenant for two weeks."

Aha. Of course. Hot Bartender Oliver is not single. He has a leggy, gorgeous, sparkly-eyed girlfriend, who is currently holding out a paper bag of groceries to Ivy.

"Some coffee, fruit, and buns for morning."

Ivy takes the bag from her. "Thank you so much. For all this kindness, for letting me stay here. I appreciate it a lot."

"Well, what else was I going to do?" Her hot-chocolate-colored eyes are wide. "Ollie told me about your situation. Left at the altar, and then your ex-fiancé shows up on your honeymoon with another woman?"

Ivy's cheeks begin to color. "Oh, um, that's not actually me—"

"I'm *kidding*. I'm sorry. He told me everything—how you're not actually Holly, you're her best friend. And she gave you her honeymoon, but her knobhead of an ex stole it out from under you." Larry looks like Eva Mendes, right down to the sexy beauty mark on her cheek—making her the perfect match for Ryan Gosling–look-alike Oliver, of course. "What a story, though. You must be livid on behalf of your friend. I told Ollie he should put hot sauce in his drink next time.

Or . . . ever hear of the melted-straw trick? I did that once to a bunch of rude frat boys in my bar. Rude frat boys are *the worst*."

"The worst," Ivy agrees. "Matt, my friend's ex, is a frat guy."

"Of course he is."

Oliver laughs and looks affecionately down at Larry, who leans her head against his shoulder. "Don't worry, Lar, I plan to mess with him as much as possible."

"I hope so, Ollie."

All at once, Ivy can't stifle a yawn. "We're intruding and keeping you up!" Larry says. "We should leave you to get settled. Before you know it, the roosters will be crowing and waking you up."

"Roosters?"

"Out on the beach. You get used to them," Larry says.

"Not a bad alarm clock, honestly," Oliver adds. "I like to get out on the ocean as early as I can, though, so I count on those roosters to get me out of bed. Okay, so the key is on the table . . ."

"And we're just downstairs," Larry finishes. "If you ever need anything, one or both of us are here for you. The bar I own is in Hanalei, a fifteen-minute walk. Come by for a drink tomorrow evening? It's called the Black Pearl."

"Okay, I will. And this place really is great. You two are the nicest."

"I'd make a reference to it being the season of giving and

all, but apparently that's a sore spot for you." Oliver shoots her a final lopsided, one-dimple grin and runs a hand through his already tousled dark-blond hair, making it even messier—until Larry reaches up and smoothes it for him.

"See you tomorrow, Ivy. Sweet dreams," she says on their way out the door.

Then they're both gone, and Ivy stands still for a moment, letting it all sink in. She doesn't have to leave Hawaii. She has a place to stay—a great place. Hot Bartender Oliver has an equally hot girlfriend—and that's not a bad thing, either. She'd have to be dead inside not to be attracted to him, and she can't spare the time or emotional energy for that.

After a fast, restorative shower, Ivy wraps herself in the fluffy white towels she finds in the bathroom and climbs into a bed with sheets that smell like they were dried on a line beside a hibiscus bush. She pulls out her phone and reads over her text exchange with Holly from earlier. When her friend had asked what the hotel was like, Ivy froze. How was she supposed to answer without lying to her best friend? She had finally typed a simple **It's great**, but knew that only told half the story. Holly doesn't even know she's not staying at the hotel now, and how is Ivy supposed to tell her that without also telling her friend the truth about Matt—which is sure to crush Holly even more?

Ivy flops back against her pillow and groans, letting her phone drop to the floor. How could Matt do this to Holly—and, in turn, to *her*? Because this is the worst feeling. Ivy has never lied to Holly; it was a promise they made to each other the first night they met, at the Christmas keg party almost a decade ago. And now she's breaking that promise against her will—and it's sure to get worse as the two weeks go on.

"Damn you, Matt." Ivy flops back and forth on the bed, struggling to calm herself, to settle into the assured embrace of the mattress. In the moonlight now flowing through the window, the cluster of ocean photographs on the wall across from the bed are gently illuminated. She finds that looking at them calms her, helps her to become more aware of her surroundings. The frenetic pace of her heart slows.

She can hear the sound of the ocean waves outside her window, smell the salty tang in the gentle breeze. There's the low rumble of a voice downstairs—Oliver's—and then the soft sound of laughter—Larry's—in answer.

This is a good place, Ivy tells herself. *I can't fix the Holly-and-Matt situation right now, so I might as well try to enjoy it as much as I can.*

6

HOLLY
December 19
Hudson Valley, New York

Holly is dreaming that a woodpecker is tapping on her frozen heart, attempting to crack it open. *Tap, tap, tap.* Her heart is a block of ice. *Tappity, tap, tap.* "It's no use," she says to the woodpecker. "Just give up. It's too frozen." Still, the tapping continues until eventually Holly realizes it's not a dream—the knocking noise is real. What's also real is the freezing cold. She's under a pile of duvets, and she still can't feel her toes.

Tap, tap, tap.

"Holly! Are you in there? Everything okay?"

Oh, *crap.* Holly hops out of bed and sees from her vantage point in the sleeping loft that Aiden is standing on the snow-covered front deck, in the morning sunlight filtering through the evergreens. She checks her watch: 9:15. She overslept, and now Aiden is here with the new rental contract.

"Sorry!" she calls out, hopping on one foot, then the other, as she pulls on her socks. "Be right there!" She finds a scrunchie and pulls her hair into what she hopes is an artfully messy bun, but has a feeling is just chaotic-looking, then climbs down the ladder.

It's only when she's nearly at the door that she remembers which pajamas she pulled on in the darkness the night before: A gift from Ivy for Holly's most recent birthday, they're printed with photos of a young Holly in various poses with her childhood cat. There's eight-year-old Holly and Mr. Snuggles dressed as twin pumpkins for Halloween. Holly grinning with braces, holding Mr. Snuggles over her head like he's Simba from *The Lion King*. Holly and Mr. Snuggles during their "adventure cat" phase, taking backpacked walks along the Brooklyn Bridge or at Coney Island.

"Good morning!" she says brightly, hoping to draw attention away from the pajamas. Luckily, the temperature inside does that instead.

"It's just as cold in here as it is outside," Aiden says as he steps through the door. "What happened with the woodstove?"

"Oh . . . I guess I slept so late it went out."

"You might want to use the main fireplace and then add the pellets after for long-term burning when the weather is like this. I should have mentioned that last night."

"I've got it. Just a sec." Holly clumsily works at relighting the fire, determined to prove she is still the capable, high-achieving girl he met in high school.

"A little kindling and some crumpled newspapers will probably help," he finally ventures.

"Kindling. Right." There's a box beside the stove filled with twigs. She reaches for a handful of it and throws them into the woodstove's maw. There's another little box filled with newspapers, so she starts crumpling up sheets and stuffing them in.

"That should be enough," Aiden says eventually. She holds the lighter to the pile until some of the newspaper catches, then the kindling. Moments later, the woodstove is ablaze, and she lets out a little cheer.

"Second time I've ever done that," she says—and sees him frown. "Aiden, I have to admit something to you. I have never stayed in an off-grid cabin or lit a fire in my life."

He smiles now, still looking bemused. "So I was gathering. I love seeing someone so happy to get a fire going, though."

"A true accomplishment for me. If we were still in high school, I probably would have tried to turn hybrid stove lighting into some kind of competition. You were very kind yesterday, but I was a little . . . intense as a teenager."

He's looking at her closely. "I didn't see you that way," he finally says. "However," he continues, "the Holly Beech I knew in high school didn't really seem like the roughing-it type."

"And she still isn't. But I won't be a burden to you while I'm here. I promise. Now that I've figured out how to light a fire, I'm pretty much set. I don't really plan to do much for the next couple of weeks except . . ." *Wallow. Attempt to cry.* "Not much."

Now he tilts his head, quizzical. "But it's the holidays."

"I know it seems unorthodox to be spending the holidays alone, but I . . ." *I was supposed to get married a few days ago, and be spending my honeymoon in Hawaii right now. Except the night before our wedding, my fiancé dumped me for another woman named Abby, and if I can stop myself from googling her today, I'm going to reward myself with a pint of Ben & Jerry's Netflix & Chill'd.* ". . . am a Grinch," she concludes. This is not exactly true, but she can't confide in him about her sorry situation. "Christmas is just *meh*. I'm fine being on my own."

"Does a person who thinks Christmas is just *meh* dress her cat up as Buddy the Elf and herself as Jovie?"

Her cheeks blaze. She'd almost forgotten about the embarassing pajamas. "I was *nine*," she says.

Aiden takes a step back so he can look at all the pictures, while Holly wishes she could slide through one of the tiny gaps in the wooden floorboards. "Is that Mr. Snuggles?"

"How did you know that was his name?"

"I'm pretty sure everyone at our school knew your cat's name. Your junior-year science fair project?"

"Right." For the project, Holly had created a series of multicolored buttons on an electrically powered mat; each one played the sound of Holly's voice naming a different emotion, need, or desire when Mr. Snuggles pressed it. After months of training, she was quite confident she had successfully tapped into her cat's deepest thoughts and emotions. In front of the entire school, in the auditorium, Mr. Snuggles had hit the buttons for "I'm bored" and "I'm hungry" before sounding the "I'm getting angry" button ten times in a row, then hissing at the principal. Still, despite the drama, she'd won the gold medal for what the science fair judges called "potentially pioneering research into the inner lives of animals."

"Sadly, he died a few years ago—but Mr. Snuggles lives on in these pajamas, which were a gift."

As Aiden's eyes roam up and down her pajamas, Holly feels her cheeks flush deeper and her heart rate accelerates. Is she ever going to get used to the fact that Aiden Coleman had a serious glow-up? To cover her nervousness, she keeps talking. "When Mr. Snuggles died—he was eighteen—Ivy and I took a road trip to spread his ashes on Cape Cod because I thought he would be happiest living out his eternal life with access to so much fresh fish. That's my best friend—the one who originally rented this place from you."

He looks up. "Right. Speaking of which, let me just have you sign this new contract and I'll get out of your hair."

"You're not in my hair!" Self-consciously, she raises a hand to her messy bun. "I mean, *something* might be in there, a bird's nest, maybe. But you can come by anytime." She fans her hot face as subtly as possible while he fishes a pen out of the pocket of a soft-looking flannel under his jacket, then hands her the contract.

Holly walks over to the breakfast bar and places it down to read it quickly—the lawyer in her won't let her sign anything without reading it first, even those incredibly long privacy updates for cell phones and social media accounts. Eventually, she signs on the dotted line. "There we go," she says, handing the contract back to him. "All sorted. Again, I'm sorry we didn't tell you it was going to be me here and not Ivy."

"It's no trouble, really. It's been nice to see you again after all these years."

"It has been." As he starts toward the door, she calls out. "Wait—you said last night there's a grocery store in Krimbo, right? Is it open on Sunday?"

He frowns. "There's a grocery store in town, but it snowed all night and is still snowing now."

She gazes out the window. "You're right. It's so pretty out there."

He shakes his head. "I noticed you don't have winter tires on your car. I don't think driving in this weather is the best idea."

"I really need groceries," Holly says. "I'm sure I'll manage."

"There's a bridge heading into town that gets icy when the weather's like this. I can't let you go out there in that car in this weather. I'll take you in my truck, okay?" He glances at his watch. "I have an errand to run out here first. It won't take too long."

He shrugs on his jacket and stands waiting, and she realizes he thinks they're going to leave right then.

"I'm not quite sure I'm ready to debut my sleepwear to an entire town, even a small one," she ventures.

"Oh, right." He laughs. "You need to change. I'll wait in the truck."

Upstairs in the loft, Holly ducks down as she changes quickly into yoga pants and a gray-and-white Fair Isle sweater, feeling a small flare of irritation. Surely it's not that bad out. Couldn't she drive herself? She steps over to the mirror and attempts to tame her morning hair, finds mint gum in her purse to deal with her morning breath, and tells herself that will have to do. The pulled-together, ultra-competitive, brainy girl he met in high school doesn't seem to exist anymore anyway—and no amount of lying about her current circumstances is going to change that. Holly draws a shaky breath and shoves another piece of mint gum in her mouth for good measure. Then she pulls on her snow boots and parka and heads out across the satisfyingly crunchy snow to Aiden's truck—but just as she approaches, he opens his window.

"There are reusable shopping bags in a basket by the door," he calls out. "So you don't have to get plastic at the store."

Holly retrieves the reusable bags from the cabin and takes out her phone, quickly texting Ivy, her fingers flying across the screen. **Not that it was on the table anyway, but there will be no fling with Eco Superman**, she types. **Because: 1. This morning he saw me in my Mr. Snuggles pajamas, and not because he slept over. 2. He is the Tracy Flick of environmentalism, not to mention road safety. A bit annoying.**

She puts her phone away and gets in the truck. For a while, the only sounds as he drives are his wheels on the snowy road and the *shush* of his windshield wipers doing their job against the falling flakes. "This truck is so quiet," she finally ventures into the silence.

He glances at her. "That's because it's electric."

After another few minutes, she tries to make conversation again. "Wow, it really is coming down out there."

Aiden glances over, and it's almost as if he's forgotten

she's there. "This is just a regular day around here, which is why it's good to have a truck."

It happens so suddenly it surprises even her. "Look, I didn't plan this out!" she explodes, all the pent-up emotion she brought here from the city bubbling forth like the mountain spring Aiden showed her the night before. "I don't have a car with snow tires! I didn't bring any food! I *always* forget my reusable shopping bags when I go grocery shopping, and I didn't know what a hybrid woodstove even was until yesterday. I would love a case of bottled water because I'm pretty sure I won't be able to get water from a stream without falling in. I don't know what I'm doing! I'm not the smart girl you used to know in high school! But people change, okay?"

He doesn't say anything in response to her outburst, which makes the fact that it happened at all feel ten times more mortifying. Holly runs her hands over her face and swallows hard, blinking away the tears that have sprung to her eyes. She feels awful. But she's also aware that something amazing just happened. For the first time since Matt told her the wedding was off and she realized that the happy ending she'd been marching toward for the past ten years of her life was nothing but a mirage, Holly experienced something other than a dull, aching chasm of nothing. She *felt*.

"I'm sorry, Aiden," she says. "I'm going through a hard time right now. That wasn't fair."

He's silent for another long moment, and she worries he's

going to pull over and tell her to get out of his truck. "Actually, it *was* fair," he finally says. "You already told me you were going through some stuff and needed a quiet getaway. You're on your own during the holidays, and that can't be all that easy, but I pressed you on it when it was none of my business. I can be a little . . . blunt, sometimes." Now there's something in his tone that makes Holly wonder what *his* stuff is. She has her head so firmly buried in her own problems—but Aiden has a life, too. And no one's life is perfect. "I didn't mean to make you feel bad about anything. I guess I've spent a lot of time on my own, doing things my way."

They're pulling down a residential driveway now. It winds and meanders through dense rows of evergreens, which shed feather-like flakes of snow in the gentle wind that rustles through their branches. Aiden stops talking and negotiates a particularly sharp turn in the driveway while Holly takes in this startlingly magical new setting. Moments before, they were on a rural road, but now it feels like she's entered another world—a world out of one of the fairy tales she read as a child. The truck is approaching an old Victorian house that looks like it has been decorated with thick icing rather than snow. It's tucked into a backdrop of snowy hillsides and more towering pines that look like they're wearing cozy white fleece jackets. The brick of the home is a soft yellow-gray shade, the gingerbread trim and wraparound porch a vibrant red. It all looks straight out of a Trisha Romance painting. Holly reads a faded and peeling yellow-and-green-painted sign just beyond the house: "Plaskett's Christmas Tree Farm."

"But all the trees here are huge," Holly says, the intense moment with Aiden all but forgotten now. "Is this a Christmas tree farm for giants?"

"It's not exactly operational anymore. Carole Plaskett died a decade ago, and George kept it all going as best he could, but he's pushing ninety now—though you'd hardly know it, he's doing great. The town uses his trees for all the events we can manage where larger ones can work, in the town square, for example, but mostly this place is just a forest now."

"A Christmas tree forest," Holly breathes. "How *magical*."

Aiden is smiling. "Everyone in town agrees with you on that, which is why we all do what we can to help George stay out here, where he's happy. We've had a few town meetings about it, and everyone is unanimous that he should stay in the house as long as he can—in part because care homes don't let in cats, and his cat, Mrs. Claws, is the other love of his life, since Mrs. Plaskett died. So we've basically divided up his care. He has a trusted live-in personal support worker—Drew Winchester, from town—and then we also make sure he gets at least one visitor per day. We've got a rotation going. Which makes it sound like work, and it isn't. We all love George."

"You have town meetings about how to take care of someone? That's really sweet, Aiden."

"It's just what the town is like."

He shuts off the engine and turns to her. "Holly, before we go in, I want to finish the conversation we were just having. We're adults now, not kids, and life has happened to both of us. In many ways we aren't the same people—but for the record, I still feel sure you're the smartest woman I've ever met. I'm sorry if I did or said anything yesterday or today to make you feel otherwise."

His words catch her off guard. But he doesn't appear to need or want her to respond, even if she could think of something to say. With that off his chest, he reaches into the back seat and pulls out a small doctor's bag while she feels a sensation that is growing familiar: that of her heart being slowly but steadily warmed by his presence. "Okay, let's go. George will be happy to meet you. He always loves guests."

"Why the doctor's bag?"

"Recently, Mrs. Claws developed a kidney issue. Every three days, she needs what I can only describe as a form of cat dialysis. I'm not sure how that job fell to me." He shrugs. "So . . . that's what I'm here to do."

"You're here to give an elderly man's cat dialysis?"

"Yes."

"And the entire town has meetings about how best to care for this man and keep him in his home?"

"Yes."

"And you use an actual little mini doctor's bag for this task?"

Now he looks embarassed. "I know it seems silly, but George gave me the bag, so I use it."

They walk up to the house, and Aiden rings the bell, waits a moment, then opens the door. It gives a soft creak. Inside, the place is bright and homey. It smells like cinnamon and cloves, cedar and pine. Woodsmoke. There's a Christmas tree in every room, and each is decorated with old-fashioned ornaments, tin soldiers, dancing *Nutcracker* ballerinas, hand-sewn snowmen, strings of cranberries and popcorn, dried orange slices, little clementines studded with cloves tucked onto the branches.

"It smells *so* good in here," Holly says. "Just like Christmas is supposed to smell."

Aiden smiles as he leans down to take off his boots. "Yeah. This place really *is* Christmas, to all of us in town. I guess that's why we work so hard to make it a good place for George to keep living in. We do it for him—but we do it for us, too." He pauses, thinks. "We all know he can't live here forever, but it means something, to the entire town, to try to keep him here."

"Aiden, my boy, is that you?"

There's a creaking on the stairs and a man comes into view. His hair is pure white, his eyes a bright, twinkling gray-blue, his face an inviting map of storytelling wrinkles, his body slightly stooped from the years he has carried. His movements are slow and careful, but when he makes it to the bottom of the stairs, he moves toward them with a youthful vigor. "And who have you brought with you?" he asks, extending his hand.

"This is my friend Holly," Aiden says. "We went to high school together. She's staying at the cabin up on the North Service Road, and we're running our errands together today."

George's eyes light up even more. "An old high school chum, how lovely! Simply a delight to meet you, Holly. And what a festive name you have."

She's startled by a warm, fuzzy rub against her leg and looks down to see an extremely fluffy white cat with a red collar and eyes just as bright blue as George's looking up at her. "This must be the famous Mrs. Claws." Holly reaches down to pat the cat's pillowy fur. The cat flops down onto the rug and closes her eyes. A purr starts up, strong as a lawn mower's motor. Mrs. Claws stretches out her body, luxuriating in the pats Holly is giving her.

"Ah, well, I wouldn't go as far as *famous*," George says, but Holly can tell he's pleased at the idea. "She was only in the one commercial, back when she was a kitten—and that was my Carole's doing. She was as bad as one of those pageant parents, now wasn't she, Aiden?"

"Mrs. Plaskett loved this cat more than you did, which is an impressive amount," Aiden agrees.

"But at least I don't go as far as dressing her up like Carole did," George says with a chuckle. "That woman. Always made our lives fun." He lets out a small sigh, and Holly can feel how much he misses his wife. "Anyway, come in, come in. Usually Mrs. Claws runs away when you get here, Aiden, but she seems to like your friend."

They head into the living room, which has cream-and-red-striped wallpaper, a soft cream-colored rug, and a fireplace ablaze in one corner, warming the room. An ottoman near the fire is draped with a fuzzy green blanket. "Got your operating table all ready for you, as always. Thanks to Drew. Come on, missy, up you go." To Holly's surprise, the cat leaps onto the ottoman and lies down, almost doglike in her obedience. "Now, perhaps since you're here, Holly, you can save me bending down and just hold her there gently?"

Holly kneels by the ottoman and places her hands on the cat, who starts purring again.

"You seem to be a cat-lover yourself."

"I had a cat growing up—a big tabby named Mr. Snuggles." She catches Aiden's eye, and he winks at her. She strokes Mrs. Claws's forehead for a moment. "Mrs. Claws seems to be of the same ilk."

Aiden has the needle ready. Holly keeps stroking the cat and chatting with George.

"There, all done," Aiden says.

"That was fast, even for you, Dr. Coleman."

"I'm becoming an expert at this. Perhaps I should think about training to be a vet."

"You've got the brains for it. You could do anything."

"Agreed," Holly says, smiling up at Aiden. "He was the smartest person in our entire high school."

"Tied for first," Aiden says, waving her compliment away with a bashful look.

Mrs. Claws rolls over for a belly rub and Holly focuses on patting her, just for a moment, until George says, "How about a cup of tea, you two? I know the town has me on a visitation schedule like I'm some sort of feeble old person who needs to be watched over"—he winks at Holly—"but surely I can handle two visitors in one day? 'Tis the festive season, after all."

Aiden glances at Holly. "Holly *does* need to get into town to run some errands."

"I'm in no rush, and I'd love a cup of tea, George." The truth is, Holly doesn't want to leave. George's home is so warm, inviting and Christmassy in a way Holly has never experienced. She wants to soak it all in, just a little more.

"Let me fix the tea," says Aiden, and heads for the kitchen. Soon he emerges bearing a tray, and George thanks him, then turns back to Holly.

"I'm sorry I don't have anything fun to offer you in the way of snacks to go with the tea. Unless you want to eat sugar-free biscuits, which, let's face it, no one does," George says.

"Hot tea is perfect," Holly says, pouring in a little milk. As she stirs it, she gazes out the window at the Christmas tree forest. "Your home and your property are so beautiful, George. I've never seen anything like it."

George's tone is proud as he says, "Plaskett Farms is a special place indeed. Three generations it's been in my family, and it's always been a Christmas tree farm." The merry twinkle in his eyes dims a few watts. "Sometimes, I worry about what might happen to it, when I can't live here anymore. There are always developers sniffing around. I can't imagine these trees ever being gone."

"Let's not worry about that today," Aiden says, but Holly can tell from his expression that he *is* worried, probably worries about it all the time. She feels a wave of admiration for the studious boy she used to know in high school, who has clearly grown into a compassionate man. Meanwhile, Mrs. Claws hops onto George's lap, and Holly can hear purring from across the coffee table. As they continue chatting, George's eyes start to droop a little. He stifles a yawn. "How rude of me."

"Not at all," Aiden says. "We should get going. I'll see you in a few days."

"Thank you, my boy. And lovely to meet you, Holly. I hope you forgive me for not seeing you out, but . . ."

"A sleeping lap cat must never be disturbed. Especially one as sweet as Mrs. Claws."

"I hope I see you again before you go back to the city?"

"I hope so, too," Holly says, genuinely meaning that.

As Aiden's truck meanders back down the driveway, through the fairy-tale forest and out onto the main road, Holly feels a pang to be back out in the real world. She hopes she does get to return and visit with George again, and wants to say that—but Aiden seems lost in his thoughts, silent as he drives toward Krimbo. She watches his side profile, getting the sense that he doesn't ever feel the need to fill silences with needless words. It's okay to be quiet, companionable. It's nice, actually.

She sighs happily and leans back, watching the wintry scenery fly by out the window as they head toward Krimbo so she can do her shopping. Soon enough, the trees grow sparser and the village of Krimbo comes into view. They drive slowly down Main Street, passing a smattering of diners, cafés, and restaurants, a clothing store called Viola's Dress Barn, a hardware store, and a bookstore. Every establishment has Christmas lights in its windows, which add a warm and welcoming twinkle to the dull light of the winter midmorning. Aiden heads off to run his own errands, then meets her back at the grocery store parking lot.

"Thanks for today, Aiden," she says when they're back at the cabin and he's helping her unload her groceries. He puts the last bag down on the deck.

"You call me if you need anything at all," he says, and she can tell he means it.

She stays outside, waving goodbye as he taps his horn and

drives away. When she unlocks the cabin door and goes inside—the interior is still warm from the successfully lit wood pellets—she doesn't feel lonely. She has Krimbo, with all its humanity and charm. The magical giant Christmas tree farm. George and Mrs. Claws. And Aiden, an old friend, somewhere out there in the gentle snowfall.

7

IVY
December 19
Kauai, Hawaii

Ivy awakes to her phone ringing out the *Friends* theme song.

"Holly!"

Ivy holds the phone above her face in bed and blinks blearily as her friend comes into focus on FaceTime.

"I'm sorry! I woke you! I completely forgot about the time difference."

"No, it's fine. I wanted to get up early anyway. I thought the roosters would wake me, or, if not them, maybe the sound of hot sex coming from the two very attractive people downstairs."

"The people downstairs?"

"Oh, um, it's just the people below me are a super-attractive couple, and I . . . I'm just surprised I didn't over-hear them last night, that's all. So, how are you?"

"I'm good, actually," Holly says with a genuine smile.

Ivy looks at her friend more closely on the screen. "You do seem . . . kind of happy."

"I think I am," Holly says, her smile widening. "I'm having a nice time here. I take back everything I said about Aiden in my last text."

"Eco Superman?"

"He's a good guy." Ivy reclines against her pillows as Holly tells her about a Victorian Christmas manor she visited earlier that day on a now mostly defunct but truly magical Christmas tree farm, a charming old widower, a cat named Mrs. Claws.

"Honestly, that all sounds kind of romantic," Ivy says. "Are you *sure* you don't want to heal your broken heart via a rebound with Captain Ecology?"

Holly laughs. "It's Eco *Superman*, thank you. And it's good to have a friend here, that's all."

"I'm glad, Holly. Even though I definitely think you should tackle him and have some mind-blowing rebound sex, I'll try to stop bugging you about that and just be happy that you seem to be where you need to be right now."

"You will not. You're the horniest person I know."

"I love my body and I enjoy sex, what can I say?"

"Right—except for two weeks out of every year when you behave like a monk, and encourage *me* to have sex instead. Remember last year, when you sent me all those new position suggestions when you were alone at that cabin in the Catskills?"

"I had rewatched *Dirty Dancing* and gotten some ideas. I had to share them with *someone*."

"Enough," Holly says, laughing. "I'm not sleeping with him. So, what's your plan for today?"

"I'm going to sit on my terrace and draw a tree I saw yesterday, and what I can see from here. Then maybe I'll hike for a while and try to find another perfect beach and draw it all day long. My ideal day."

"I'm so glad you're there," Holly says, her tone sincere.

"*I'm* so glad you're looking so happy." Ivy ends the call and sits up in bed—but her happiness fades away as she considers all she left unsaid during the conversation with her best friend. Holly doesn't even know where she's really staying, and she certainly doesn't know about Matt and Abby's treachery. It's clear Holly is starting to feel better—and Ivy can only imagine the setback that finding out Matt came on their honeymoon with someone else would deliver. It has to be better to protect her best friend from the truth, for now.

Ivy puts down her phone, shakes off the bad feelings about Matt and her dishonesty-by-omission with her best friend, and makes coffee. She dresses in a blue-gray crop tank and cutoff shorts, so different from the trendy pantsuits she wears to her job as a senior graphic designer at Imagenue in Manhattan. She pulls her ponytail through the back of a Montreal Expos cap that she "borrowed" from her dad and never gave back, then goes out to the deck with her steaming mug to set up the portable easel she brings on these trips, placing it close to the railing. At work, her day would often start with a creative meeting, where Ivy would bring her branding ideas to the table. She appreciates that there is at least some creativity in her day-to-day life—but this is different. At work, she thinks inside boxes, according to clients' wishes, aligned with trends. On her art trip, she can be completely free.

First, she takes a sheet of canvas and draws the kiawe tree she saw at the hotel the day before, checking her phone to get the shape right, painting the colors by memory. As she swipes streaks across the page that perfectly mimic the straw yellow of the sand below the tree, Ivy is filled with satisfaction and a sense of purpose. The multifaceted shades of the tree come to life on the page next. Once she feels she has the browns and greens just right, she shifts her focus to the texture of the trunk.

An hour passes, but Ivy is so absorbed in what she's doing, she hardly notices. She finishes her drawing and starts another, this one of the beach she can see from where she sits.

She blends blues and aquamarines, shifts her focus to the froth of white where the waves hit the sand. She adds the finishing touches on the lather and spume of a wave, then puts down her pastels and stretches her arms above her head as she contemplates the mountains—which she knows she'll need an entirely new color palette for. In the now full sunlight, the fertile mountains are a patchwork not just of green but also ocher, rust, blue-black in the shadows.

"Good morning!"

Larry is standing at the top of the stairs to the deck, holding a carton of milk. "I realized I brought you coffee yesterday but no cream or milk. Do you need to borrow some?"

"Oh, that's really kind of you. But I take it black."

Larry has approached and is looking at Ivy's canvas now, her mouth a surprised O. "This is gorgeous! You did this?"

Ivy feels suddenly shy. All she can say is a humble "Yes."

"This is spectacular!"

Ivy is blushing now. "It's not quite done."

"But it's still wonderful." Now she sees the drawing Ivy did of the tree, held down by stones and drying on the patio table nearby. "And that one. *Wow.* I know exactly which tree that is! Down by the hotel tiki bar, right?" Ivy nods. "You are *so* talented."

"Thank you," she says, ducking her head and pretending to focus on putting away a few pastels that have fallen from the box.

"So, is this an art trip for you?"

"Yeah. I try to take one once a year, although I hate that I'm here because of my friend's heartache."

"At least something good is coming out of it," Larry says. "Where do you show your work back home?"

"I don't," Ivy says. "This is just for fun. I'm a graphic artist by day—*that's* my real job."

There's a sound on the stairs, and Oliver's tousled hair appears, then his face and the rest of his body, clad in a black wetsuit that makes Ivy's blush from all of Larry's compliments intensify—because he looks exactly as good in a tight wetsuit as she'd imagined when she was crouched behind the bar yesterday. "Morning, Ivy." He flashes his dimple at her. "Larry, I just wanted to let you know I'm heading out surfing."

"Before you go, check this out! Ivy is secretly a talented artist," Larry announces.

Oliver crosses the deck to the tree drawing, and when he looks up into Ivy's eyes, she sees surprise in his expression—but something else, too. "Wow," he says. "This really is great. You drew this of the tree at the hotel yesterday, the one you were taking pictures of?" Ivy nods. "It's perfect."

"Thank you," Ivy says, "but really—"

Oliver now crosses the deck to the easel, standing behind Ivy to examine her drawing. She has the sudden urge to ask him where he buys his cologne, because even with his girlfriend standing right there on the deck, she wants to reach out and touch him.

"Ivy says she just dabbles, that her actual job is graphic designer," Larry says.

"That true?" Oliver looks down at Ivy again, a question in his eyes.

"Yes," Ivy says, keeping her voice firm even though her heart is racing and her palms have gone all sweaty. She feels like she's making a school presentation she didn't prepare for. "My pastel art is just for fun. But thank you both for all the compliments. And hey, can you guys recommend any beaches for me to go to that might be great for drawing, or is basically everything drop-dead gorgeous around here?"

Larry laughs. "Oh, you've asked the right person. Ollie is his own walking Hawaii tourism board." She puts her hand on his shoulder, and Ivy tries not to feel jealous that she gets to touch him whenever she wants. "Hon, I'm going to come surfing with you, okay? Maxi is opening the bar for me today, and I'm closing. I just need to go change. You give Ivy some tips on good beaches, and I'll meet you downstairs?"

When Larry is gone, Oliver picks up a small notepad from beside Ivy's easel. "Can I use this?" She nods and hands him a pencil.

"Okay, so you want to go to Ines's Secret Beach," he says, writing it down. "It's about twenty minutes up the coast." He sketches a map. "Then Lumaha'i Beach, which will take another hour to get to. You can hike that. Those two would make the perfect day trip, and when you leave here, you can go to Hanalei to get picnic supplies."

Next, he draws another map, writes "Glass Beach," and looks up at her. "Heard of it?" She shakes her head. "It's a stretch of beach made entirely of sea glass, instead of sand. It's spectacular—but you have to go at low tide."

"A beach made of glass—how is that possible?"

"There used to be a glass factory, years ago, and apparently, after it was abandoned, it all just happened that way. Little rounded pieces of multicolored glass strewn everywhere eventually took over the beach. Normally human intervention is a real bummer, but in this case, it's absolutely stunning when the tide is low and the sun is setting. The colors, the textures—you'll love it. You'll want to draw it all day.

"Do you drive?" She nods. "There's a car-rental place near the market, and they have great rates. Ask for my pal Kalei." He draws a map now. "It's about an hour's drive from here, and very straightforward. You just take 56 and 50." He rips the sheet of paper off the pad, hands it to her, then starts on another one, upon which he writes down "The Blue Room."

"Is that a club?"

His one dimple shines at her like a flashlight as he smiles. "Sounds like it, right? But it's a cave, not far from here.

Twenty minutes' drive, near Tunnels Beach. You have to go when the water level is high. The water in the cave turns this shade of blue that's like . . ." He trails off, at a loss for words. "You'll think you dreamed it," he concludes. "You shouldn't swim in the caves, although some locals do—and I might have done it, a time or two—but you can swim at Keʻe Beach down the road. Calm, serene, perfect spot for a contemplative back-float. And the best poké you'll ever have is at the restaurant on that beach."

"Oliver, are you actually currently employed by the tourism board?"

He laughs. "Nah. I just really love it here."

"How long have you lived here?"

"Oh, I don't live here full-time. But this is my third winter. It's a great place to avoid ever having to see snow."

"You don't see the beauty in snow? I'd think someone who is such a Christmas enthusiast would be right into the white stuff."

He shivers as if someone has just tossed a snowball down the back of his shirt. "I hate being cold," he says. "I chase the sun all year long and I'm going for a record. If I can avoid snow and cold for the next . . . decade or so? I'll be happy. What I'm after is the opposite of that line in Narnia, you know the one? 'Always winter but never Christmas'? I think an ideal world for me would be always summer but *always* Christmas."

"I love being warm, and this place is heavenly for sure, but I love winter, too."

"And yet Christmas you find . . . just okay?"

"You're never going to drop that, are you?"

He bites his lip, then lets it go and laughs. "Nope. Named Ivy, best friend is Holly, yet somehow thinks the festive season is *just okay*. You're a riddle wrapped in an enigma, Ivy." He holds her gaze for a moment before turning his toward the sea. "I need to get out on the waves before I run out of time," he says. "But it was great to see your art—it's really good, Ivy. See you later?"

"Thanks for the tips, Oliver."

"Can't wait to see what you draw today."

When he's gone, Ivy walks to the edge of the deck and looks down. In the distance, she sees Oliver carrying a butter yellow surfboard. Larry is behind him in a powder blue wetsuit, her long hair flowing down her back, her surfboard coral pink. Oliver has an orange dry bag on his back, and it shines bright in the morning sun as he turns left and moves across the sand with long, purposeful strides.

What would it be like, Ivy wonders, to lead a life like his? He works as a bartender, surfs, lives in a beach house in paradise when he feels like it, with a beautiful lover, and chases the sun and waves with her. Would Ivy want to be so free? *No*, she tells herself, even as the very thought creates a sense of longing in her. It's not realistic. People like Oliver are a lot of fun to be around, but also likely have Peter Pan syndrome, a refusal to grow up that inevitably gets tiresome. She's dated guys like him and it never lasts. At some point, you *have* to grow up. And part of being a grown-up is carving out time to do the things you love rather than letting them overwhelm your responsibilities. It's okay for those passions to be a hobby, not a career, though. You can still lead a fulfilling life while paying the bills regularly—with actual money instead of barters, the way her parents do.

Ivy finishes packing her bag for the day—a break from reality, but not her real life. She *has* a real life, and it's in New York City, not here in a fantasy paradise. But then she catches one last glimpse of Oliver and Larry. As Larry tilts her head toward Oliver, then laughs up at the sky, Ivy is forced to concede that those two make an easy, free life seem like a simple choice to make—that it could be more than just a lot of fun.

8

HOLLY
December 20
Hudson Valley, New York

The next day is sunny and the roads are free of snow, so Holly decides to venture into town on her own. She parks her vintage baby blue BMW in front of an antique shop in the middle of Krimbo, gets out of her car, and stands for a moment, taking in the shop's window display: Santa's workshop, featuring a collection of vintage toys, hobbyhorses, music boxes with dancing ballerinas on top, a cranberry-and-popcorn-strung tree with brown paper packages crowded at its base. Holly came to the Hudson Valley and Krimbo to get away from Christmas because it only reminded her of her wedding that wasn't, but the holiday season in this charming town is different from any of her memories. She enjoys herself as she walks slowly along the street, peering in shopwindows at seasonal displays as she goes.

When she sees a store with a bright yellow sign that says "Krimbo Home Video," she decides she has to go in and look around. She thought video rental stores had gone the way of telephone booths and landlines—but also recalls a small TV-DVD combo at the cabin.

Inside the video store, the shelves are lined with VHS and DVD cases, and she can't seem to figure out what the organization system is. When she passes *It's a Wonderful Life*, *A Christmas Carol*, *The Lemon Drop Kid*, and *White Christmas*, she finally realizes every single movie on display is a Christmas film, all shelved by decade.

She moves along to another aisle: There's *Benji's Very Own Christmas Story*, and a terrifying-looking holiday-themed horror movie called *Bloody Night*.

In the '80s section, there's *Ernest Saves Christmas*, *National Lampoon's Christmas Vacation*, *Scrooged*, and more. She starts snapping photos to send to Ivy, who immediately texts back asking to see more. **Have you time-traveled? Are you in a . . . movie rental store?**

All editions of "Home Alone" have their special section, look! All decorated with tinsel and Christmas lights.

Holly keeps walking through the tiny aisles, snapping photos for her friend and smiling to herself.

Christmas horror? who knew that was a genre? she texts Ivy.

You have to rent at least one scary Christmas movie. I insist.

Do you think someone staying alone in a secluded cabin should be renting horror movies?

Go to the eighties section. Eighties horror movies are more like comedies, you know that. Also, you promise you're renting the Nicole Kidman one you just sent me called "A Bush Christmas"?

Holly snorts with laughter just as she rounds a corner—and runs straight into Aiden. His pleasantly familiar woodsy-spicy scent hits her nostrils just as the electricity of his blue-eyed gaze zings through her mind. She's almost certain her heart skips a beat.

"I heard someone laughing back here and had to see who it was," he says.

"You're in here renting videos, too?"

He suddenly looks shy. "Actually, no," he says. "I was across the street and saw you come in here. I wanted to say hi."

This makes Holly feel inordinately pleased. Standing near Aiden, she feels like her entire being is at attention. He leans down, lowers his voice. "Honestly, I don't know how this place stays in business, but a lot of people in this town love renting movies. Most of those people are over sixty."

Holly laughs. "Don't knock it," she says, holding up *A Bush Christmas*. "I'm renting one for tonight."

"You'll have to tell me how it is."

"I'm sure it's full of eighties corniness. I can't wait."

He waits while she rents the movie from a clerk who looks like a real-life version of Comic Book Guy from *The Simpsons*, and they walk outside together. The day has turned gently overcast; fluffy snowflakes are starting to fall. The snow globe effect turns the little town even more festive—but Holly frowns at the snowfall, remembering her lack of winter tires.

Aiden seems to read her thoughts.

"I promise, I'm not giving you a hard time about not having snow tires—but I have an idea."

She raises an eyebrow. "Snowmobile? ATV? Probably not my thing."

He laughs. "Nope. When I first moved back here from Boston, I had a sedan. I still have the winter tires in my garage. I'm sure they'd fit on your car—and there's a garage in town that can put them on. I can give Ellie a call right now to see if she has time this morning?"

"Really, you'd do that?"

"The tires are just sitting there. Someone should be using them. Hang on." Aiden calls the mechanic. "Ellie says to bring the car and the tires right over," he says when he hangs up. "I just need to run home and get them—I'm five minutes away—and I'll meet you at the garage."

"You're *sure* it's not too much trouble?"

Aiden waves off her protests and gives her directions to the garage—while she becomes more certain than ever that Krimbo is a town where helping one another is just part of the daily routine, and that kindhearted Aiden fits in perfectly.

"Want to grab lunch while you wait for your car to be ready?"

"Absolutely, I'm starving," Holly says. She and Aiden walk side by side, companionably, down Krimbo's Main Street and soon reach a café with a quaint red, white, and green striped awning and an artfully painted sign that says "Seventh Heaven" in cursive script.

Inside, holiday music is piping from the stereo, and there are delicious smells emanating from the kitchen. "Coffee?" Aiden asks, walking casually behind the counter and reaching for the pot and two mugs.

"Guess you're familiar enough with the owner?"

Holly hears the light tinkle of a laugh. "You could say that!" A willowy woman with high cheekbones, wide-set dark eyes, and a welcoming smile pushes her way through the forest green swinging doors leading from the kitchen into the café. She's carrying a tray of cookies.

"Hi, I'm Sidra." Her smile widens. "Aiden's sister-in-law. I own this café with Aiden's sister, Alexa."

"And this is Holly Beech—an old high school friend," Aiden says. "She's renting the cabin up on the North Service Road for the holidays."

"Nice spot," says Sidra.

Aiden pours two steaming mugs of coffee and hands one to Holly with a jug of cream. Holly stirs, sips, says, "Wow. This might just be the best coffee I've ever had."

"Sidra roasts the beans herself," Aiden says proudly, taking a sip of his own brew. "Where's Alexa today, Sid?"

"Mondays are her enforced day off," Sidra says with a smile.

"And she's *actually* not here? You're sure she's not hiding behind the door in there?"

"I left her at home with the weekend *New York Times*, which she of course didn't get to over the weekend, and strict instructions to relax."

Aiden and Sidra both laugh, as if the idea of Alexa relaxing is highly unlikely.

"What can I get you two?" Sidra asks. "Daily sandwich?"

Aiden turns to Holly. "Sidra and Alex bake their own bread, raise their own chickens, pickle their own everything. Whatever the special is today, you're guaranteed to love it."

Sidra heads back into the kitchen and soon emerges with

two sandwiches on white plates dotted with a holly-berry pattern. "It's your favorite today, Aiden. The Krimbo Klub."

Two customers have entered and taken seats, waving hello to both Sidra and Aiden. "Two specials?" Sidra calls out. "Coming right up!"

Sidra busies herself with a few more customers as Holly takes a bite of her sandwich. "What is *in* this? It's incredible—and not just because I'm starving."

"The Krimbo Klub has turkey, turkey bacon, avocado . . ." He's counting the ingredients off on his fingers, and pauses. "House cream cheese, pickled onions, peperoncini. Their secret sauce, which my own sister won't even tell me the ingredients for—all on their home-baked sweet French roll."

"You sound like a sandwich board."

"I would wear a sandwich board for this sandwich."

They eat in silence for a while, watching townspeople walk by in the soft snow. Most people either wave in greeting or come inside. Everyone orders the sandwich of the day, and either coffee or hot chocolate—and most people cast curious glances over at Holly.

When Holly crumples up her wax paper, Aiden asks if she's ready for dessert.

She groans. "I'm stuffed, but also totally down for dessert."

"That's the right attitude."

"I'm a team player, Aiden."

He laughs and stands. When he goes behind the counter,

he effortlessly serves a few customers in the increasingly crowded café, pouring coffees and using rose gold tongs to place cookies and pastries on little plates before returning to their table holding a plate with two cookies. They're thick, dark chocolate, coated in icing and covered in red and green sprinkles.

"I just ate an entire hoagie," Holly says, eyes wide. "I'm not sure I'm ready for a cookie of that size."

"Just one bite, see how you feel."

She goes ahead.

"I love this cookie," she says. "I want to marry this cookie. I want to make an honest cookie out of it. What is it?"

He laughs. "It's a peppermint snowdrift." He thinks for a moment. "Basically, dark chocolate cookie batter around a peppermint patty. It's my grandma's recipe. If there's a better cookie in the world, I don't know what it is. Except they have, like, a dozen other flavors at the café, and they're all comparable. The cookie flavors, like the sandwiches, rotate. So you never know what you're going to get from day to day."

"It's so good." Holly dabs at the corners of her mouth with a paper napkin. "Do I have frosting on my face?" she asks.

He shakes his head and laughs.

"So, when did you move out here to this perfect little town?"

"My grandparents always lived in Krimbo, but my parents came out here in my senior year. My mom got sick."

"Oh—is that why you didn't come to grad, your mom was sick? I'm so sorry, Aiden."

"You noticed? That I wasn't at grad?"

"Of course I did. I was dying to get your SAT scores out of you, remember?" She raises an eyebrow, but he shakes his head.

"Still not giving them up. But, yeah. Krimbo has always felt like home base because we spent a lot of time out here when my mom was in treatment. Moving here was just a formality."

"And she's doing okay now?" Holly asks with concern.

"She's doing amazing. She had breast cancer, but she's had clear scans every year for the past seven."

"That's great, Aiden. My nana was diagnosed with cancer two years ago, and she fought so hard."

"Fought?" Now Aiden's eyes are the ones clouded with concern.

"She passed away last year."

"I'm so sorry, Holly."

"Thank you. We were close; it was hard. That's her car I brought here. She left it to me because we used to go on a road trip together in it every year. Such good memories in that car. I should have rented something else to drive, I know that—but I always find it so comforting. It still smells like her. Chanel No. 5." Holly's smile is wistful now.

"I think I remember your nana from school plays and events. She looked just like you, and always sat right up at the front."

There's a lump in Holly's throat as she nods and says, "Yes. That was her. My favorite person in the world." She looks down at her empty plate, blinks away tears. "My family aren't the warmest people. It's always about acheivements and status. That's probably why I was so competitive in high school. But Nana was the one who always reminded me I was enough—just me. Not all the things I did."

"You're definitely enough, Holly," Aiden says, his blue eyes bright, his voice suddenly husky with emotion. "You always have been."

Under his gaze, Holly feels as if time has stopped—or perhaps gone backward. All at once, it's like she's spinning, her body flooded with adrenaline that feels like joy. She looks away from him, breaking the intense connection and feeling bereft after she does. "Thank you for listening." She looks back up at him when she's sure she has her emotions under control. "Should we help Sidra out by carrying these empty plates back to the kitchen? It's still pretty slammed in here."

They both get up from the table and, to what Holly is certain is her relief, the confusing moment between them is over.

Back at the garage, the tires are on Holly's car and it's ready for the snowy conditions—and Ellie the mechanic won't accept payment, forever cementing Krimbo in Holly's mind as the nicest town in America.

Aiden walks her to her car, parked out in front of the garage, and they stand looking at each other for a moment as the peaceful snow falls between them. All at once, Holly feels an impulse she can't resist. "Aiden, would you like to come over for dinner and a movie tonight? As a thank-you for the tires and for all your help?"

She can't read his expression, and hopes she hasn't made a fool of herself. "You really don't have to do anything to thank me," he says.

"But I want to."

He smiles, and his ice-blue eyes turn warm. Her insides turn warm, too. "Then I'd love to."

"Seven o'clock give you enough time to work up an appetite again after that lunch?"

"Perfect."

Holly only brought yoga and sweat pants, T-shirts, sweatshirts, and heavy knits on her trip to the Hudson Valley—but after taking a freezing-cold shower and thawing out her hair, she still finds herself agonizing over what to wear for her evening with Aiden. It doesn't matter, she finally tells herself. He's just an old high school friend coming over for ramen noodles, which she plans to doctor up using a recipe she and Ivy developed in college.

She grabs the first T-shirt she can find, one Ivy bought her as a souvenir from her last art retreat—it's as bright pink as the interior of a watermelon and says "Nobody Puts Baby in a Corner" on the front, and "Catskills, NY" on the back. She pulls on her one pair of yoga pants that sort of, *maybe* don't look like yoga pants. She didn't bring any makeup, just skin-care products, so she swipes on lip balm and smoothes it over her brows, too. "This is not a date," she says to the mirror. The woman staring back at her may or may not agree.

She hears a *beep* from her phone and picks it up. It's her brother, Ted. **Checking in, sis. You surviving out there? Have you gone full-on Laura Ingalls, built your own smoker, are you out hunting on the land for protein sources?**

Ha ha ha, she texts back. **For your information, I managed to bag a hoagie today. Roughing it isn't that bad.**

A pause. **You're okay, though? Sure you don't want to come back and join us for Christmas? Mom's pretty agitated about the whole thing.**

My Christmas present from you is that you handle Mom this year. I'm staying where I am. And I'm fine. Ivy and I have a big table booked at Alice on NYE. You and Ming can come to that, and I'll see you then. xx

She's in the cabin's little kitchen performing the minimal amount of prep work required to make the dish she's planning—chopping ginger and garlic, washing and chopping spinach and kale—when she hears Aiden's truck rumbling up the snowy driveway. As the pace of her heartbeat picks up, Holly tells herself she's just excited to see another person, that's all.

"Hello!" Holly opens the door wide and invites Aiden in. He takes off his snow boots and jacket, then holds up a little cloth bag. "I come bearing gifts. 'Tis the season, after all."

"I'm the one who owes *you*. That's what this dinner is for."

"You don't owe me anything, Holly," he says, his expression suddenly grave.

"Well." She finds herself caught off guard. She's used to Matt, she supposes, who always makes a joke of everything, who voices his every fleeting thought, even if it's inappropriate or rude. She can tell Aiden never does that. "I'm still very grateful."

"I was happy to help." He follows her toward the kitchen. "I wasn't sure what would go with what you were making, so I brought craft beer." He pulls a six-pack from the bag. "This is from my favorite local brewery."

"Looks great."

"But then I also didn't necessarily peg you for a beer person, so I also grabbed a pinot gris"—he pulls out a bottle—"from a winery in the Finger Lakes, not far from here."

"This is far too generous of you." She picks one of the beer bottles out of its cardboard case. "I feel like I have to try a beer called the Kringle Krusher, don't I?"

He laughs. "Right? They also have an Abominable Winter Ale, but the Krusher is my favorite. And I brought a jar of hot sauce made by my grandma's friend Nell." He reaches into his cloth bag again and holds up a jar hand-labeled Nell's 5-Alarm Sauce. "She also has twelve-alarm," he says. "But no one in town has ever tried it except Nell's husband."

"That's perfect. I'm making Dr. Ramen, and it always needs hot sauce."

"I've heard of Mr. Noodles, but . . ."

"It's a recipe Ivy and I came up with in college. It involves doctoring up Mr. Noodles with . . ." She uses her fingers to count off the ingredients. "Ginger, garlic, butter, sesame seeds, soy sauce, and a ton of spinach, kale, or whatever greens you have on hand. Hot sauce or chili crisp and a frizzled egg on top. Elevated ramen."

"That actually sounds pretty good."

"Well, you're about to find out."

Holly pours them each a beer, then takes a sip. She looks down at the label. "I have a soft spot for festive alliteration—I met Ivy at a college keg party called the Columbia-U Christmas Kegger, which is playing fast and loose with the concept of alliteration, I guess." Briefly, she tells the story of how she and Ivy met—but finds herself leaving Matt out of it altogether. "By the end of the night, we knew we were meant to be. We've been best friends ever since."

"I'd love to meet her someday," Aiden says. "Where did you say she was spending the holidays?"

Holly's throat goes dry, and she takes another sip of her beer. "Hawaii," she manages. "Artist's retreat."

She slides a small dish of pistachios toward him. "I'm afraid I don't have much in the way of appetizers to go with our cocktails, sorry. Pistachio?"

Aiden laughs. "Cocktails," he repeats.

"What's so funny?"

"I don't know. We're in a tiny cabin in the middle of nowhere drinking beer, but I guess you're more used to fancy cocktail parties."

"I wouldn't say I like them, though. This is much more fun." She isn't sure what has happened, but she feels suddenly off-kilter. She hasn't seen Aiden since high school, but it feels like he knows her well.

"So, tell me more about your life in Krimbo," she says, hoping to distract from her blushing cheeks, disconcerted by how frequently being near Aiden is making her feel this way. "Your grandparents and parents were out here, your sister followed suit, and you . . . ?"

"I didn't mean to move here, actually. It just sort of . . ." He thinks for a moment, but all he says is, ". . . just sort of happened. I've been officially living out here for a year."

"And before that, you were at MIT. So, you lived in Cambridge?" He hasn't been offering a ton of detail about his life, and she can't help but press now, her curiosity about what he's been up to for the past ten years growing the more time they spend together.

"Right, I was in Cambridge for a couple years. But—" His eyes have darkened, like a shadowy storm cloud has passed over a blue sky on a perfect day. "Actually, I'm an MIT dropout. I didn't finish my degree."

She feels like she's channeling her mother as she tries to deflect the awkward silence that follows by standing up and saying chirpily, "Guess I'd better get started on dinner." As she melts butter in a skillet and turns the water on to boil the noodles, she changes the topic, hoping to lighten the mood. "Do you keep in touch with anyone from school?"

"Not really," he says. "Do you?"

"Do you remember Josie Cheng and Lachlan Schneider? We get together every spring and go to Coney Island, just for old times' sake." She thinks for a moment. "Actually, the last time we got together, they told me Ricky Exeter had been indicted on corporate fraud charges. Apparently he developed a Ponzi scheme he couldn't get anyone to go for, so he took it to Palm Springs and his gran's retirement community."

Aiden winces, then nods. "That tracks. Ricky fancied himself a diabolical genius." He sips his beer, tilts his head. "Actually, I do have something. Did you hear that Mr. Abrams, the math teacher, and Ms. Malla, the art teacher, left their respective partners and married each other?"

"Nooooo way!" Holly squeals, feeling like a teenager again—feeling the way she does around Ivy, she realizes. Relaxed, like she can be herself. "I always thought it was weird how much time Ms. Malla spent in the math room! How did you find that out?"

"I ran into them last summer at a restaurant in the city." His expression grows serious again, the way it had before. "I know gossip is wrong, but why does talking about people you used to know feel *so* good?"

She laughs. "It's pure entertainment, but you feel a connection to it. Imagine hearing gossip about your best friend or a family member. Terrible feeling. You'd have to tell them. An old schoolmate, though? Someone you once knew, but don't anymore. Feels like catnip."

They keep chatting as she stir-fries the garlic and ginger in the butter, then adds the greens and soy sauce. She boils and drains the ramen noodles, then puts them in the pan, mixing them up with the rest of the ingredients.

"It smells *amazing.* I can't believe this is all happening with a few packs of instant noodles."

She pushes the noodles to the side, and adds sesame oil and the hot sauce Aiden brought. When it sizzles, she cracks two eggs and fries them until the yolks are just set. She scoops the noodles and greens into soup bowls, tops each bowl with an egg, and sprinkles sesame seeds on top.

"That looks like it came from a restaurant."

"Don't be too impressed. It's literally the only thing I can cook."

"Well, I *am* impressed."

"Want some wine with this?"

"Sure. Here, let me open it. Juice glasses okay?"

"Perfect," Holly says.

When he takes a bite of the noodles, he closes his eyes, a blissful expression on his face. "These are amazing."

She smiles at the compliment, then pours the wine and passes him a glass.

He takes a sip, then another bite. "*So* good. Alex and Sid should start serving this at the café. In fact, these are so good, I think . . ."

"You think *what*?"

He has a mischevious expression on his face. "I think if you tell me yours, I'll tell you mine."

She squeals. "You mean our SAT scores?"

He nods.

"2160," she says.

"Impressive score," he says, poker-faced.

"It's okay, you don't have to tell me. 2160 is a tough act to follow," she says with a wink.

"You're right," he says, his expression still unreadable. "It is."

"Aw, come on!" she erupts. "Fair's fair. You agreed."

He laughs. "Hey, you just said I didn't have to."

"I was trying to apply reverse psychology. I've been dying to know your score all these years."

"Have you really? All these years, you've wondered?" There's something to his words she still can't quite decode. His expression is changing again, softening. She finds herself drawn closer to him, leaning toward him in her stool.

"I have!" she insists, reaching over and touching his arm under his soft flannel shirt, not quite sure why she can't stop herself from doing so.

A long pause. She waits.

"2300," he finally says quietly.

"Excuse me? Can you repeat that?"

"2300," he says louder, and with a grin.

"Aiden! That's a great score! You left me in your dust. Congratulations."

"I'll admit it, I *really* wanted to beat you. It started to become a point of pride to do better than the legendary Holly Beech, when I was at college on scholarship. All these years later, though . . . it hardly seems to matter."

"Oh, come on. Look at your face. It totally matters."

"You're right." He smiles mischievously. "It totally matters. Hey, are you done with your food?" She nods and he stands, clearing the plates as she thinks about what he said earlier, about being an MIT dropout. With an SAT score like that, why didn't he finish college? But as comfortable as she is with him, she doesn't feel she can ask. It seems like a sore spot, and she doesn't want to pry.

"You're my guest. You don't clean up," she says, jumping up from her stool.

"Out of the question. I was raised to do the dishes when someone else cooks. You have to let me, or my mom will find out and ground me. One of the perils of living in the same small town as your parents."

She laughs. "Okay then—but you have to let me dry."

After they wash and dry the dishes, Aiden declines another glass of wine because he has to drive, but says yes to a coffee to go with the movie. Teenage Nicole Kidman manages to save Christmas and her family's farm, but they're chatting so much they barely pay attention, and soon the movie's credits are rolling.

"I have an early morning," Aiden says, and she thinks he sounds regretful. She knows she is. She doesn't want the night to end. "I should get going. But this has been a great night, Holly. Thank you."

Holly walks him to the door. "Thank you, Aiden. For everything." She steps out onto the deck with him, into air so cold it sparkles in the moonlight with tiny flecks of snow. She looks up and sees all the familiar constellations hanging above the evergreens. "Wow," she breathes. "I know these stars are always here, but I can't see them in the city. This place is exactly what I needed."

"This is the best spot for stargazing."

But when she looks away from the sky, she sees that Aiden is watching her, not the stars. His eyes are bright in the darkness. "I won't pry," he says. "But I *will* say that getting outdoors in winter always helps if something is bothering me."

"You mean eating ramen noodles, sleeping in, and watching holiday movies is not the solution to all life's problems?"

He laughs. "No, those are amazing choices, too. But so is fresh air. Watching stars—or, when it's light out, there are some maps to hiking and ski trails in the guidebook. And snowshoes, cross-country skis, and skates in the shed. The code to unlock it is 'SNOWY.'"

"I love to skate," Holly says. "I haven't in ages."

"There's a pretty good outdoor rink in the town square—but to be honest, the best skating around here is on the river. Only you can't do that alone. It's not safe."

"Oh. Well . . ."

"I can take you," he says quickly, almost sounding relieved at the idea. "I'm tied up tomorrow, but the afternoon after that?"

Holly doesn't know if he's asked her to go skating on the river because he feels sorry for her, or because he actually wants to—all she knows is the invitation has created a warm bloom of happiness in her chest. "I'd love to, Aiden."

"Great. Midafternoon okay?" She nods. "The skates in the shed may need a sharpening and a tune-up, so let's meet at McLaren Sports, five doors down from the grocery store, at three. Good night, Holly."

He continues to look down at her, thoughtful. She has the sudden image of herself standing on her tiptoes to reach his lips, brushing hers against his. What would that feel like? But she can't. She's like a statue. And then he's turning away, waving when he reaches his truck.

He waves again through the windshield, and then he's gone.

9

IVY
December 21
Kauai, Hawaii

Ivy is satisfyingly weary after an afternoon spent exploring and sketching. The day before, she discovered Ines's Secret Beach to be a true hideaway, empty of tourists when Ivy got there, sheltered by immense, palm-tree-lined sea cliffs and featuring a beach of shell pink sand softer than any mattress Ivy has ever slept on. She sat on a pillowy dune and sketched for hours before eating her picnic lunch, then making her way farther along the coast to Lumaha'i.

There, she snapped a photo and sent it to Holly—**The beach from "South Pacific"! Picture Mitzi Gaynor washing that man right outta her hair!**—but decided against going swimming. The waves were high, and she had read online and been warned by Oliver that this beach recorded the highest number of drownings per year because people underestimated the pull of the tide and the power of the ocean.

Instead, she spent the rest of the afternoon at Lumahaʻi in the shade of a row of fragrant hibiscus, sketching contentedly before eventually taking a short nap on a beach blanket she had tucked into her backpack. She awoke feeling decadent, rested, sun-warm—*happy*. She'd shaded a drawing of the beach she had been working on before her nap, waited for the soft pastel to dry enough for her to slide it into her portfolio folder and then into her backpack, and prepared for the hike back to Hanalei, making sure to leave herself enough time so that she wouldn't be walking in the dark.

As the scenery gets familiar, she cuts up from the beach path. Soon, she finds herself walking through the streets of the town as dusk begins to fall. There's a buzz in the air, and many people about. She sees a sign for a juice bar up ahead and gets in line so she can buy a drink to quench her thirst after the long hike. Then she'll find a good spot to get dinner, she decides.

She's nearly at the front of the line when she hears an unwelcomely familiar voice behind her. *Shit.*

"Think they have any rum to put in this juice, Abby Bo-Babby?"

Matt. A delighted giggle—at least *someone* likes him. Ivy doesn't catch Abby's reply through the sudden angry rushing in her ears. They're right behind her. She has the urge to duck out of her spot in line and hide somewhere—but it's Matt who should be hiding and ashamed, not her! So she asks for a "santol-ade"—a drink made with the juice of ripe mangosteens—and pulls her Expos baseball cap lower over her face as she waits, the nauseating reminder of Matt's betrayal of her best friend washing over Ivy like a pailful of dirty water. She considers for a moment what it would feel like to confront Matt, to call him out in front of Abby, the way he deserves.

But doing that would add yet another huge event she would have to keep from Holly. *How was your day?* Holly might ask her, and Ivy would have to leave out the fact that she dumped a santol-ade on Matt's head in a tiny Hawaiian town.

"Ugh!" Ivy takes her drink and walks away, all happiness from her exhilarating, productive day gone. She skulks around the back of the juice stand and kicks at a boulder, and of course badly stubs her toe on it. "*Ow.* Shithead!"

"Now, what did that rock ever do to you?"

Ivy turns to see Oliver, lanky and handsome in the khaki shorts and fitted black golf shirt of his bartending uniform.

"I saw you getting juice, but when I came over to say hi, you'd snuck around back here."

"Matt is here," Ivy mutters.

"I saw him. I figured that was why you took off. I see you decided to kick a rock." Even his one-dimpled smile does nothing to cheer her.

"A big part of me wanted to just kick him in the shins and run away."

Oliver laughs, then stops himself. "I'm sorry. This is *not* funny."

"It's *not*," Ivy says. "I'm lying to my best friend. I'm the *worst*. I've never felt so horrible, so dirty in my life."

"Hey, Ivy?"

She looks up at him. "Yeah?"

"Sounds like what you need is a friend," he says, all mirth gone from his eyes. "So, it's good you ran into me. I think I know something that might cheer you up."

"Nothing can cheer me up," she says darkly.

"Tonight's the Hanalei Christmas-tree-lighting ceremony. And I know, I know, you're lukewarm on Christmas. But this is more than that. It's really special. I promise you."

"You were right about the beaches you recommended," Ivy says. "They were great. But a parade?"

"It's not a parade," he specifies. "It's a Christmas-tree-lighting ceremony."

"Sorry, sorry, tree-lighting ceremony."

"It starts at the pier, where everyone watches as they bring the town Christmas tree in on a barge—huge shipments come by steamer every year and get dispersed around the island since, obviously, Christmas trees don't grow here. Then Santa and Mrs. Claus roll in on their outrigger canoe—"

"Santa and Mrs. Claus have an outrigger canoe?"

"In Hawaii they do. And it's pulled by dolphins." Her mouth drops open. "I *told* you. You have to see this." He has a kid-at-Christmas look on his face, which has, of course, coaxed his cute dimple out again. She can't help but smile now, his enthusiasm contagious. "Then everyone follows the tree, with the Clauses leading the way, of course."

"That sounds a bit like a parade . . ."

He ignores her. "And *then* the ceremonial lighting happens in the middle of town." His sea green eyes are dancing with true delight now. "It's my favorite thing on this island, and I have very high standards for favorite things. The evergreen gets decorated and lit up, *and* all the palm trees in town that have been decorated in advance light up, too. It's a sight to see, Ivy, I swear—guaranteed to soften even the hardest heart."

"Hey, I do not have a hard heart," Ivy says.

"I know that." Oliver's tone is thoughtful now, serious. He's looking at her closely, the way he did when they first met—as if he's trying to decode her, figure her out.

Ivy lifts her chin and says, "I'm sorry, I can't go back out there. I have to avoid Matt."

"See, that's what I don't get," Oliver says. He rubs one

hand over the golden stubble on his jaw, and his shirt rides up, but she manages to keep her eyes on his face and not his chiseled abs as she reminds herself of how very much she likes Larry. "Why does this guy get away with messing with your friend's life *and* ruining your holiday? Why are you letting him?"

"I'm not *letting* him," Ivy says, defensive now. "If I could avoid him completely, I would."

"I'll keep an eye out. If we see him, I'll hide you."

"What, are you going to magically turn into a giant hedge?"

He grins. "Maybe? You don't know my superpowers yet, Ivy." He reaches down and lowers the brim of her Expos cap so it covers more of her face. "There. You're in disguise. I'll be your invisibility cloak, okay? No one sees you unless you want them to. I've got you, Ivy."

Ivy and Oliver fall into easy step, staying close beside each other in the crowded, bustling town.

"So, I think you'll like this story," Oliver says as they walk. "Today, Matt asked me for an island breeze, and I told him I was out of pineapple juice. He said he'd take it with orange juice, and I told him I was out of vodka. Then, when I happened to walk past him at the pool, I 'accidentally' spilled his blue lagoon all over his Tommy Bahama floral button-up."

Ivy laughs. "Thank you for actively participating in a vendetta even though you barely know the parties involved. I appreciate it."

"Well, I wouldn't say I barely know *you*," he says. "And I know what he did to your friend."

They've arrived at the beach. A group of children are already gathered on the sand, all of them abuzz with anticipation as the holiday tree comes into view, then makes its way across the bay on a barge towed by a catamaran. The tree is greeted on the shore by cheers and whistles, then hauled onto a flatbed by a waiting crew.

"Just wait," Oliver whispers as the jubilant crowd turns back to the ocean. "Santa and his wife are a local couple," he explains—his whispers in her ear sending tingles up and down the length of her body, no matter how hard she tries to fight the sensation. "They dress up in the costumes year after year, delighting the kids on the island as they're drawn across the bay in the outrigger canoe. Santa rings a bell and yells 'Ho ho ho,' and the kids run into the surf to meet them."

"Wow," Ivy breathes. "They *are* getting pulled by dolphins."

"You see? This is pure magic, isn't it? I wish I'd brought my camera so I could take a photo of you right now."

The idea of him taking her photo makes her heart do a treacherously excited cartwheel, but luckily, she's distracted by Santa and Mrs. Claus climbing out of the canoe and wading to shore as the canoe and dolphins are driven back the way they came. They don't seem to care that their festive outfits are now half soaked. They greet the children enthusiastically, delivering pats on heads and "Ho ho hos" and cries of "Have you been good this year?" as they lead the crowd through the town, following the path of the tree on the flatbed. The streets are loud with singing and laughter, but it's a pleasant kind of loud that fills Ivy's ears like the rushing noise inside a seashell.

In the center of town, the tree is lifted up onto its heavy stand by as many as are able to help, and strung with a cavalcade of lights in mere moments. Cheers rise up into the air again as a traditional Hawaiian band sets up on the platform beside the tree and starts playing carols. The crowd sings along in Hawaiian to familiar tunes like "The Twelve Days of Christmas" and "Deck the Halls."

A reverent silence falls. Ivy watches as a woman dressed in red robes, a filmy yellow mantle across her shoulders, takes the stage. Her long, dark hair falls to the middle of her back. A leafy crown sits atop her head.

"That's one of the Hanalei kahunas," Oliver whispers, his breath warm in her ear. "Sort of like a town shaman, a healer."

The kahuna raises her arms, and the tree illuminates as if she has conjured the light, all dazzling and golden. Across the town, palm trees strung with Christmas lights are lit up, too; the world is a kaleidoscope of color. Ivy *oohs* and *aahs*, along with everyone else, completely caught up in the moment.

"Be the light," the kahuna says to the children below her, a sort of benediction.

Ivy stands still for a moment, letting it all wash over her. Oliver is watching her again, a huge smile on his face now.

She looks up at him. "That was awesome, Oliver. It really did cheer me up. Thank you."

Just then, a family with three young children jostles past them, and she's knocked closer to Oliver. He catches her by her waist so she doesn't fall. Instead of letting her go, he gazes down at her.

"What?" she asks, self-conscious.

"You had fun," he says. "Admit it."

His hands are still on her hips. His touch feels warm, and she suddenly has the urge to reach down and hold his hands against her, feel how smooth his skin is.

She's so intent on trying to brush these physical longings away, she hardly notices when there's a crash of thunder overhead. But milliseconds later, rain begins to fall in sheets, and she is brought back to reality. Oliver drops his hands from her hips and grabs her hand. "Come on!"

They run toward an empty market stall to take shelter—but just before they reach it, Ivy grinds to a halt. It's Matt and Abby, heading for the same shelter. "No," she says. "We have to go somewhere else."

Oliver sees them, too, and, taking his cue from Ivy's stricken expression, grabs her by the waist, pulls her close, and stares into her eyes as if he's about to kiss her. Ivy's body feels electrified, by the suddenness of this action, she tells herself, but she knows that's not all. The rain is falling so hard her clothes have soaked through, but all she can feel is the touch of his hands. *Get a hold of yourself, Ivy. This is not some romantic, cinematic scene in a rainstorm. He's just trying to hide you from someone you don't feel like facing right now. And. He. Has. A. Girlfriend.*

"Are they gone?" she manages.

"They're under the shelter, and they're not looking at us right now," Oliver says, his lips so close to hers she can almost taste him: she imagines citrus and coconut, a little bit of mint. "They've turned in the other direction." She stares at him through the rain. His pupils are dilated; she can only see slender green rings at the edges of his irises. They continue to stand perfectly still, staring into each other's eyes—and now Ivy feels like she couldn't move if she wanted to. He's the one who steps back, running one hand through his soaking wet hair, releasing a shaky breath.

"I know somewhere we can dry off," he finally says. "Larry's bar."

Right. Larry. His beautiful, incredibly kind girlfriend. Ivy forces herself back to a reality where she and Oliver are not, in fact, the only two people on the planet, the way it felt seconds before, and follows him.

❀ ❀ ❀

"Here we are." They've reached the Black Pearl. Its sign swings above their heads, a carved wooden oyster with a radiant black orb inside. Oliver pulls her through the front door, and they stand in the entrance dripping, laughing at themselves.

"Hey, come on in, let's get you two dry!" Larry calls out. She reaches under the bar and comes up with a handful of towels. Crossing the room, she hands some to Ivy, then turns her attention to Oliver. She stands on her tiptoes and rubs his hair with her towel so it stands up wildly in all directions.

"Hey," he says, patting it down. "You're messing with the do."

"Honey, the rain messed with the do. Nothing could make it worse. We've been friends a long time, so I feel I can be this honest with you."

Ivy feels a twinge, watching them together. They seem to have that rare combination of deep friendship and romance that Ivy didn't think existed until she met them. But as Oliver grabs a towel from Larry and snaps it as she dances lightly away, Ivy knows it does exist. "What am I going to do with you?" Larry says over her shoulder as she heads back behind the bar.

Whatever spark she felt earlier with Oliver was surely one-sided. He had promised to shield her from Matt, that was all. And Larry is an angel. Ivy will not allow herself to feel jealous, will not indulge a wish to steal her boyfriend. Ivy is not that person. She takes off her soaked baseball cap, gathering her long, sopping hair into a ponytail, which she attempts to wring out into the towel.

"Please, just wring it out onto the floor," Larry calls out with a friendly smile. "Your hat, too. Go ahead, it's fine. I'll mop it all up in a sec."

Once Ivy and Oliver are some approximation of dry, Larry runs a mop over the floor while telling them to take a seat at the bar. Ivy takes in her surroundings. Larry's bar is quirky and inviting; the walls are papered with vintage postcards depicting scenes from the South Pacific and various Hawaiian vistas. Strings of lights shaped like pineapples, surfboards, and palm trees are strung haphazardly across the top of the bar and from the ceiling, too. A record player sits behind the bar, and there are shelves beside the bottles stocked with vinyl.

Larry is currently spinning Janis Joplin's *Pearl*; Janis is singing about a guy who fills her like mountains, fills her like the sea.

"You two drowned rats look like you could use a cocktail," Larry says. "Bartender's choice?"

"Sure," Ivy says. She glances over at Oliver, who has a weird look on his face. "What?"

"Oh, you don't know what you're signing up for," Oliver says as Larry pulls a jar of juice with a big red skull and crossbones on it out of the fridge. "You see?" Oliver declares. "Skull and crossbones."

Ivy feels mildly alarmed. "What is that?"

"My special jalapeño-pineapple juice. Can you handle hot stuff, Ivy?"

"Of course," Ivy says, and now Oliver's sidelong glance seems to turn flirtatious.

"Yeah?" he says lightly, and she feels that one word zing like an electrical jolt that lands at the base of her pelvis, where heat begins to spread.

Maybe Holly is right. Maybe the idea of two weeks of sexual deprivation is too much for her libido—but she *has* to rein these feelings in, and now.

"I like spicy food," Ivy says primly, turning away from him and focusing on the decor again as Larry stands before them, mixing up their drinks. There are framed photos behind the bar—some of Larry and Oliver, Ivy notices, both smiling and looking blissfully happy, and others of Larry, Oliver, and another woman, or just Larry and the woman.

"Great photos," Ivy says. Larry's smile grows wider.

"Aren't they? We had just gotten engaged in that one." Ivy hates that her heart plummets when Larry says this. *They're engaged?* She hopes her expression isn't betraying her, that her smile doesn't look as pained as it feels. "After we're married, we'll finally live together full-time and not do this long-distance, all-over-the-place stuff." She tilts her head. "Although we still haven't quite figured out how that's going to work." Then she shrugs and smiles again, as Ivy thinks about what Oliver said to her when he was showing her the apartment—about how he only winters here in Hawaii, and has a serious case of wanderlust. "We will, though." Larry mixes mezcal and Malibu rum with the spicy juice in a cocktail shaker. She's more straightforward than Oliver is as a bartender; she doesn't toss the shaker or showboat around behind the bar, just does her job steadily while singing Janis Joplin at the top of her lungs.

"When's the wedding?" Ivy asks, directing the question at Oliver.

"Did you guys set an official date yet?" Oliver asks Larry, to Ivy's confusion.

"Shira's still waiting to hear from a venue in LA, but I'm hoping I can convince her to do it here, on the beach. Who knows, maybe we'll just have two ceremonies?"

"Wait—who's Shira?"

Larry pours the concoction into martini glasses, tops it all off with prosecco, and garnishes it with jalapeño rings, which float like little lifeboats in the sunny yellow cocktail.

"There you go. The Hawaiian bonfire. My jalapeño-infused pineapple juice will make you forget all about being caught in the rain. And what do you mean, who's Shira?" She points at one of the photos, one with just Larry and the woman, who has a blunt blond bob, amber eyes, and a smile just as infectious as Larry's. "She's my fiancée."

Ivy looks between Oliver and Larry. "But I thought . . ."

"You thought *what*?" Oliver says, a slow smile stealing over his face.

"That you and Larry . . ." Ivy feels embarrassed now, and it doesn't help that Oliver seems delighted by her mistake.

"That *we* were a couple? I thought I mentioned to you that Larry is my best friend."

"I thought you were one of those smug couples who says you're also best friends," Ivy mutters, and Oliver laughs, then clinks his glass against Ivy's, takes a sip, sputters dramatically. "Whoa, this is your hottest batch ever, Lar."

"Shira is a film director and lives in LA, but she'll be here for Christmas. She gets here tomorrow." Larry hops up and down now. "I'm so excited. And no, Oliver is not my boyfriend."

Ivy takes a sip of her own drink to cover up how flustered she is. She tries to ignore what she suspects is relief coursing through her body at the fact that Oliver and Larry aren't a pair. *No flings on art holidays*, she reminds herself, but her inner voice is already growing weak.

Larry is wiping the counter and singing along to the Janis Joplin record again. "Hey, Lar, you're a great singer and all, but it's the holiday season!" Oliver says. "Tonight was the tree lighting! Don't you think you should be playing carols?"

Larry looks at Ivy and rolls her eyes. "Honestly, he's like a child this time of year, right? No, I do *not* think I should be playing bland Christmas carols, thank you very much. Me, Janis, and Bobby McGee here are perfectly fine."

"Agreed," Ivy says, and she finds herself smiling as Larry starts singing again—because her joy is infectious, but Ivy knows there's something else behind her own happiness. Now Oliver leans his head close.

"Hey," he says as Larry goes off to serve a small group of patrons who have come through the door, as rain-soaked as they were. She turns her gaze toward him, feeling that electrical zing again, this time causing a tantalizing throb between her legs. If all he has to do to make her feel that way is look at her, Ivy can't help but wonder what sort of magic would happen if they actually touched.

But no. *No.* She will not.

"Did it bother you, when you thought Larry and I were a couple? Were you disappointed, by any chance?"

"You think highly of yourself, don't you?" Ivy says, taking a large sip of the spicy drink, grateful that the hot sensation on her lips and in her mouth gives her something else to focus on other than him.

He shrugs, flashes his dimple at her. "I guess I'm just trying to think about how I would feel, seeing you with a guy I thought you were with. I think I'd be a little jealous. I like you, Ivy."

This must be how he does it, Ivy thinks. He's probably getting laid left, right, and center, with his good looks and extreme confidence. Who just comes out and says, *I like you, Ivy?*

Exactly the kind of guy you're most attracted to. The sexy, self-assured kind. The kind who would probably, if you gave him the go-ahead, push you against this bar and kiss you like you've never been kissed before.

He had spoken the final words close to her ear, and the soft rumble of his voice sends another shiver through her body. *What the hell, Ivy? He's just a guy. Get a hold of yourself.* "I like you, too," Ivy says, her voice schoolmarm-prim, somehow, when it could just as easily be full of the desire she can't seem to get control of. She takes another fortifying sip of the spicy cocktail, while Oliver raises his eyebrow, making her feel like he can read her mind and knows exactly what she wishes they could do, possibly right against this bar. "But these two weeks every year are sacred to me. I don't have room for anyone or anything other than my art."

He leans back and nods. "Right. You only make those gorgeous pastel landscapes once a year, for some reason."

She looks away from him and back at the photos behind the bar. Beside the personal ones of Larry, Oliver, and Shira, there are other, professional-looking photos, all framed, all very similar to the photographs of ocean waves at the apartment. "Those are spectacular photos," she says, hoping a change of subject will make her feel less powerless against her attraction. "I saw some like that at the apartment. Who's the photographer?"

Now, all at once, Oliver's expression changes. And Ivy knows that sort of look. "Wait a minute," she says. She raises herself on her barstool, leans over, and squints at the images in the framed photo, and, all at once, sees the tiny silver signature at the base of each one: "Oliver Donohue." She turns to him. "*You* took those."

He waves a hand as if it's nothing that he's so talented.

"Oliver, come on, these are great. Like, good enough to be in *National Geographic* or something. I've never seen waves and water captured like that. It feels like they could come right off the paper. The movement, yet the stillness. They're perfect."

He looks even more bashful now. "Well, actually, my photos have been in *Nat Geo* a few times. I'm working on a photo-essay for them right now. That's what I was doing this morning."

So he isn't just a bartender-surfer. He's a bartender-surfer-photographer. Which, unfortunately, means her attraction to him is now in overdrive. "The amount of patience it must take to catch the waves like that," she says. "I've never seen anything like these." Maybe if she can keep the talk centered around art, she'll be okay.

He leans over the bar and points at the top one, a photograph of a wave curled tight like the top of an intricately carved violin. "You're right that it takes patience. It usually takes me at least five or six hours to get just one perfect shot of a wave. That one, I think, took about ten. My entire body was a prune." He settles back down onto his stool. "I also take a hell of a lot of pounding and have been almost concussed more than once. The ocean is the boss, and you'd think I'd know better by now, but I get taken for a ride every single time."

"I can tell from the way you're talking about it that you love it, though."

His grin widens. "*Adore* it. That moment I know I've got *the* shot—and I always know, even before I look at it—it's the absolute best feeling. Nothing like it in the world."

"I get that, in a way," says Ivy. "I mean, I'm not getting my head pounded into the sand of a beach, but I have to be patient when I'm doing my landscapes, wait for the light to be just right. I know I could take a photograph and draw from that—and I do, sometimes. I did that with the tree, for example. But there's nothing like being immersed in the perfect, most beautiful, natural moment—and creating it on a page at the same time. I feel one with it, if that makes sense? One with my entire life."

"Makes perfect sense," he says. During their conversation, he's moved his stool closer, and their arms aren't touching, but almost. She can feel the now familiar sensation of the hairs on her arms standing up, almost as if they're straining to reach out and touch him. "I feel it, too. That I'm one with the wave, maybe even the whole ocean. That it has a message, and I'm the conduit. I chase that feeling." She notices that this close, and in this light, his ocean green eyes have a ring of indigo outlining the iris, and that at night they look more green-gray than green-blue. She thinks of the shades in her favorite box of soft oil pastels. Maybe transparent blue mixed with light gray. No, English gray and charcoal blue.

He tilts his head, quizzical. "Is there something in my eye?"

"I'm sorry—I do this a lot. Sort of forget I'm in the real world and start trying to figure out the colors I'd use to draw things. My best friend is used to it, but for other people, it takes a little time."

"What are you thinking about drawing?"

Her throat goes dry and her pulse speeds up. "You," she says, trying to make it sound like she says this sort of thing to people all the time. "Your eyes, specifically."

The sexy smile dimple has made an appearance. "You'd want to draw me?"

It feels like it takes far too much effort to drag her gaze away this time. "Sure, why not?" she says. "Something tells me you're a bit like a wave, though. Might be hard to get you to sit still for long."

"I'd sit still for you," he says. "For as long as you wanted me to."

Ivy breaks his gaze, puts down her drink, and decides to be frank. "I can't do this," she says.

Oliver looks confused. "Do what?"

"I can't keep flirting like this. I'm sure if we got together we'd have a lot of fun. But I'm sort of an all-or-nothing person. I can get very focused. And I can't spend a night with you"—as she says those words, she feels that pulse between her legs again, so intense this time it almost makes her squirm in her seat—"because, as I said, I've made a commitment to myself and to my art. I have to focus."

Now his eyes are lit up with blue-green fire. "What makes you think it would just be a onetime thing?" he says.

"Isn't that what you do?" she asks him. "One-night stands with tourists?"

He frowns and stays silent. Larry is approaching again, and Ivy doesn't tell her not to when she starts preparing her a refill.

"Hey, you know, Larry," she says, turning her attention as firmly as she can away from Oliver. "I think a case can be made for Janis Joplin's 'Mercedes Benz' actually being a Christmas song, right?"

Larry laughs as she adds the final touch of prosecco to Ivy's cocktail glass, then mixes Oliver another drink, too. "You're absolutely right. It's like a Christmas wish list. A new car, a color TV, a night on the town—it's positively festive. Hey, are you guys hungry? All I have here are bar snacks, but I'm starved. Ollie, would you go across to the Manapua Man truck and get us some dumplings? Pretty please?"

Oliver hops off his stool. "One of my Oliver's Tourism Board highlights. Come on," he says to Ivy. "You can help me pick."

The food truck is a Westfalia van, parked across the street, with a sign on top that says "Manapua Man." The savory smells emanating from the van's window make Ivy's mouth water immediately. She forgot how hungry she was.

"Hey, Noa." Oliver greets the man leaning his head out the window, wearing a red hat that says "Manapua Man" in yellow writing, with a hibiscus flower beside it.

He glances at Ivy. "What do you feel like?"

"Tell me what's good."

"Three four-packs of faux char siu steamed, and three of veggie baked, please."

The big, fluffy dumplings are ready quickly, nestled in compostable cardboard boxes. Ivy takes three of the six boxes and they cross the street again, but just outside the door of the bar, Oliver turns to Ivy and looks down at her. "Hey," he says. "I'm sorry. I was being really forward in there. I get the importance of keeping your creative time sacred. I really do. I won't do that again, okay? Friend zone from here on out. I meant what I said—I like you—and I'd still like to hang out while you're here. Cool with you?"

"Of course," Ivy says. "I am living in the same house as you, so it's going to be pretty impossible to avoid each other."

"Exactly," he says. "And why would we want to?"

That thump of desire hits her again, but she's almost sure it's fainter than it was before. Or maybe she's just getting used to it.

Back at the bar top, Ivy takes a bite of one of the faux char siu dumplings. It's delicious, the filling a silky fermented bean curd bathed in sweet-salty sauce. "*Mmmm.*" She finishes it in two bites.

"I take it you like them?"

"Love them," Ivy says, eating her way through the rest of the box and starting on the baked veggie. During a lull in bar patrons, Larry takes a break and eats with them, and says, "Okay, as a thank-you for dinner, I will put on a Christmas album for you, Ollie."

His face lights up like one of the light-strung palms outside. "Really?" He turns to Ivy. "This is huge. She never lets me listen to Christmas music. I don't even know what to pick, but think I have to go with the festive classic Bing Crosby's *Merry Christmas*, right?"

Ivy laughs and shrugs. Larry puts on the album and goes to serve some new customers as Bing Crosby begins to gently croon "Silent Night."

"I'm almost sure I've never met anyone as into Christmas as you are," Ivy says. "Why is that? Did you have the most excellent celebrations when you were a kid?"

All the joy suddenly leaves his expression, as if she's snuffed out a candle. "Not exactly," he says. "But I always knew what I wanted my Christmases to look like when I got older. I'm more about making my own traditions than looking back at the past."

She can tell she's inadvertently hit a nerve. "I'm sorry," she says. "I touched something raw there."

"No, no, it's really okay. I didn't have the best childhood, but I've moved past it. My dad was kind of the worst. But I'm okay. Really. I have the therapy receipts to prove it."

Larry approaches with a tray of shot glasses. "Those women in the corner asked for snowballs and I accidentally made polar bears. You two game?"

"Sure," Ivy says, accepting a shot and clinking her glass against Larry's and Oliver's before downing the chocolaty-minty concoction. "Honestly, Larry, you are the best bartender ever."

"Hey," Oliver says, feigning hurt feelings.

"Come on, Ollie, you can't have everything. You get to be the best photographer, let me keep my class A bartending skills," Larry says. She also pours them pints of water, and crosses the room to serve a new table.

Oliver is staring at Ivy again—intently, at her lips. "Hey," Ivy says, swatting at him.

"You have some crushed candy cane on your lips, from the side of the glass. That's all." He points to her cupid's bow.

She licks the bit of candy cane off and hops down from her stool. Her resolve is wavering. She needs to put some space between them again. "You know what? This album is actually pretty catchy." Bing is now singing about Santa Claus coming to town, and Ivy shakes her hips. "Makes me want to dance."

He watches her for a moment, his expression inscrutable, before hopping off his chair, too. "Finally," he says. "It just took festive cocktails to get you in the spirit. But I'll take it." He grabs her hips, sending a shower of sparks up and down her skin, and they dance together for a moment while she tells herself she can handle this—she can have fun with a guy she's this attracted to, be friends with him. It doesn't have to go any further.

His one-dimpled smile is full of mischief now. "Come on, let's see how mad Larry gets if we dance on the bar. She should know better anyway—Christmas music always gets me *way* too excited." Ivy laughs and follows him as he shimmies onto the bar top, while Larry shrieks at them good-naturedly from across the room and fake threatens to kick them out. No harm is being done here, Ivy tells herself. She's having a great time. She'll get back to work tomorrow. For now, it's perfectly okay to be in the moment, dancing on a bar, laughing up at the light-strung ceiling.

10

HOLLY
December 22
Hudson Valley, New York

Holly uses the code Aiden gave her—"SNOWY"—to open up the shed, finding several pairs of skates, including one in her size. She loads them into her car and drives into town, following Aiden's directions to the winter sports shop. She's early and he's not there yet, so she gives the skates to the tall, curly-haired older man behind the counter, who tells her with a smile that his name is Martin McLaren, he's been sharpening skates his entire life, and they'll be ready "in a jiffy"—which in Krimbo speak, he says, is about twenty minutes.

She decides to go to Seventh Heaven to get a coffee while she waits. Bells tinkle merrily above her head as she enters the café. She's greeted by the aroma of fresh bread, and something sweet and spicy baking.

Just as she approaches the counter, Aiden's sister-in-law, Sidra, today in a crimson apron, her dark hair swept up in a tousled topknot, pushes open the green swinging doors leading from an industrial kitchen. She's carrying a tray of cocoa-brown cookies with crinkled edges and a glossy chocolate coating.

"Holly," she says with a smile, blowing tendrils of hair out of her face as she puts the tray down. "So glad to see you back. What can I get you?"

"Just a coffee today, thanks."

"Are you sure? I've got fresh Lebkuchen: a ginger-cookie base, heavy on the spices, with a thick buttercream filling and a cinnamon-chocolate glaze."

"That sounds incredible," says Holly. "Okay, I'll take one, please."

Sidra's smile widens as she uses the rose gold tongs to choose two fresh cookies for Holly. Then she pauses, tongs aloft, and adds another cookie. "You seem very enthusiastic about our cookie-of-the-day program. So I'm throwing in one extra on the house."

"Who's getting cookies on the house?"

A second woman bustles through the swinging kitchen doors, a forest green and red plaid kerchief covering her brown hair. Her eyes are vibrant blue, just like Aiden's. She's carrying a tray of sandwich buns.

"You must be Alexa, Aiden's sister. You look so much alike."

"I guess. And you are . . . ?"

"This is Aiden's high school friend," Sidra says. "The one I was telling you about, staying out at the cabin on the North Service Road?"

"Holly Beech, nice to meet you," Holly says with a smile—but Alexa doesn't smile back.

"The one who loved the peppermint snowdrifts," Sidra prompts, hands on hips, her smile now full of good-natured teasing. "Which I *told* you were perfect." She turns back to Holly. "Alex is a cookie perfectionist, and she was worried Friday's snowdrift batch wasn't up to her usual standards. She forgot to add the green and red jimmies to the icing, you see. A travesty, according to her."

"The jimmies are very important for color and texture," Alexa explains, like she's talking about a lifesaving brain-surgery technique and not holiday cookies. "It's a key step in the peppermint snowdrift baking process, and I forgot."

"It was the best cookie I've ever had, I swear," Holly says. "Jimmies or no jimmies."

"Thank you," Alexa says curtly, picking up a bread knife and beginning the work of splitting the buns on the tray she has just put down. "So, you know Aiden," she says as she cuts. Holly nods. "You went to that snobby private school he got the scholarship to?" She looks up as Holly stops nodding. "Where no one would give him the time of day or invite him to any parties and so he kicked every single one of their asses academically and proved he really did belong there?"

"Oh, well . . ."

Sidra puts her hand on Alexa's shoulder and gives it a gentle rub. "Holly, my wife has zero filter. It's normally a cute quirk—but honey, we are dealing with a new customer, not someone who already knows and adores you." She says this last bit out of the side of her mouth. Alexa just rolls her eyes, but she does smile at Sidra. Her expression turns somewhat frosty again when she turns back to Holly, though.

"Well, sure, she's a customer, but she also said she's an old friend of Aiden's, right? And you were just giving her cookies on the house, which is a practice reserved for close friends only—or we'd go out of business. So, she's sort of a customer hybrid." Alexa sets down the knife and tilts her head, thinking. "Wait." She snaps her fingers. "Holly *Beech*. I do think he mentioned that name back in the day. Weren't you the one whose grades and scores he was always chasing? He called you his pacesetter. But you barely knew he existed?"

"Alexa!" Sidra's tone is sterner now. "Please accept my apology," she says to Holly. "The local retirement home's annual holiday luncheon is today, and then the Snowflake Dance, and we're working double time to make sure we have enough cookies—"

"Which is why I don't understand why we made it the special *and* why you're giving them away," Alexa mutters as she sets back to work.

Sidra just slides another Lebkuchen into the bag and presses it into Holly's hands. "We do hope you come back again soon."

"No, really, I'll pay," Holly says, but neither Sidra nor Alexa makes a move toward the cash register, so she takes out a ten and shoves it in the tip jar.

"Phew," she mutters as she exits. Alexa and Aiden might look similar, but they couldn't be more different.

She heads back to the sports shop and is trying on the newly tuned skates when Aiden comes in.

"Nice socks," he says by way of greeting, his blue eyes sparkling.

She laughs. "I honestly thought I was going to spend two weeks without seeing another human being, let alone showing off my fuzzy novelty Bumble the Yeti socks," Holly says.

"Let me guess, a gift from your friend Ivy?"

"Correct!"

"I feel like I know her already," he says as she takes the skates to the counter to pay.

Outside, Holly offers to drive to the river, and they walk toward her car. Inside it, she turns on the heaters and invites him to find a local radio station. He spins the old-fashioned radio dial and settles on a station playing

Christmas music. As the car fills with the sound of Dolly Parton's voice singing "With Bells On," Holly pulls the paper bag of cookies out of the canvas bag she brought to town. "Hey, want a cookie? Pre-skating sustenance? I was in the café earlier, and Sidra gave me a few extra."

Aiden takes the paper bag and looks inside. "Uh-oh. Sometimes Sidra has to launch a diplomatic mission with free cookies—and that's a lot of Lebkuchen. Was Alexa in a mood?"

"It sounds like there are a lot of town events going on today. She was . . . a bit stressed?"

"You're being kind. My sister is . . ." He pauses and considers his words, and Holly finds herself smiling as she pulls out of her parking spot, at his habit of mulling over everything he says so carefully. "When she and Sidra lived in San Francisco, Alexa worked for a multinational bank and finally admitted she'd become a workaholic about two years after we'd all figured that out already. She suffered severe burnout. This move to Krimbo was good for her mental and physical health—but she still acts like multimillion-dollar accounts are hanging in the balance on busy days at the café."

Holly laughs. "Okay, that's definitely the vibe I got. She was very serious about leaving the jimmies out of the peppermint snowdrifts yesterday."

Aiden laughs. "Sounds accurate. You get used to Alexa, and *then* you love her. But it's a process."

"Maybe I need to give these free cookies back and take some of the pressure off her."

"If you've got free Lebkuchen in that bag, hold on for dear life—except for the one you're going to give me." He takes a bite and talks with his mouth full. "Because no one says no to Sid and Alex's Lebkuchen."

Aiden gives directions, and soon Holly drives down a short dead-end road leading to an opening in the trees where the river is visible. They step out of the car into complete wintry stillness. The evergreens are heavy with snow; the birches are pale, stately and shining with ice. The frozen water of the river curves out of Holly's view like an undone ribbon on a present. "Gorgeous," she breathes. "I love the way everything feels so silent, so peaceful, after a good snowfall. Like the world is extra insulated. Safe."

"When I'm here in winter, sometimes I wonder if there's anywhere in the world that could be more peaceful," he agrees.

They sling their skates over their shoulders by their laces, and Holly follows Aiden to a fallen tree log a few feet from the riverbank. He clears it of snow so they can sit down and put on their skates, and as the Bumble the Yeti socks make another appearance, Aiden catches her eye and smiles.

Skates on and tied, Holly tentatively steps down onto the ice and glides for a moment. The pleasant sound her blades make on the ice reminds her of childhood, when her nana would take her skating at Rockefeller Center during every

Christmas holiday. Aiden skates ahead a bit, adding the sound of his skates to hers. As he does a figure eight, Holly laughingly calls out, "Show-off!" But she increases her pace, too, and soon they're racing down the ice together. As she chases after him, overtakes him, and then he chases after her, Holly is reminded of how he used to make her feel in high school. The way she always wanted to keep up with him. But maybe it wasn't a bad thing, she suddenly thinks. Maybe Aiden always brought out the best in her.

They slow at a bend in the river and begin to skate along beside each other in companionable silence. Holly takes in the towering pines, the white-clad hills and mountains visible in the distance through breaks in the trees, the riverbanks covered in snow that glitters in the sunshine. They glide under a quaint stone bridge, then around another bend. "It's perfect here," Holly finds herself saying.

"Isn't it?" Aiden says. "This is one of my favorite things to do, and I rarely make the time—so thanks for saying yes to going skating with me."

"I'm so glad you asked."

Around another bend, the river narrows, and leaf-bare maple trees crowd in close, their limbs frosted with snow and ice that shines blue-white in the sun filtering through the forest canopy. There are more evergreens, too, and every one of them is perfectly shaped, like the vintage ceramic ones in the window display of the antique store in

Krimbo. Up ahead, bright color catches Holly's eye: one of the evergreens has been decorated with red and gold balls, hung with tree lights. She gasps. "Who did that?"

"People in Krimbo *really* love Christmas," Aiden says. "You never know when you're going to happen upon a fully decorated tree—even in the middle of nowhere."

"I love that," Holly says happily, marveling at how easy it is to love Christmas in a magical place like this.

At a section of the river covered in blown snow, they're forced to slow down, then turn back. Holly hits a small crack in the ice, wobbles, and nearly falls, but Aiden grabs her mittened hand with his gloved one. He holds her steady as they skate back the way they came. He doesn't let go, and neither does she.

"Aiden?" she finally says as the log where they first put on their skates comes into view. He releases her hand, and she wishes he hadn't.

"Yes, Holly?"

"I'm having such a good time out here." They slow to a stop at the edge of the river and turn to face each other. His eyes are an even brighter blue than usual, his cheeks vibrant from the cold.

"Me, too," he says. "I'm so glad *you* turned out to be Ivy Casey."

She wants to say something more, wants to tell him that every moment with him so far has been one she doesn't want to end. But she's too nervous, too uncertain of herself. They take off their skates and get back in her car, but she still has the same sensation, one she doesn't know what to do with.

As she starts the engine, his phone sounds a text message notification, then another. He pulls it out of his pocket to check. He looks up at her. "It's Sid. She says she's really embarassed about how Alex acted earlier. She wants me to apologize to you—and tell you Alexa is great. It's just—"

"A process," Holly says, waving a hand. "It's fine."

But Aiden's expression is now clouded with concern. Holly turns up the car's heat and waits for him to say what's clearly on his mind. "Don't get me wrong, Alex is . . . she's a lot at the best of times. But she seems to be veering toward a burnout again, when this move to Krimbo was supposed to take away stress. And Sidra is her person, you know? But lately Alex seems all about pushing her away." He bites his lip and looks down at his phone before putting it away again—while Holly feels touched by how much he clearly cares for his sibling and sister-in-law. "My parents make it look so easy. My grandparents, too. But marriage, long-term releationships, they aren't all that easy." He shakes his head. "Sorry. You're not my therapist. I'll save this for my next session."

"Aiden, you can talk to me. And I agree with you. Relationships are complex. Marriage or a long-term commitment . . . that's a a big step." The word "marriage" feels like it rasps against her throat on the way out like stone against stone. She fiddles with the car's heat again, even though it's the right temperature, and thinks about what it might be like to tell Aiden everything. About Matt, and how she thought she was going to get married and live happily ever after, but was so very wrong. About how even just a few days away from Matt has made her realize how firmly she put on blinders in her quest to reach her life goals. Tears suddenly threaten, and she finds herself blinking them back with force. She's having a really nice day, and she wants to keep it that way. So she bites back the emotion she's feeling, looks up at him, and smiles. "But Sidra seems so great. I'm sure they'll work it out."

He's looking at her, thoughtful again. "Yeah," he says. "Thanks, Holly." But he holds her gaze, clears his throat. "So, uh, you know how part of the reason Sidra and Alexa are so busy today is because of the Snowflake Dance, right?"

"Yes, they mentioned that."

"It's at the high school and is pretty much what it sounds like, a holiday-themed dance, but for the whole town, not just teens." He tilts his head. "Do you want to come?"

"Aiden, you don't have to take me all over the place and invite me to everything just because I'm on my own during the holiday season. I'm fine, really. You don't have to feel sorry for me."

"I don't feel sorry for you. That's not why I asked you."

She couldn't look away from him if she tried. The lure

of his gaze feels magnetic, and being near him makes her body buzz with the kind of excitement she hasn't felt in ages—maybe ever. Is this what a rebound feels like? Should she be doing this?

She wants to, she realizes. It feels good. So she says with a smile, "How fancy is this dance? I only brought yoga pants and cozy sweaters."

"You'd look great in anything," Aiden says, and his cheeks flush as he finally looks away. "People do tend to dress up, though. But truly, yoga pants and a sweater will be fine."

"It's just, I may never get invited to a school dance again— so I want to do it right. Any clothing shops in town?"

"There's Viola's Dress Barn, which is my grandma's favorite shop, if that tells you anything." He grins. "She's stylish, but still . . . she's also in her eighties."

"Okay, so no to Viola's."

"And there's a thrift shop, Bebe's Bargains. It's the last store before Main Street ends."

"I love thrifting," Holly says. "It'll be fun to see what I can find."

His answering smile causes a flutter in the pit of her stomach, and she thinks of how it felt when he held her hand as they skated down the river. Rebound or not, bad timing or not, she *likes* him. He makes her forget about who she is now, all she's been through, and remember who she used to be—and right now, that's the best feeling in the world.

11

IVY
December 22
Kauai, Hawaii

The rooster's crow at dawn feels like an aural ice pick in Ivy's temple. She grabs a pillow and holds it over her head, but the shrill crowing continues. Memories from the night before swirl in her head like she's hit the start button on a blender. *Janis Joplin. Bobby McGee. Spicy pineapple juice. Mezcal. Manapua Man. Oliver. Larry. Trying to forget. Bing Crosby. A mop in my hand.*

Had she . . . danced on the bar at one point the night before? She remembers a delighted Oliver finally getting his wish and Larry putting on a Bing Crosby album. Larry had whispered to Ivy that she always let him do this when she wanted the bar to clear out a little so she could go home early, but they had ended up staying late, hanging out and drinking a few more of those strong, spicy cocktails. Eventually, Ivy remembers telling Larry that she likes to clean while drunk—which is patently not true; she just needed something to occupy herself so she didn't stand staring at Oliver, besotted and googly-eyed in her drunken state, despite her promise to herself to keep this trip focused on art only.

She has a dim memory of stumbling back home with Oliver and Larry, laughing as she stumbled up the stairs to her apartment. She sees that her clothes are strewn from one end of the apartment to the other. A glass of water, half empty, sits beside the bed—good intentions, at least. The blinds are wide open and the early-morning sun streams through. But, she tells herself, she's not going to close the blinds and go back to sleep, because that is not why she's here. She's here to *work*—and that's what she's going to do, regardless of her hangover, or her confused emotions for a guy named Oliver.

Ivy stands, and the room spins for a second, but she makes it to the bathroom, where she brushes the taste of the spicy pineapple bonfires away with minty toothpaste. In the shower, she lets the water run icy cold at the end, and emerges feeling much better.

In the kitchen, she brews her coffee as strong as possible, and—after two cups, gulped straight—the hangover releases some of its grip on her. But she's still feeling too rough to attempt an ambitious day trip, so she packs her art supplies with some water and fruit, thinking she'll simply wander down the beach until she finds scenery that inspires her.

She's halfway down the steps to the beach when she hears a male voice.

"Morning, sunshine."

She looks down and sees Oliver through the slats in the steps. He's sitting on the terrace of the apartment below at a small table covered in breakfast remnants: a coffee carafe, an orange juice jug, pastry crumbs, a butter dish, a pot of jam. Larry, wearing a short black silk kimono robe, steps out onto the terrace holding a water jug and two glasses. Her bed-mussed black curls tumble down her shoulders; her tanned legs go on for days.

"Ivy!" She flashes a delighted, toothy smile. "You look gorgeous. This is not fair. You do not look like someone who consumed several of my bonfires last night *and* danced on my bar top."

"Oh, boy. I was kind of hoping that was just a dream," Ivy says.

"Meanwhile, I—" Larry shakes her head and laughs, swiping her hands up and down her gorgeous self. "I'm a disaster."

She is decidedly *not* a disaster. She looks like she's just stepped off the runway of a Victoria's Secret show, and Oliver, in his white T-shirt and rumpled beige linen shorts, looks like her extremely sexy consort. But he's not. They are not a couple, just two very attractive best friends. And now that Ivy doesn't have the Hawaiian bonfires as armor, thinking about Oliver and the night before causes a flood of nerves to wash over her. She forces a smile she hopes doesn't betray her way-too-complicated attraction to Oliver. "Cold shower, strong coffee, tons of water. That's my hangover cure. And I'm sorry, I hope I wasn't too much last night."

"You were *the most* fun," Larry says. "Also, you insisted you love to clean while drunk, and so I had the bar closed in a fraction of the time I usually do. I appreciate it. Gave me more time to hang out with you." Another smile. "Now, come, sit. Let me show my gratitude by sharing some of our malasada pastries. I promise, all the sugar, butter, and cream will be the final nail in the coffin of your hangover."

Ivy glances at Oliver, whom she notices is being very quiet, just sitting still, smiling at her weakly from behind his Ray-Bans. "I don't want to interrupt . . . I was planning to go down the beach and do some drawing."

"*Please*, Ivy. We're stuffed, and the cream filling means these are never as good day-old."

Ivy sits opposite Oliver, and Larry pours her water and offers her juice or coffee.

"Larry, we're not at your bar," Oliver says. "You're at home. You don't have to serve everyone."

"I know that, Ollie," Larry says. "But I like Ivy, and I want her to be happy."

Meanwhile, Ivy notices that after he speaks, Oliver rubs

his temples. Larry follows her gaze. "He's regretting his nightcap last night. Or perhaps I should say night-*caps*. You were wise enough to say no to one and take yourself to bed."

"I barely remember doing it, so I'm not sure 'wise' is the right word, but you're right that I seem to have fewer regrets today than you do, Oliver."

"Good bourbon is never a bad idea," Oliver says, accepting a tumbler full of water from Larry after she pours Ivy's and drinking half of it in one gulp. "But apparently, sometimes it *is* a bad idea."

"Yes, well, you were talking my ear off before bed," Larry says dryly, glancing at Ivy.

"I'm sure it was just gibberish," he says quickly. "No need to discuss anything I may have said in present company. Anyway, I've *got* to get myself feeling better for work." He rubs his head again and groans. "This is an important day."

"Busy day at the hotel?" Ivy asks.

Oliver shakes his head. "I'm off for the next two days. I've got a camping trip planned at Nā Pali, a state park. I need one more shot for my *National Geographic* assignment. I've got all the wave images I plan to include, but there's a water-fall there I've been trying to catch the perfect image of for years. Maybe I'm just used to getting pounded by waves, but it's elusive, and it was part of the pitch to the magazine."

"I keep telling him the shots he has are incredible, but Oliver is a perfectionist—which is probably why *National*

Geographic is always beating down his door with assignments."

"I need *the* shot, not just *a* shot," Oliver insists, gulping more water. He stands. "I also need Advil."

He ambles inside, still rubbing his head. Larry watches him go, then turns back to Ivy. "What did you say your plan was for today? Just walking up the beach, looking for inspiration?" Ivy nods. "You should go with him! Talk about inspiration. Nā Pali is gorgeous." She grabs her phone from the tabletop and scooches her chair closer to Ivy's. "Hang on, let me find the album from the last time we camped there." She scrolls for a moment before turning the screen toward Ivy as she thumbs her way through photos of jagged cliffs and pristine beaches with otherworldly colors as Ivy looks on, dazzled.

"Wow," Ivy exclaims as she looks at a photo of a cliff range that appears to have been hand-carved by some mysterious god. The sharp angles rise into peaks that resemble castles; the colors tumble and pitch from deep forest green to sunshine yellow. "I've never seen anything like this. Not even here, and I've seen a lot of beauty on these beaches already."

"Nā Pali is really something else."

The next photo is of a waterfall that flows down the side of a cliff like the water is made of delicate spiderwebs. It's not especially big or powerful, but the way it flows is almost ghostly. "And here is Oliver's waterfall."

"The water looks like strands of silk. I can see why he might be finding capturing it so challenging."

"He's become a bit obsessed, but I don't blame him."

Ivy imagines what it might be like to try to draw those spun-silk strands of water, let alone capture them in a still photograph. She'd love to try, she realizes.

Larry scrolls to the next photo; it's of a campsite at the edge of a cliff overlooking the ocean. Shira is there, holding up a tin camping mug. Larry has her arm around her, and they've both been caught mid-laugh. "You know, I can't believe I ever thought you were with Oliver," Ivy says with a laugh. "You and Shira are clearly perfect for each other."

Larry smiles down at the image fondly. "I can't wait to see her—she's been back in LA, finishing postproduction on a film. She's a director. Her arrival is why I can't go camping with Ollie. I have to work so I can hand the reins over to a few of my staff and take some time off to be with her over the holidays." Larry is scrolling again through the photos. "Look at that view, Ivy. That's the Hanakāpīʻai Valley. It's beautiful here near Hanalei, yes, but being out on this more rugged coastline is a once-in-a-lifetime opportunity."

"I can't," Ivy says firmly.

"Why not?" But then Larry stops scrolling through photos and puts her phone down on the table. "Sorry. I shouldn't pressure you. Shira is always saying that just because my ideas seem great to *me* and I think everyone should always do what I say so the world would be a better place"—she laughs and so does Ivy—"does not mean that everyone else has to agree."

"No, it really does seem like a great idea. I just . . ."

"I get it. You don't know Oliver well enough to want to go off camping in the wilderness with him."

"I guess so," Ivy says, but she knows this is a half-truth, that she's always been an adventurer and that she feels she knows Oliver well enough to go camping with him. "It's not that."

Larry's voice is soft now. "What is it, then? Are you okay?"

"Sorry. Those cocktails are coming back to haunt me. My head's a bit foggy." She sighs. "But no, I'm not okay. I'm being a bit ridiculous about something. And I need to quit it. Nā Pali looks like a landscape artist's dream. When else will I ever get the chance to draw scenery like that, from real life?" She reaches for Larry's phone again and looks at the kaleidoscope of colors in the state park, the waterfalls, the streams, the breathtaking cliffs. She can feel her fingers tingle and itch with a yearning to translate all that onto paper with her pastels. It would be her best work, and she knows it. *Maybe* even good enough to want to tell the gallery owners who still call her sometimes that she has work she wants to show.

The next photo she scrolls to features a flock of seabirds flying through the sky as a lone fish jumps out of the dawn-flat ocean below.

"Wow, that's a *great* shot, Larry!"

"Every once in a while I take some of the stuff I've learned from being friends with Oliver and catch something special on my phone's camera," Larry says. "He's right that it takes patience. And a bit of luck."

Ivy gazes down at the photo—and all at once, a line comes into her head from the one romantic movie, other than *Meet Joe Black*, that she has always had a weak spot for: *Ever After*, the "Cinderella" retelling featuring Drew Barrymore.

She can see Drew's lovely, sweet, heartbroken face, hear her voice as she utters the line "A bird may love a fish, but where would they live?"

But she's not in love with Oliver. That's ridiculous. They've just met. It's chemical, a physical attraction. That's *all*. Okay, maybe a tiny bit intellectual, too, and maybe he's turning out to be one of the sweetest, weirdest, quirkiest, most thoughtful men she's ever met. And maybe she also likes his sense of humor. And his dedication to his art. But she can fight it.

Can't she?

Perhaps a night camping in the middle of nowhere with him could serve as some sort of inoculation against her feelings, she tells herself—could help ensure that she gets through the rest of the trip keeping him at arm's length.

"I think it's a really good idea, actually."

"What's a really good idea?" Oliver is back. "Ivy, you

looked like you were very deep in thought just now. My head was hurting just looking at you."

"I suggested Ivy go with you on your camping trip so I can be sure you don't slip on a rock in your hungover state and tumble down a cliff, never to be heard from again," Larry says.

Oliver shrugs. "Sure. You're welcome to come along." He seems to have almost no reaction to this idea, which makes Ivy feel somewhat relieved. Maybe last night was all in her head. Maybe Oliver is just a harmless flirt.

"I really wouldn't want to impose," Ivy says. "I don't have any camping gear—"

"No worries, you can use mine," Larry says. "I have doubles of everything for when Shira is here—most of it is practically brand-new because she's more of a five-star-hotel girl, though she's always game to humor us and try new things."

"I'd be happy to bring you along, Ivy," Oliver says. "You'll love it. You won't be able to draw fast enough. I'll be working the whole time, trying to get that damn shot, so I can't promise to entertain you personally—but I *can* promise you'll get what you came here for."

She pulls her gaze away from his blue eyes and looks down into her water glass. *What you came here for.*

"Okay. Sounds great." But she finds she can't look at him again, because she's afraid of what he might see in her eyes.

Larry leaps from the table. "I'll grab my gear. And *thank you*, Ivy—I think I would have just worried about him out there on his own—"

"I'm not a kid, Larry," Oliver protests. "I've camped alone dozens of times."

Larry waves a hand at him as she walks inside. "And you shouldn't. No one should camp alone. Thanks again for being my wing-woman on this, Ivy. I can't wait to see what you come back with."

Ivy dashes off a text to Holly, checking in and telling her she's going camping off-grid for a couple days with a friend she met. She decides to wait until later to unpack why she hasn't mentioned anything about Oliver. There's no time, anyway.

"Ready?"

"Yep." Ivy tucks her phone in her pocket and throws her pack into the back of Oliver's rust-speckled Jeep Wrangler before getting in. He unrolls the windows, and the warm breeze tousles her hair as he starts the engine.

Larry stands on the deck and waves goodbye to them as Oliver reverses down the driveway. Out on the road, he turns on the satellite radio, which is tuned to a Christmas music station. Ivy finds herself smiling at the incongruity of the sun-dappled ocean, lapis lazuli sky, and lush greenery all around—as Trisha Yearwood and Garth Brooks sing a duet about a marshmallow world, and Oliver sings along happily.

Oliver glances at her sidelong. "What's so funny over there? The world *isn't* your snowball?"

"This is just one of the most unusual holiday seasons I've ever had, that's all."

He turns left onto a dirt road. "Unusual in a good way?"

She thinks for a moment. "Yes, actually. It's nice meeting new people. New friends. Larry seems great, and you . . ."

"Yes? I'm waiting." His eyes are on the road, but he's grinning, and she can see the dimple out of the corner of her eye.

"I'm glad we met," Ivy says. "It's great to have another artist friend on a trip like this, someone who is just as serious about their work as I am." But as soon as those words are out, Ivy feels something creep over her. Something that almost feels like shame or embarrassment. Oliver senses the shift in her mood.

"Hey, what's up? You okay?"

Ivy sighs. "It must have sounded a bit ridiculous for me to say I'm just as serious about my art as you are. *You're* working on a big assignment for *National Geographic*. I'm just . . . doing little drawings for the sake of it."

"And that makes your art less meaningful than mine? Just because mine is for public consumption and yours isn't? On the one hand, I think maybe that makes your art purer. On the other, though . . ."

Now Bing Crosby is crooning about being home for Christmas.

"On the other, what?" she prompts.

"Ever since you explained to me why you were on this art honeymoon, I wondered why you had to compartmentalize things so much. Why *can't* your art be a bigger part of your life? Why does it have to be confined to two weeks per year? That first moment I saw you, you were standing in the shade of that tree you love at the hotel, looking like you wanted to memorize it—looking like you were in love with it. I've thought about that a few times, how passionate you are about your work."

They're driving down the highway now. On one side of the vehicle are the verdant green mountains; on the other, sand and glittering ocean as far as the eye can see. To Ivy, all at once, the vastness of the scenery, the almost incomprehensible beauty of it, compares to the way she feels about art. How big a role it could play in her life, if she could only let it. *Too* big. It would take over everything. "It's hard to explain" is all she is able to offer him, her tone closed and curt. He doesn't press her further, and she is silent and thoughtful for most of the rest of the drive to the state park.

Ivy wipes her brow with a bandana she tucked into the back pocket of her jean shorts, and takes a long swig of water. "Well, I think I may have found the ultimate cure to the Hawaiian bonfire hangover—a fourish-mile hike to a campsite in the Nā Pali park."

"Yeah? You think you're cured?"

"Absolutely. I was either going to be cured or die somewhere back there."

He laughs and swigs water, too. "You're right. I feel like a million bucks now, out of pure survival instinct."

They get to work setting up camp, and Ivy finds it just as satisfying as drawing. She likes the way she knows exactly what to do, from years spent camping as a child and teen, as she sets up her tent and then helps Oliver find a flat rock to set up their camp stove, solar-battery-powered cooler, and a plastic bin filled with their provisions.

The sun is high in the sky by the time they're finished.

"Hungry?"

"Yes! Especially after that hike."

"Hang on, I packed some sandwiches and fruit in the cooler. Let's have those, and then let's both head off and get to work."

She watches him as he sorts through the cooler. He seems perfectly at home out here, too, and incredibly happy. He's got a bandana tied around his hair, and his flannel shirt-sleeves are rolled up. Music is playing on the small speaker he brought—not Christmas music this time. She recognizes the same Leon Bridges song that was playing the day he showed her around the apartment.

"Can I help?"

"Nope. I'll just be a minute."

"Thanks, I'm just going to go change, then."

In her tent, Ivy peels off her sweaty hiking clothes and puts on her favorite Roots sweatpants and the only T-shirt she brought, from John's of Bleecker Street.

Oliver grins as she emerges from her tent wearing it.

"John's! The best pizza in the Big Apple."

"Glad you agree. Holly and I go back and forth between John's and Joe's, but I think John's wins the prize on ambience alone."

"Makes me miss NYC, seeing that shirt. I'll have to get out there for a visit next year."

She sits down in a camping chair he's unfolded and accepts a small plate with a sandwich and some cut-up pineapple.

"Wow, if this is roughing it with you, I think I like it!"

"I've never understood why 'roughing it' means freeze-dried food or jerky to some people. I even have wine for tonight, to go with my famous campsite pasta," he says, pulling a soft-sided flask from the cooler box near his chair, then two foldable glasses, which he unfolds and shows off. "Still ice-cold. That is, if you'll be able to handle it after last night." He puts the flask and glasses back into the cooler.

"Last night," Ivy repeats. "It actually feels like that was days ago. I think I've hiked enough and sweated enough that my system is entirely reset. Bring on the wine."

"*After* we get our work done."

"Exactly. The perfect reward."

"Glad Larry convinced you to come out here yet?"

"I've been glad since the moment we set off. This place is incredible."

"It is. I've learned over the years that Larry's ideas are generally good ones."

"How long have you two been friends?"

"About a decade," Oliver says. "She came to Hawaii for a surf trip once—she's from Mexico City—and decided to just stay. I admire that so much. She saved up, bought the dive bar she worked at, and made it into something awesome, earned enough to buy the house. She's tough and resourceful. She's been a godsend for me over the years, making sure I have a home base when I'm here, rather than just wandering around the world, aimless."

She listens to what he's saying, nodding along—but with every word, the more she learns about him, she finds herself growing more attracted, and it goes beyond the physical. The electricity is back, just the way it was last night. It wasn't just the strong cocktails, or the cozy bar setting, or the mood she was in. It's him. She likes him—way too much. She gets up from her chair and takes his plate from him, brushing it off with a napkin along with hers before putting it back in the cooler.

"Should we get a move on? I'm eager to get to work."

"Absolutely. Hey." Oliver stands up, too. "Here." He leans down and pulls something out of his pack: it looks like a bulky black plastic watch. "You'll need this."

"What is it?"

"It's a solar-powered satellite communicator. It means we can track each other's location, and you can find your way around." He turns it on, and a flashing beacon appears on a tiny map. "And we can communicate." He holds up his own device and presses a button. "Basically, it's a walkie-talkie, and means neither of us is ever really alone out here. I'd hate to lose you in the wilderness," he says. "Also, these are fun." He hits the communication button, then speaks into the watch in a comical growl: "Hello, Jovie 92, this is Buddy 90."

She laughs. "You are *such* a Christmas junkie . . ."

He ignores her. "I've got an APB on a mynah bird at eleven million lat and 8.3 trillion longe. Please confirm you see it, too. Roger."

Ivy hits her own button. "You're an idiot," she says.

He speaks into his device again. "That would be, 'Copy that, Buddy 90, this is Jovie 92, I read you loud and clear *and* you're an idiot. Over and out.'" They both laugh, and then he explains to her that there aren't any dangerous snakes or predator animals in Hawaii; it's mostly just the terrain she needs to be careful of.

"So, I'm going to hike out to the waterfall now and see if I can get a few shots in this late-afternoon light. You could head here." He points to a location near the ocean on her map. "It takes a bit of effort to get there because of the elevation, but it's worth it for the views. You might like those elevated spots as a start for your drawings."

"Actually, I'm kind of dying to see that waterfall, too," she says. "Mind if I just come along with you?"

"Oh . . ." He looks away. "Ivy, would it be horrible of me to say no? I've *really* got to focus this afternoon, and I think I might just need to be alone for a bit."

She feels her cheeks grow warm with embarrassment. "Of course. No problem at all. I totally get it."

"See you later, okay?"

He can't seem to get away from her fast enough, calling over his shoulder that he should be two to three hours, and they can meet back at their campsite for dinner later. "My famous pasta is on the menu, don't forget!" he adds over his shoulder, and then he's gone.

Ivy sighs, then turns and starts to hike in the direction he showed her—but as she walks, she can't help but think of their conversation in the truck on the way to the park. Oliver is clearly a true artist, and she's a hack in comparison. Which is supposed to be fine with her. Only now she doesn't like the way she feels. Oliver has made her question why she needs to compartmentalize the thing she loves most in the world into a mere two weeks every year—something she has forced herself to ignore for a long time.

Because that's the way it has to be, she tells herself as she hikes toward the lookout point Oliver recommended.

This place of otherworldly beauty doesn't *really* exist in her life. She wishes she could talk to Holly, who is always a steadying influence, but there's no cell service out here. *This is all just a fantasy*, she tells herself. *This is not real life. I don't want to live the way Oliver does, flying like a dandelion seed in the wind, not really grown up, not really accountable. I have a life in New York City, and that life relies on my having a steady job, a steady paycheck. Maybe I don't love my job at Imagenue, but I also don't hate it. I like my life. This is all just for fun.*

12

HOLLY
December 22
Hudson Valley, New York

Buy something short and hot. Forget Matt ever existed, even if it's just for one night.

Holly can't text her best friend about the school dance, but she knows exactly what Ivy would say. She pushes open the door to the thrift shop and is immediately greeted by the familiar, slightly musty smell of secondhand stores everywhere, as well as the festive-sounding tinkle of a door chime made of tarnished silver bells tied with red ribbon.

"Hellooooo?" calls out a high-pitched voice, and a person wobbles around the corner carrying a pile of Christmas sweaters so high they're completely obscured. "I can hear you, but I can't see you!" the voice trills, and the person totters past with the sweaters. "I'm Bebe. If you need anything at all, just holler. And if you want to try anything on, there's a changing room—more like a changing *closet*, really, but we make do—at the back, just to the left of the rain slickers and galoshes."

"Thank you," Holly says to the walking pile of sweaters.

She flicks her way through flannel shirts and leather jackets in varying shades of red, teal, taupe, and gray. There are garage coveralls with names like "Bob" and "Annie" emblazoned on sewn-on name tags, caftans, cardigans, and, finally, festive-looking garb: sequined tank tops and faux leather jeggings, cocktail dresses that have seen better days, and a few dresses that look more suitable for a prom. Holly takes out one of the sequined tops and a pair of the faux leather pants.

"Good choices, good choices." Bebe has materialized behind Holly. Now that she isn't carrying a mountain of sweaters, Holly can see that she has curly white-blond hair and twinkling amber eyes. She's holding a pair of black, high-heeled, pointed-toe booties. "And these would be adorable with that outfit. You don't happen to be a size-eight shoe, do you?"

"I do, actually," Holly says, taking the boots. "I mean, none of this is what I'd usually wear, but—"

Bebe waves a hand at her. "*But* it's the holiday season! Sparkle, shine, and pleather leggings with the perfect boots are exactly what's called for."

Holly steps out of the dressing room moments later feeling like a different person—feeling more like Ivy than herself. Bebe is now holding a shiny black claw-clip, which she effortlessly uses to secure Holly's long hair in a surprisingly sophisticated, soft updo. "Perfection," she breathes.

"You're good at this," says Holly.

Bebe shrugs, but looks pleased. "I used to be a stylist in the big city, then I traded in my Prada for a simpler life here in Krimbo. I don't miss it, but it is fun to get clients glammed up once in a while. I assume this is an outfit for the Snowflake Dance? Only event for miles that requires any sort of fashion sense—and most people in this town don't seem to get the memo." She adds a rhinestone cuff bracelet to the ensemble and steps back, nodding her head. "You'll be the belle of the ball. Give me two shakes, and I'll steam the clothes for you, freshen them up a little."

Once Holly has changed back into her sweats, Bebe disappears into a back room and quickly returns with the outfit and accessories tucked into a garment bag.

"Twenty even," she says. "Cash preferred."

"I can't believe all this is only twenty dollars," Holly says. "You're sure?"

"Absolutely positive. Now, you enjoy—and I'll probably see you there at the dance. I'll be the one in the golden caftan pushing the punch on everyone! Happy holidays!"

As Holly returns to her car, her phone chimes its text

notification. She smiles because it's Aiden: **Did Bebe sell you on the gold caftan she had in the window last week?**

Holly smiles and texts back, **Nope, she's saving that for herself.** She pauses, then types, **What time are you picking me up?**

See you at seven, he replies within seconds.

Can't wait. As the reply text whooshes its way into oblivion, she feels that electric frisson again—and instead of fighting it, she decides to go with it. *Just for now*, she tells herself, *I'm going to live in the moment and see where it takes me.*

The Snowflake Dance theme is "Winter Wonderland": Ropes of tinsel crisscross the high school gym ceiling, each one woven with a bounty of fairy lights. The floor sparkles with glitter that appears to have been tossed everywhere, and there are real Christmas trees in every corner, filling the gym with the festive scent of pine. "Wow," Holly breathes. "This is just . . . magical."

Aiden smiles. "Isn't it? The rest of the year, it's just a regular school gym, but the dance committee really goes all out every year, and they do an amazing job of transforming it."

"Are those trees from George's?"

"Absolutely. A group of us went out there to help cut them down and drive them into town in our trucks. In the spring, we'll plant seedlings and start the process all over. And we'll mulch these trees, use them for people's gardens."

She smiles at his obvious excitement.

"Gorgeous, just gorge-ee-usss!" a familiar voice trills. Bebe is approaching, her golden caftan resplendent in the holiday lighting. She's carrying a large, cauldron-like bowl. "Holly, wonderful to see you. And you, too, Aiden. I've just finished mixing up the first batch of snowflake punch. Try a glass, let me know if I've missed anything?"

Aiden puts his hand lightly on Holly's back as they follow Bebe to a large table covered in Christmas cookies. There's a space in the middle for the punch bowl, and Bebe sets it down, then reaches for two glasses, which she fills to the brim. Holly accepts a cup and so does Aiden. He taps his glass against hers and raises an eyebrow.

"Brace yourself," he murmurs.

Holly takes a sip and has to force herself not to sputter it out.

"What do you think?" Bebe chirps.

"It's . . . incredible. Really. What's in it?"

"Trade secret. But do you think it's missing anything?"

"It is absolutely not missing a thing," Holly manages.

"Wonderful. Punch is up, everyone! Come and get it!"

"Take a cookie," Aiden says in a low voice. "Actually, take two. You need a base of something in your stomach before you have any more of that punch."

"What is in that punch?" she asks before she takes a bite. "Mm-*mm*." She tastes the soft yet flaky cookie in her first bite, the sour and unexpected tang of the melted Jolly Rancher filling in the next.

"Good, right? And I don't think the question should be what is *in* the Snowflake Dance punch, but rather what's *not* in it. Pretty sure Bebe just goes around town asking people for whatever they don't want in their liquor cabinets, then dumps it all in a punch bowl and adds a few cloves, cranberries, and cinnamon sticks. She insists she uses a recipe, but every year it tastes different."

Holly ventures another sip. "I think I taste brandy? But also gin."

He takes a sip, too. "Definitely brandy and gin. Possibly also Kahlúa?"

"Frangelico. Crème de menthe. How many of these do you think it's safe to drink? Because it's actually kind of growing on me."

"Honestly, probably zero. But it's the holiday season." He takes another sip, then puts his down on the table. "I'll make you a deal. You can have as many as you want. I'll be the designated driver and make sure you get home safely."

All at once, Holly hears the familiar opening bars of Smokey Robinson's "Christmas Everyday," and she freezes.

"Holly? You okay? You look like you've seen a ghost."

Holly struggles to regain her composure. This is the song

that she and Matt had been practicing a cute ballroom-style choreography to for their first dance as a married couple. She looks down at the punch glass in her hand and, slugs it back, then reaches for his.

"Whoa, Holly. Do you want some water?"

"No," Holly says, feeling her head grow pleasantly fogged from the strong drink. "I want to dance. Do you want to dance?"

She leads him out to the dance floor and finds herself feeling bold and sexy in her glittery top, formfitting pants, and high heels. She forces the choreography out of her mind and dances in a different way, swaying her hips and looking up into Aiden's eyes. "I just love this song," she says. "I haven't heard it in a while." The uncertainty in his expression disappears, and soon he's dancing along with her, and they're laughing. She grabs both his hands in hers and shimmies her hips, and he does the same. And then the song abruptly changes, and all at once, Judy Garland is singing mournfully about having yourself a merry little Christmas.

"Martin McLaren from the sports shop DJs every year by putting his iPod on shuffle," Aiden explains. "You really never know what you're going to get."

Holly isn't quite sure how it happened, but she and Aiden are now close, staring into each other's eyes. Aiden's hands are on her waist, and hers are around his neck. What her best friend insists is the saddest Christmas song ever has suddenly become incredibly romantic. A lock of Aiden's hair has fallen into his eyes, and Holly finds herself reaching up and smoothing it away from his forehead before she even fully realizes what she's doing.

"Sorry," she says. "I hope that wasn't too . . ." But she doesn't know how to finish the sentence. Perhaps it's the two glasses of punch, but she's feeling lightheaded and happy. She holds tighter to Aiden's shoulders and his presence steadies her, as does his gaze.

"You all right? You downed that punch pretty fast."

"I'm really good," Holly says, and knows this is the truth. She's happy right where she is, with Aiden close. His touch, his smell. "Aiden, I . . ." She presses her lips together. What should she say? How does one do this? *Should* she be doing this? Just days ago, she was engaged. Now she's in the arms of a man from her past, someone who has quickly become a touchstone in her life. A source of joy. A friend—but more than that; she's smart enough to know this. She likes him. A lot. Suddenly, it's as if a mini version of Ivy is standing on her shoulder, whispering in her ear, *Then tell him that, silly.*

"I like you," she blurts, then feels herself blushing. "Oh, wow, that sounded so high school of me. I'm mortified."

"Well, we *are* in a high school gym," Aiden says. "And we did go to high school together. And . . . maybe you're just going along with the vibe you're getting from me. Because I like you, Holly. The truth is, I always have." He pulls her a little bit closer. "In fact, I have a confession to make. I had the biggest crush on you in high school. To the point that I wrote you an incredibly sappy Christmas card and slid it into your locker."

Holly stops dancing and stares up at him in shock. "Wait a minute, that was *you*? I still have that card! I swear, those were the sweetest things anyone has ever written to me! I memorized it!"

"Please tell me you did not. I think it was a bit maudlin."

"It wasn't. It was sweet." She closes her eyes. "'I'm writing to wish you a very Merry Christmas—and to profess my deep affection for you.'" She opens her eyes. "That was really you?"

"It was me. I did think you were the best girl in the entire school. I thought you were really pretty, and I was a teenage boy, so of course I focused on that." He smiles a sweet smile. "But you were so much more. Not just smart, not just kind . . . but totally unique. You were funny and kind of weird. And yet also sophisticated. There was no one like you. There still isn't." He has her in his arms again, and they're swaying to the music.

"It was really special to me, Aiden. That card made me feel like I was someone other than just . . . Holly Beech. I always wondered who wrote it. Always. I can't believe it was *you*."

His shoulders are broad and firm beneath her fingers. His appealing scent, of soap and cedar and wood shavings, is all around her. His hands on her waist, his touch, send tingles in every direction, over every inch of her skin. What she wants, she realizes, is to kiss him. And she very much does not want to do that in front of an audience that includes almost all of Krimbo.

When the music switches gears again, this time to "Frosty the Snowman" by the Ronettes, Holly says, "Do you want to get out of here, by any chance?"

"Let's go," Aiden says, and there's something in his voice that warms her to her core. She can barely resist reaching up and pulling his face and lips to hers right then, but instead lets him take her hand and lead her from the gym without a word to anyone else.

"What would you like to do?" he asks once they're outside the gym and in the bracing cold air. Holly doesn't think twice about it. With her high heels, she doesn't have to stand on her tiptoes to reach his full, warm lips. She tilts her head and reaches for him, pulls him close and parts her lips.

"Kiss me," she whispers, and he does. His lips are smooth and firm, and he tastes like cinnamon, sugar, a hint of mint. His tongue is gentle at first, then more exploratory, and she finds her hands exploring his body, too, running her fingers over his muscled back, down to his hips, over his ripped stomach.

"Aiden," she whispers, "I like kissing you."

"I like it, too," he says, his smile both shy and sexy as he looks down at her, then pulls her in for more. She wants more, to go further. Would it really be okay to tell him so? She knows Ivy has done this many times; that if her best friend wants something, she asks for it, makes her needs and wants very clear. Holly has always gone a different route. A safer route.

What would it be like to act like someone different?

"I want you," she murmurs, and is excited by the way this causes him to kiss her more deeply, to pull her closer. "Let's go somewhere."

He pulls himself back and looks down at her, his expression now searching. "Go where?" he asks.

"Show me your place? I haven't seen it yet. I want to." She hopes he gets her double meaning—because she knows she does want to. That she doesn't want to *think*; she wants to just feel, and *do*. Yes, she's had two strong glasses of snowflake punch, but she's not drunk, just buzzed—and it's giving her courage. Aiden is the one who wrote her that card, all those years ago. The one she has cherished without even knowing who it was from. His words have always reminded her that once, someone really saw her. It's even more intoxicating than the punch. She reaches for his hand, and they walk toward his truck. He opens the door for her—but before she can climb in, he takes her hand and tugs her back, pressing her against the open door, one hand cupping her cheek and the other firm on the small of her back, pulling her tightly against him. He slowly lowers his mouth to hers, millimeter by millimeter, until she shivers, from anticipation and desire and from the cold of the night.

"Let's get you warm," he says, brushing his lips against hers, just once, before helping her up into the truck. He goes around to the driver's side, gets in, and turns on the engine, then the heat. She scooches across the seat toward him and reaches for him again, and he lets out a low groan. "Holly, you're driving me crazy. You always have, but especially tonight." They move closer and closer until she throws caution to the wind and straddles him, steering wheel at her back, hands in his hair as they kiss with abandon. She feels the hard ridge of him pressing against her. She is certain she has never in her life wanted anyone more—but then the sharp honk of the truck as she accidentally digs into it with her backside startles her and she collapses into his shoulder, laughing.

"I guess we really aren't in high school," she murmurs, flopping back onto her own side of the seat, breathing hard, "and therefore might be past the point of making out in cars?"

"It was incredible, though," he says, his eyes intense, pinning her to her seat.

"Let's go," she breathes. "Your place." It feels good to say what she wants. To *know* what she wants. He keeps one hand on her thigh during the drive, but they don't speak. She's not sure she can—not sure that anything she wants to communicate to him now involves words at all.

Aiden lives in a large log cabin just outside of town, all barn beams and warm-stained wood, masculine furnishings like a red plaid couch, flannel blankets. His smell is everywhere, intoxicating her even more. "Do you want anything to drink, maybe a snack or something . . . ?"

"Aiden. I want *you.*"

She takes his hand and pulls him toward the couch, but he shakes his head and says, "Holly Beech, you are not a couch girl." He leads her down a hallway, to a bedroom with a large window overlooking acres of snow-draped pines.

She pulls him down on the bed, relishes the feeling of his body on top of hers. *Finally.* She thinks she says this in her head, but realizes she has said it aloud. Realizes she has been waiting a long time—her entire life—to feel this way. Swept away. Levitating. "Aiden . . ." She reaches down to unbuckle his belt, to slide her hands past the waistband of his boxer shorts, to feel the length of him in her hand. He's sliding her pants down her waist, and she helps them along, then lifts the sequined top over her head and tosses it to the floor. She wasn't wearing a bra, so now she's in the center of his bed in just her underwear. And he's staring at her, his eyes intense, hungry.

"You're so perfect," he says. "So beautiful. Just the way I always imagined. I've never wanted anyone the way I want you, Holly. All of you."

He touches her hair, runs his hand down the side of her face, her neck. "Your hair," he says. "Your skin." His fingers run along her shoulder, the side of her arm, and she feels all the hairs stand on end, feels her body electrified by his touch. "All so perfect. Your lips." He kisses her, and she pushes him down on his back and straddles him, looks down at him from this new position, feeling sexy and beautiful and powerful and *wanted*. And she wants in return. Needs him. She kisses his lips, nibbles his ear, runs her mouth along his neck and to his chest as he groans with pleasure.

He asks her softly, "Do you want this?"

"Yes."

"You're sure? Because you had a lot of the punch . . ."

She laughs. "Two glasses—but I swear, I am in full control here." She knows the Holly she usually is probably wouldn't be in Aiden Coleman's bed with her clothes off if she hadn't had those two glasses of punch—but she also knows it's true that this is what she wants. That she's in control. That she's not going to regret this.

"I'm sure," she says. Then she pauses. "Are you?"

He laughs, and it's a sexy, ragged sound. "I am so *fucking* sure," he says, his voice a low growl. "But just one second."

As she lies still, waiting for him, she feels her body practically vibrating with longing. He rummages in his bedside table and comes back with a condom. He rips it open, and she takes it from there, sliding it along the length of him before wrapping her legs around him—knowing she's exactly where she wants to be, doing exactly what she wants to be doing. He's staring into her eyes, his expression full of pleasure. She's on top of Aiden now, and he's reaching forward, sliding his hand down and touching her, turning her pleasure into a quest just as important as his. His touch electrifies her, makes her gasp and moan along with him. She moves her hips against his. He doesn't stop touching her, or looking at her in that hungry way. She can see the pleasure she's giving him, the want she's fulfilling. And he's doing that for her, too. She feels lightheaded, sees stars and sparks and fireworks. She's so close—and then he gasps and shudders beneath her, and she realizes what has happened.

It's instinctive for her to say, "It's okay, I'm fine, that was great," the way she always had with Matt. But he holds her fast when she tries to open even an inch of space between them, slides his hand down again so it's between their bodies, and continues to touch her, gently at first, then with a sultry intensity as the pleasure that had already been building reaches its steamy crescendo. "Aiden," she moans, and the shooting stars and fireworks are back, and she's glad that all that's outside his window are trees, because she's quite sure she has never been so loud in her life. Her cries ring out in the room; her body floods with pleasure—and when she looks Aiden in the eye after her orgasm, he has the sexiest, most triumphant look on his face, as if he derived just as much pleasure from giving her satisfaction as he did from getting it.

She falls back on the pillow. "That was . . ."

He turns and buries his face in her hair for a moment, then falls back on his own pillow. "Unbelievable," he says, kissing the side of her head, then leaning up on his elbow and kissing her lips. His breath is still coming fast. He's staring into her eyes with that searching expression of his. "Holly?"

"Mmm-hmm."

"Were you about to say to me that it was okay, that you were fine, after I came?"

She feels suddenly embarrassed, and he clocks her expression and says, "No, *no*, please don't think you did anything wrong, because you did *everything* right—but I just need you to know this: When you're with me?" She nods. "It's never going to be okay for you not to get just as much out of it as I do. Ever. Got that?"

Holly laughs and pulls him to her. "Aiden," she says, "maybe you really are Superman."

He looks confused. "Superman?"

"Never mind, *that* was the punch talking." She pulls him

to her again, and their kisses soon become just as exploratory and full of desire and passion as they were earlier in
the night, outside the school gym.

"You know," he says, rolling her on her back and beginning a tantalizing trail of kisses down her body, toward her
navel. "It's lucky for you that I had hardly any of that punch.
I could go all night if you want me to."

She pulls him close and wraps her legs around him again.
"Oh, trust me, I want you to."

13

IVY
December 22
Kauai, Hawaii

At Nā Pali, time passes quickly as Ivy sits on a rock at the lookout point she found and draws the view, one she is sure she will never tire of. The jagged surfaces of the mountains and cliffs are even more exquisite in person than they were in the photos she saw on Larry's phone, and the colors present a unique challenge in every case. When Ivy does her pastel work, she often makes her colors extremely vivid, far surpassing what a vista might actually look like. But here, her task is to get the colors vivid *enough* to do the scenery justice.

Her fingers are cramping and her back is sore when her satellite communicator goes off.

"You all good, Jovie 92?"

"Yes! Great! You?" She stops herself. "Sorry. What I meant was, 'Roger that, Buddy 90, this is Jovie 92, all good. Season's greetings. Over and out.'"

A staticky pause, and then Oliver's voice is back. "Ivy? Stay where you are, and I'll be there in a few minutes to get you. You need to see the waterfall. I'm sorry I said no earlier." A pause. "Buddy 90 out."

A few minutes later, Oliver arrives in the clearing. He runs his hand through his hair, making it stick up wildly, and sighs a long sigh she can hear even from several feet away.

"I couldn't concentrate," he says. "I felt so bad, telling you that you couldn't come see the waterfall. All I could think the entire time was *I wish Ivy were here to see this.* So, I came back to get you."

"It was fine, really, Oliver." But she's touched by the fact he came back for her, and finds her heart feels suddenly light, when without him around before, it felt a little heavy, even as she enjoyed her work.

"I promise, I won't be a distraction. You can still get your shot," she says as they walk.

He slows and gives her a long look, his expression more serious than she's ever seen it. The dimple is nowhere to be found. "I'm not so sure about that, Ivy," he says. Then he speeds up again before she can question why he said that. "Do you have a swimsuit on under your clothes?"

"Yes."

"Perfect. It's a bit of a hot hike, and the pool below the falls is great for a refreshing swim. It's where I've been standing for the past few hours, pruning up my toes and fingers, but not getting anywhere. I need a break."

He's right—she's sweaty and tired by the time they reach the waterfall. But she forgets all about her physical state when she sees it. "*Oliver.*"

For the first time since he came back to get her, he smiles and looks relaxed again. "I know. It's perfect. Come on."

He peels off his shirt, and she looks away from his smooth, tanned skin and the trail of golden hair beginning just above the waistband of his board shorts. She lifts her own T-shirt over her head, discards her faded jean shorts on the rocks, then chases him as he runs lightly down the dirt path toward the water and does a cannonball into the pool below the falls. She does a slightly demurer scissor jump. The water is cool and refreshing around her.

"Ahhh, this is heaven," she says. She swims alongside him, then treads water and stares at the falls. "I want to draw this. So badly."

"Absolutely," Oliver says. "Let's dry off."

They swim back to the edge and climb out. Ivy dries herself with her T-shirt before putting it back on. She gets out art supplies while Oliver pulls his waterproof SLR from his bag and slips back into the water. She watches for a moment as he swims over to the opposite edge of the waterfall pool, where there's a shallower place for him to stand, just beneath the feathery wisps of water.

"I hope I'm not in your way?" he calls out.

"No, you're good!"

For the next while, she keeps her head bent over the page in front of her, looking up only to examine the falls again, or search for a better, creamier shade of white to get the wispy strands of water against the pewter gray of the rocks just right. She's trying hard not to focus on Oliver, not to look at him at all, but she finds that the proximity to him has made her entire body feel like it's buzzing, more alive than usual. Eventually, he steps out from beneath the falls and swims back toward her. He's got that serious look on his face again.

"How'd you do?" she asks.

"Not great," he says as he climbs out of the pool and comes to sit cross-legged beside her.

"No?"

"I still don't feel like I have it. I might have to settle for one of the shots I already have, and I'm sure once I decide on one, I'll let this go. But for now, I have this image in my mind of the shot I want to get, and it keeps eluding me and that's"—he rubs his damp hair—"frustrating."

"I think I understand," she says. "There are times I want to draw something and the light isn't right, or I can't seem to get the right angle, and I can waste entire days on that. But I have a lot more control over my medium than you do. I can just draw something the way I want it to look, or mix a color myself from my imagination. You're at the mercy of nature."

"Exactly. And don't get me wrong, I love it—the challenge of it, because that moment when you get it, there's nothing like it. But it's also the bane of my existence. Anyway." He turns away from the waterfall and looks at her. "I'm glad you got to see it."

Ivy scoots forward to hang her legs over the side of the rocks and dips her feet into the cool water. "I love this place," she sighs.

He smiles. "Yeah. Me, too. Not how you usually spend the holidays, huh?"

"Actually, I normally spend them alone." She explains more about her yearly art retreats, which happen while her parents travel—as well as her parents' hatred of corporate greed, which they associate with the commercialism of Christmas.

"Really, your parents don't use actual money?"

"For almost everything, they barter. Dad hasn't figured out a way to barter for flights yet, and he and my mom do like to travel. But truly—almost literally everything."

"What's the craziest thing he's ever traded?"

Ivy thinks for a moment.

"Two of our prize pigs for a pickup truck. He had tears in his eyes—he loved those pigs. Hmm, what else. He dragged me to a Comic-Con convention when I decided I didn't like comic books anymore—I went through a Catwoman phase—and we traded a box of old comic books for my Halloween costume that year."

"And your Halloween costume was?"

"I wish I had been more original, but I was the Pink Power Ranger."

"That's adorable."

"Stop it, I wanted to be taken very seriously as a preteen."

"Oh, I take you very seriously, Ivy." Suddenly, he's not smiling anymore. Their eyes lock, and Ivy finds herself leaning toward him. She decides to slide back into the water, hoping the cool of it will help clear her head. He follows and they swim alongside each other.

"So, how about you?" she asks him.

"How about me, what?"

"Your family? Your embarrassing childhood stories." They're facing each other now, treading water. "I'm sure you must have some."

"I didn't exactly have an idyllic upbringing."

"Sorry, right, you mentioned that . . ."

"Yeah, my parents split up when I was pretty young, and I kinda helped raise my little sister a bit—then took off as soon as she was safely in college." They've reached the other side of the pool, and there's a rock ledge to stand on. He stays in the water but leans against the rocks, and she does the same. "Now she's just as much of a wanderer as I am, so I honestly can't remember when the last time we spent Christmas together was, although we do try to link up at least a few times a year."

"And your mom?"

"Gone."

"I'm so sorry."

He shakes his head. "Yeah. She was a single mother, and she worked hard. And then she got sick. Ischemia, stress-related." He sighs. "I always wonder what would have happened if she hadn't had to work that hard, you know?"

"Oh, Oliver." His sea green eyes contain a pain she suddenly wishes she could take away.

"It was tough. But I'm okay. I guess after that, and after getting Cecelia off to college, I just didn't want to be tied to any one place anymore. And maybe I was trying to outrun my grief."

"Did it work?"

He laughs, but it's still a sad laugh. "Not really. Sort of? I think it was probably better than the alternative, which was rot in Indianapolis working at some dive bar for the rest of my life, possibly turning into the father I never knew. I don't know for sure—but what I do know is I've done what I felt I had to do with my life. Sometimes, though . . ." He trails off. He doesn't say anything more, and she feels waves of emotion as she processes all he has just told her. She had assumed, when she first met him, that he was a roving photographer and bartender because he refused to grow up, that he was irresponsible, hell-bent on having fun to the exclusion of all else. But it turns out he just grew up way too fast, and the life choices he made had nothing to do with irresponsibility at all.

"I really admire you," she says. "I think I made some assumptions when we first met and they didn't turn out to be true."

He turns toward her. "Oh, yeah? What sort of assumptions did you make?"

"I guess I just thought . . . this sounds shitty, but that you weren't a serious person. I'm sorry."

She pushes herself off the rocks, floats on her back, and looks up at the sky. He joins her in the water, and she can feel his presence, floating nearby.

"And now?" he says, his voice muffled by the water in her ears. "Do you think I'm a serious person?"

She keeps floating, keeps looking at the sky. Ivy has made it a practice to be an honest person for so long that what she's really feeling and thinking has crowded into her mind and can't be ignored.

"Yes" is all she says.

She decides to let the water decide what's going to happen next. A soft push and she's by his side. One more, and their hands are touching. They float there in silence, then both turn over at the same time so they're facing each other in the water.

"You're a real distraction, Ivy," he says, his voice low.

"I'm sorry," Ivy says. "I know how much you want to get that photo."

His gaze is intense, and she wants to get closer to him, wants their bodies to be touching again. *Maybe just one kiss*, she tells herself. *Maybe that would be enough to get him out of my system.*

The water has brought them together again. Their faces are just inches away.

"Ivy . . ."

"Oliver . . ."

"I want to kiss you," she says, her tone frank. "I think we should. Get it out of our systems." Her voice is a whisper, and his laughter in response is low and sexy.

"Okay, let's try that."

Ivy has had good kisses before. She's had great kisses. Lots of them. But she has never in her life had a kiss like this. The water between them is a soft embrace, as are his arms, reaching for her under the water. His lips against hers are strong and searching; his tongue tastes like salt water. The kiss leaves her panting and filled with a want that veers toward need. Almost blindly, they swim together to the side of the pool, where they can rest their feet on the rocks and give themselves to exploring each other without having to worry about sinking. Clearly, this was not going to be just one kiss. Her willpower, the shred of it that was left, disintegrates like a puddle of water in the hot sun. *Poof.* Gone. She feels like she's been dying of thirst for days, and is finally getting the water she needs. At some point during the kissing, they slide down into the pool together again, their legs entangling under the water as they float.

"Okay, we should stop," Ivy eventually says, placing her hand on his chest, gasping for breath, treading water again.

"Right," he says. "We were just getting that out of our systems. And we did. We're good now. Right?"

"Right?"

He swims away, pulls himself out of the water, and shakes the water out from his hair. "Out of our systems," he repeats. "Now, let's head back to camp before it gets dark."

14

HOLLY
December 23
Hudson Valley, New York

Holly?"

She opens her eyes and finds herself staring directly into Aiden's bright blue ones. He smiles down at her from where he sits at the edge of the bed. "I'm really sorry to wake you so early. But . . ." She thinks he's about to pull her into his arms again, for a repeat of some of their most passionate moments from the night before—and earlier that morning. But then she realizes he's fully dressed, hair still damp and shampoo-fragrant from a shower. "I have somewhere I need to be. So . . ."

"Oh. Of course." Holly tries not to show how mortified she

is as she pulls the sheet up around herself and crosses his bedroom, picking up her clothes as she goes. Is this what a walk of shame feels like? If so, she never wants to do this again.

"How are you feeling after the punch? Can I get you a coffee? Water?"

"I'm fine," Holly calls out, scuttling toward his bathroom and closing the door firmly. She peers at herself in the pine-framed mirror, and is dismayed. The night before, she felt like a sexy vixen. Now last night's mascara is pooled under her eyes. When she wipes it away, dark circles still stare back at her. She splashes water on her face and swishes some of Aiden's toothpaste in her mouth. But then she has to put on her sparkly tank top and ultra-tight pleather leggings that seemed so perfect for the dance—but feel all wrong today.

In the kitchen, Aiden is waiting with a large glass of water and a steaming mug of coffee. "I know you said you were fine, but I wanted to give you something."

"Thanks," Holly says, still bleary-eyed. He's wearing his customary jeans and flannel shirt, making her feel even more out of place in her outfit from the night before.

This is why I've never had a one-night stand, Holly thinks regretfully. *This is way too awkward. This is* not *me.*

"You know what?" Holly says. "I think maybe you should just take me home. I can have coffee at the cabin. Let's just go."

❄ ❄ ❄

Holly stands at the window, watching Aiden drive away and feeling the ache in her chest she hadn't felt for a few days returning full force as soon as he's gone. She groans. "What did I *do*?" She retreats to the couch, where she sleeps fitfully for a few hours, but when she wakes, her mind is still racing. She gets up and, in the kitchen, she brews coffee in the French press. As she waits for it to get strong enough, she texts Ivy.

Help. I had rebound sex with Eco Superman and now I'm freaking out.

Less than a second later, her cell phone rings.

"Oh, thank goodness! You're back in the land of cell service! I'm so relieved you answered," Holly says. "How was your camping trip?"

"It doesn't matter. Good, fine, whatever. You had sex with Eco Superman!"

"Yes," Holly says.

"I'm going to need a lot more than yes. Details, details! I need details."

"Well, Aiden and I had the most perfect skating date yesterday afternoon. And we had amazing cookies—"

"Can we get to the sex part, please?"

"Okay, so then he asked me to a school dance in town—"

"That is the sweetest thing I've ever heard, but I thought you two weren't in high school anymore?"

"Not exactly a school dance, but an annual Christmas dance that takes place at the high school. And I somehow managed to thrift the sexiest holiday party outfit possible, and I got slightly tipsy on some extremely strong punch, tipsy enough that I started feeling quite brazen."

"Holly!" Ivy sounds delighted.

"Then he told me he was the one who wrote me that card, back in high school."

"What? The one you always cherished?"

"Yes. *He* wrote that for me. It was Aiden."

"So you jumped him, right then and there."

"We ended up outside, making out in the snow. And then . . ."

Ivy is now gasping with delight.

"And then . . . we had the most amazing sex of my entire life at his cabin in the woods. All night long. I'm *exhausted*."

"Wait. All this is why you don't know if you're okay? You're amazing! Holly, I'm so happy for you!"

"Yeah, but I haven't gotten to the bad part. This morning, he was already dressed when I woke up. He could not get me out of there fast enough. He said he had somewhere he needed to go, and vaguely mentioned having to drive to the city for a meeting. He made me coffee but then basically tapped his fingers against his kitchen counter waiting for me to be done, and finally, I said to just take me home because I could not stand the awful morning-after awkwardness anymore." This isn't exactly a true account of events, but the exaggeration about Aiden tapping his fingers makes Holly feel even more vindicated in her agony. "That's not the worst part, though. *The worst part* was when he dropped me back off at my cabin." She squeezes her eyes shut at the memory. "He gave me a hug instead of a kiss."

"Hmm," Ivy says. "That is a little odd. You didn't try to kiss him?"

"I didn't get the chance. He went straight in for the hug and said he'd call me later."

"Okay. So, he'll call you later."

"But what if he doesn't? What if he never wants to see me again?"

"I highly doubt that. Mind-blowing sex is generally a two-way street. Maybe he's just feeling shy this morning. Maybe he has this meeting to go to and he wishes he didn't. He said he'd call you later, and I'm sure he will. And I'm sure it's all going to be fine."

"I've never done this before, though. How do you put it out of your mind? My body feels like a ball of electricity."

"That's a good thing. The ball-of-electricity stuff, that's kind of why I do it. It feels good." Holly thinks she hears her friend let out a little sigh, but then she keeps talking. "You don't regret it, do you?"

Holly pauses to consider how she feels. "No regrets," she

says. "I did what I wanted to do in the moment. It was one of the best nights I've ever had, on every level."

"And you found out he's the sweet guy who wrote a card you always cherished. Be happy about that, Hol. Try to enjoy it—maybe even for what it was. Because even if it was just a great night between old friends, how can that be a bad thing? It could have been exactly what you need right now."

"I needed this pep talk," Holly says, and she does feel a little better already. "Thanks for being there."

"Of course. Is there anything you can do today to get your mind off him?"

Holly thinks for a moment. "There are cross-country skis in the shed. I think I still remember how to Nordic ski."

"That's a great idea."

"Plus, it was a super-late night. I could have a nice long nap."

"Sounds like a perfect day to me."

"So, how's it going there? And who is this friend you went camping with?"

"Just someone I met at the hotel," Ivy says as Holly hears voices in the background. "I'll tell you more later, but I have to go." As Ivy hangs up abruptly, Holly feels a twinge. She's thousands of miles away from her best friend—and although she insisted she needed to be alone and that's why she came to the Hudson Valley, the distance feels suddenly vast.

She pours herself a coffee, and feels somewhat better

after she drinks one, then another. She dresses in her warmest clothes and heads to the shed to find the cross-country skis, determined to have a good day—on her own. Aiden might call, and he might not. Either way, Holly tells herself, she's going to be fine.

Holly hasn't Nordic skied for a few years, but once she has the boots and skis on, it all comes back to her. She moves easily along the drive and out onto the road, following the signs for the hiking trail.

At first, the path is narrow, and she *shushes* along in silence beside skinny birch trees covered in icing-like layers of snow. But eventually, the path opens up, and the trees morph from birches and elms to formidable evergreens. They tower above her, their snowy tops barely visible as they reach toward the sky. The trail widens even more, and Holly turns a corner—then gasps at the beauty of it all. The valley is laid out below her like someone shook out a blanket covered in picturesque mountain ranges and evergreen trees, all topped with lacy snow. The sky above is a brilliant blue, with fluffy clouds floating across it.

Holly stands still and takes it in, feeling the anxiety about Aiden start to dissipate. Another breath of the winter air and her head is almost clear. She thinks of what Ivy said, about how he might call or he might not. And she'll be fine. She did what she wanted to do. She had a great night.

Even if they don't end up getting together again, she knows

she'll always have a special place in her heart for him, especially knowing he was the one who wrote her the card she's treasured.

She glides forward again, feeling the power those long-ago words have always given her, as simple as they were. They make her remember who she used to be—who she is around the people she feels most comfortable with.

The sun is almost down by the time Holly turns the corner onto the driveway of the cabin again, stomach grumbling, thinking over what she might make for dinner—but all thoughts of food fly from her head when she sees Aiden shoveling the cabin path. He stops when he sees her.

"Hey!" he calls out. "I saw the tracks in the snow, so figured you'd gone out for a ski. I decided to wait for you. Hope that's okay?"

She stands by the shed and pops off the skis, then walks toward him along the path he's shoveled for her, her shy smile growing bigger the closer she gets to him. It's cold out, and getting even more so as the sun goes down, but Holly doesn't feel the cold anymore. Her entire body feels warm, and her heart is pounding.

"More than okay," she says. "I'm happy to see you."

"Oh, yeah?" His smile is slow and sexy—and this side of him is new, the side of Aiden that isn't just sweet and nice but also extremely hot. He steps closer to her. "Even when I acted like a total weirdo this morning, when I kicked you out of my bed and took off on you?" He shakes his head. "I'm so sorry about that. I did have a meeting in the city, but the truth is, I think I might have needed a little time to process what happened between us last night. I could have handled it better."

She looks up at him and tilts her head. "And? How did that processing go?"

His smile grows bigger. "All I could think, all day long, was *I must be the luckiest guy in the world*. And the stupidest one, for leaving." He reaches out, puts his hands on her waist. "Which is why I drove out here the second I got back into town. I couldn't wait a minute longer to see you."

Holly reaches up and touches his stubbly cheek, runs a finger along his chin, pulls his face to hers. Their lips meet in the twilight, and their kisses quickly grow fervent.

"Come inside," Holly says, leading him to the door. Inside, she can't get out of her winter clothes fast enough, and neither can he—and soon, they've fallen together onto the couch, lips locked, limbs entwined, exactly where they both want to be.

15

IVY
December 23
Kauai, Hawaii

Oliver's arm brushes against Ivy's as they load their tents into the back of his Jeep—but, as she has grown used to doing, she forces herself to ignore the shower of sparks his touch sets off on her skin, to push away how his proximity makes her feel. Not think about how it felt to kiss him in the waterfall pool. Definitely not think about doing that again.

Despite the tension Ivy feels, they listen to music and chat easily during the drive and are back at Larry's villa by noon. As they're unpacking their camping gear from the back of the Jeep, Larry comes outside with a phone message: a colleague of Oliver's from the hotel has a sick kid at home and is looking for someone to cover her shift. Oliver looks concerned as he heads inside to call her back.

Moments later, he comes out again and hastily helps Ivy unload the rest of the gear.

"Paula's a single mom," he says to Ivy. "I try to help her out as much as I can, and today, she's in a real spot. So, I told her I'd take her shift, meaning I need to shower and get to the hotel. But I had a great time, Ivy." A smile steals over his face and she wonders if he's remembering the kiss. "Didn't get the damn shot, but it was still a lot of fun." He looks at her a moment longer, and then he's gone, back inside the villa. Ivy stands still, unable to think of anything else now but the way his lips felt on hers. So much for getting it out of her system. If anything, the kiss has just made things worse.

But Ivy has always been disciplined. Now that Oliver will be at work, she'll have time to get her head back where it should be: firmly focused on her art. She can do this.

Later that afternoon, Ivy walks slowly back up the beach, her hands stained with pastels and her heart happy after a catch-up chat with Holly and finding a cove filled with driftwood that provided the perfect inspiration for a series of pastel drawings. As she slows her pace to watch the sun sinking low over the water, she hears someone calling her name.

Larry is standing on the bottom terrace of the villa, waving at her. Ivy speeds up toward her.

"Great, you're back! I started making dinner for myself, but I always make too much—and tonight, cactus enchilada for one has turned into cactus enchilada for about . . . maybe ten. Would you like to join me?"

"I'd love to," Ivy says, and goes to put her art supplies upstairs and change.

When she comes down, she can hear Larry in the kitchen, humming a song as she cooks. Ivy taps lightly on the side of the screen door, then walks in. The apartment is similar to the one upstairs, but bigger. There are more of Oliver's photographs on one wall, and Ivy walks toward them, examining them one by one. "He's so good," she says.

"He's amazing at what he does." Larry pops the cork on a bottle of white wine and also takes a bottle of sparkling water from the fridge as she accepts Ivy's offer of helping to set the table on the terrace.

Back inside, as Larry takes the enchilada dish out of the oven, Ivy is drawn again to the wall of Oliver's photographs. "Why doesn't he do this full-time?" she asks Larry.

Larry looks up from chopping cilantro. "I think he's got a pretty good thing going, with the way he's set up his life. I think he likes not putting too much pressure on his art." Larry sprinkles the fresh cilantro over the enchilada dish, then picks it up. "Come on outside," she says.

On the terrace, Larry serves Ivy a heaping plate, then pours them both glasses of wine.

Ivy sips the Sancerre and stares out to sea.

"You okay?"

"I guess I'm just wondering what it might be like to do this all the time—live in a place like this. Travel around."

"Can't you do that?"

Ivy shakes her head.

"Why not? Is there a reason you have to stay in New York City?"

"Well, my best friend is there. And my job. That's kind of a big one, work."

"What is your job?"

"I do brand consulting at a big advertising firm."

"Do you love it?"

"Definitely not love. I like it, though. It pays the bills."

Larry tilts her head. "You'd have a lot fewer bills to pay if you didn't live in New York City."

"True, but I just"—Ivy shakes her head—"always imagined my life a little more grounded." She explains how her parents were always happy, but her childhood was unsettled. "I never knew where we were going next, or if I should get comfortable anywhere. I was always switching schools, or getting homeschooled. I guess I've just always craved stability."

Larry is pensive. "Oliver always has, too, you know. His childhood wasn't exactly what you would call stable."

"Yeah, he told me."

"But I also guess what his mom's life taught him is how dangerous it is to give up on your dreams. You only get one life, and you never know how long it's going to be."

Ivy sighs, then takes a bite of the enchilada and is momentarily distracted. "Larry, this is amazing."

"Thank you. My abuela's recipe, from back home in Mexico City. The secret is using *nopales*. Prickly pear cactus. They aren't native here, but my mom brought me a plant the last time she visited, and I use that. They're bastards to prep"—she holds up her left hand and shows off a bandage on one finger—"but worth it for the flavor and texture."

Ivy takes another bite and ruminates as she chews. "The 'you only live once' thing—I guess that's why I make time, every year, for what I love to do."

"Your art."

Ivy nods.

"But you don't feel you could make time for it more?"

"I just don't see a future in it."

"You mean, financially?"

"I guess so. Like I said, I've always craved stability, and art . . . it's never stable."

"Has meeting Ollie made you feel differently about that?"

Ivy freezes with her wineglass halfway to her mouth. "What do you mean?"

Larry holds Ivy's gaze. "You know what I mean. The chemistry between you two is palpable. My hair gets frizzy just being near you. I sent you off camping together, but you clearly haven't gotten it on yet. What's wrong with you?"

Ivy can't help but laugh. "Trust me, I want to, okay? But I always promise myself that these art trips are for art only. It's important to me. And . . ." She hesitates. Should she be talking to Larry this way about Oliver, her best friend? But Ivy feels a sense of trust, so she continues.

"When I first met him at the hotel bar, I thought he was just some fun-for-now guy. But he's not—he's talented, and serious about his work. Plus, he's kind, and smart, and . . . I like him a lot."

"Why do I feel like you think this is a problem, that Ollie is a better guy than you thought he was? You two, you're like"—she claps her hands together, then clasps them as if in prayer—"*kismet.*"

The fact that Oliver's best friend is saying this fills Ivy with a warm buzz, but she still tries to fight it. "I don't know about that . . ."

"I sent you out into the wilderness together, the chemistry zinging between you like you're a pair of science lab beakers, and you . . . *what*? Just kiss?"

"How did you know?"

Larry laughs. "He told me, of course. We tell each other everything. Hope that's okay."

"Yeah, of course. I tell my best friend everything, too—although I haven't told her about Oliver yet."

"What are you so afraid of?"

Ivy tries to explain it. "I have no problem getting physical with the men I meet. I think sex *can* just be for fun—and I've had a lot of fun over the years, always on my own terms. But with Oliver . . ." She trails off, thoughtful again.

"It wouldn't just be for fun, necessarily."

"Right."

"And that's a problem because?"

"Well, because I only have a week or so left with him. Plus, my art. I wanted to focus on other things. All this—" She waves her hand in a circle, trying to encompass the little table, the beach, the ocean, the sky. "It has an end point."

"In my experience, life is what you make of it. You can do anything you want, Ivy. *You're* in charge. You can have love, and sex, and art. You can have it all." She lifts her glass. "And by the way, Ivy, I promise: Everything you just said is sacred, I will not repeat it to Ollie. You have my word. I'll stop pushing my views onto you and let you enjoy the time you have here. More enchilada?"

"Yes, *please.*" She smiles. "I can see why he's best friends with you, Larry. You're kind of amazing."

She winks as she serves Ivy more food. "I know," she says lightly.

Larry's phone *bings*, and she picks it up, reads the text, and smiles. "That's Shira, telling me how excited she is to see me tomorrow."

"I'm looking forward to meeting her."

"I've told her all about you. She's keen to meet you, too. We're going to have so much fun. On Christmas Eve, there's a lūʻau down at the beach by the hotel. Everyone goes. You have to come, obviously. Amazing food, dancing, you'll love it."

Ivy thinks about being at a beach party with Oliver, and finds she can't resist the idea. "That sounds like fun," she says sincerely.

"It will be," Larry says, her easy, animated chatter back after their more serious discussion moments before. "The four of us are going to have an amazing time, I promise. It's going to be the best Christmas ever!"

16

HOLLY
December 24
Hudson Valley, New York

Holly wakes to the sound of Aiden downstairs in the cabin's kitchen, whistling "Silver Bells" as pots and pans clatter. She stays in the loft bed for a moment, smiling up at the skylight as clouds float past in the winter-blue sky. They've been spending every possible moment together, mostly remaining in bed before finally going out for a walk in the twilight, then making dinner in the cabin. When they'd cuddled up by the woodstove together as night fell again, she told him she didn't want him to leave—so he didn't.

She puts on the first thing she finds—his red-checked flannel shirt—and climbs down the ladder.

"Good morning," he says with a smile. He's wearing nothing but bright red boxer shorts covered in prancing reindeer as he cooks. "Merry Christmas Eve, Holly."

She rubs her eyes. "Wow, it is Christmas Eve already, isn't it? I feel like we lost a day there." She pulls a stool up to the breakfast bar, and he pours her a cup of coffee.

"Yeah. But it was one of the best lost days of my life."

Her cheeks heat up as she thinks of how many times they made love, and how good it was, how perfect, every single time. "I'd get lost with you again and again," she says.

"Hungry?"

"Starving." He flips two over-easy eggs onto a plate, adds a piece of toast, and brings her the plate, kissing her as he gives it to her. She knows as she runs her hands over his smooth muscled chest and down toward the waistband of his boxers that if this kissing continues, she'll gladly skip breakfast to go back to bed with him. But he's got two more eggs in the pan sizzling behind him. He groans a little as he pulls away from her, finishes cooking, and pulls his stool close, kissing her nose as he pours out more coffee.

Once he starts to eat, he looks thoughtful, glancing at her from time to time but not saying anything.

"I've gotten used to the fact that silences with you aren't awkward," she says. "But you look pretty serious now. What's on your mind?"

He laughs. "I like to think things over before I say

them—but sometimes people see that as being a bit emotionally closed. And I swear I'm not."

"By 'people,' are you talking about exes?"

A rueful smile. "Well, one ex," he says.

"Care to elaborate?"

"I was dating someone all through MIT—her name was Toni—but she said I was a workaholic, so wrapped up in what I was doing professionally that I didn't make any time for our relationship. So it ended. She wasn't the right person for me, but I'd hate to repeat those mistakes in another relationship, so I did try to take some of the things she said to heart."

"I can't really picture you as a workaholic," Holly says, swirling egg yolk around on her plate with a crust of toast. "You seem pretty relaxed out here, managing the eco-properties."

"I don't just manage them, I own them," Aiden says. "I bought them with the proceeds from selling my company."

Holly looks up at him, surprised. "*Your* company?"

"It's called Air Works."

She nearly spits out the sip of coffee she's just taken. "*Air Works!* Aiden, that was your company? Wait, the AirClean Tower was your invention?"

He looks bashful now—but proud, too, she can tell. "You've heard of it?"

"I read about it in the newspaper. It turns smog particles

into jewelry. It's the most amazing invention for dealing with air pollution. You're a genius. Why didn't you tell me?"

"I didn't mention it because—well, I guess because it feels a bit like bragging. And because I don't own it anymore. It's not really a part of my life now."

"But *you* thought of that technology."

He looks down at his plate. "I did. When I was at MIT, I just became so disillusioned with the way so many of my classmates talked about working for huge corporations when they graduated, coming up with technology or ways of investing, formulas designed to make money, more and more of it for the people who didn't need it. The smog tower was an idea I'd been toying with since high school—"

"I remember, you did a rudimentary form of it as a science fair project one year!"

"Yeah, but back then it didn't work, so I lost to you. And Mr. Snuggles." He smiles good-naturedly. "Anyway, I just decided to go for it. I found an investor, and when it actually worked this time, I ended up dropping out of MIT to work on it. I guess that's when Toni started to get a little upset. We were on a certain trajectory together. We had a life plan." Holly nods, because she knows exactly what this is like. "But I just . . . got off the train." His expression is faraway. "And I *loved* it. I was so happy. I felt like I was doing what I was meant to be doing and making the world a better place at the same time—but I woke up one day, and Toni and I had broken up, and I hadn't spoken to my family in months, except by text or voicemail—and my mom was having an important scan that week. I started thinking about how I would feel if she got sick again. And . . . I just decided to sell. I got a pretty good price on it, bought a few properties out here, and this is my life now."

Holly stares at him, processing all he has just said to her and feeling a wave of pride in his accomplishments that she hopes he feels, too. "I think that's brave. You thought up such a meaningful idea—but you knew when it was time to step away. I'm so impressed by you."

His smile reminds her of the shy, smart high school boy she knew. They kiss again, and this time she knows their breakfasts will go unfinished. "Should we celebrate the fact that you think I'm a super genius by going back to bed?"

"I thought you'd never ask." She hops off the stool, and he carries her across the room fireman-style while she laughs. At the bottom of the loft ladder, he pauses and sets her down.

"Wait. We never did talk about what I was thinking about back there, though."

"Oh, right . . ."

"Would you like to join me and my family for Christmas dinner tomorrow?"

"Are you sure? I don't want to impose."

"I want you there, Holly. I want you to meet my family, too."

She smiles. "Tell me about Christmas with your family in Krimbo."

"First there's a town parade, right at sunset every Christmas Day." His blue eyes are alight with what she's sure are years of happy Christmas memories. "My parents live on Main Street, so we set chairs up on the sidewalk and watch. My dad and grandpa cook a Christmas dinner with all the fixings. I act as sous chef, and my mom, Sidra, and Alexa— and this year, you—get to sit around drinking mulled wine and teasing us about all the dishes they're going to have to do later."

"While I *do* somewhat resent the fact that this social engagement means you're going to have to put on some pants and not just reindeer boxers," she says, tugging at his waistband, "that sounds like the perfect way to spend Christmas, Aiden. I'd love to. Now, can we go back to bed?"

They can't get up the ladder fast enough.

17

IVY
December 24
Kauai, Hawaii

The night of the Christmas lūʻau, tiki torches create a glowing runway leading to the beach in front of the hotel. Ivy, Oliver, Larry, and Shira follow the beacons toward a team of hotel dancers doing a fire dance. The bass thrums through Ivy's body, and she feels excitement coursing through her as they arrive. She slips off her sandals so she can feel the sand beneath her feet.

Oliver ended up working another shift for Paula, so she hasn't seen much of him. She went to Glass Beach on her own to draw, but found herself filled with anticipation all day not just about the lūʻau, but also about spending time with Oliver. She's been turning her dinner conversation with Larry over in her mind constantly. She doesn't have any answers, but she knows one thing: Oliver is just as much of a distraction when he's not around as when he is. She can't simply pretend her feelings don't exist.

"Mai tais for everyone?" Shira says. She's as outgoing as Larry, and Ivy took to her immediately. She's loved listening to Shira's Hollywood stories about the adaptation of a mystery book she's directing.

Shira and Larry walk toward the bar hand in hand, and Oliver and Ivy are left alone.

"Hey," she says, suddenly shy.

"Hey. I feel like I haven't seen you in ages," he says. "I've missed you."

"Me, too," she answers honestly, looking up at him.

"So, I know that kiss we had was supposed to get it out of our systems, but I haven't been able to think about anything else since."

"It was a really great kiss," she admits.

"One for the ages."

"But just because we had a really great kiss doesn't have to mean we're . . ." She trails off.

"Doesn't have to mean we're what?" he prompts.

"I don't know, falling for each other or anything."

He takes a step closer. "Right. Falling for each other," he repeats. "Or anything. Who says?"

"Exactly. No one."

He reaches for her hips, pulls her closer, stares down into her eyes. "So, who says that the second I saw you standing under the tree near my bar, I got déjà vu, like I had met you before, not just in passing—but a thousand times before. That I felt not just like I knew you, but like I *would* know you." Ivy's lips part as she stares up at him, mesmerized by his words, his voice, his touch. "Who says that the first time you touched me, it sent electricity through the rest of my body. I . . ." He stops.

"You what?" Ivy asks, practically breathless.

"Look, I know I said I wouldn't do this. But I have to let you know." His voice is a beacon, his whispers landing on her lips, making their way through her body, to her heart. "Ivy, you, with your artistic soul and your incredible talent, your strength, your heart, your casual sexiness, your beauty that comes from inside you, too . . . I feel like you're exactly the person I've been looking for." Now he kisses her, slowly, gently. "So, who says we're falling for each other? Well, I'm falling for you. Hard. And I had to say that to you."

He holds her hand against his heart. She feels it beating under the firmness of his chest, and her mind fills with things she wants to say. About how she felt the same when she first saw him, despite the bleakness of her situation. How, as much as she has tried to deny it, she has thought of almost nothing *but* Oliver since the moment they met. How when she sits down to draw, even when she's surrounded by more beauty than she's ever seen, she still returns to his face, his eyes, has to force herself to draw anything but him. The way she feels like she's falling, too. How hungry she is to know everything about him. But as he keeps gazing into her eyes, she becomes aware that she doesn't have to say any of this to him, not right now. She just has to allow herself to feel it.

"Give me your phone!" Larry shouts over the music.

"Why?" Ivy asks her.

"You two are adorable. Look at you, dancing and kissing. *Finally.* There needs to be photographic evidence of how completely enamored with each other you are, and the fact that you've finally admitted it!" She takes Ivy's phone and snaps a few photos, then hands it back. Oliver swings Ivy around playfully, and as he does, she catches a glimpse of another couple dancing behind them.

Matt and Abby. Ivy freezes. Oliver looks down at her. "Hey, you okay?"

Then he sees who she's looking at. "*Oh.* Hey, want to dance into them and fake accidentally spill your drink on his shirt? Wait . . . I already did that." His face is close to hers. "Do I need to hide you? I can really kiss you this time." His lips are almost on hers again, and as much as she wants another kiss, all at once she also needs this game of cat and mouse with Matt to be over.

"I'm not hiding from him anymore," Ivy says. "I'm done. I'm going to talk to him."

"I'm right here if you need backup," Oliver says.

Matt has left Abby on the sand and is heading to the bar. Ivy follows behind him, then stands waiting as he orders his drinks. He turns to walk back to the beach and does a double take when he sees her, puts down his drinks, rubs his eyes. "What the . . ."

"Matt." Ivy's greeting is as flat and devoid of emotion as she can make it—but inside, she's a boiling cauldron of rage.

"What are you doing here?"

"I could ask you the same thing."

"It's my—"

"Please, don't. *Do not* say, 'It's my honeymoon.' What the hell, Matt? You brought your new girlfriend on your honeymoon? This is over the top, even for you."

"Hey! Don't insult me on my—"

"Honeymoon?" Ivy rolls her eyes. "You're the worst, Matt—and I guess the one good thing about the way you hurt Holly is that I finally get to say that to your face."

"But why are *you* here?"

"Because Holly, in her infinite kindness and generosity, insisted I go in her place. Logically, she never imagined you'd be here with someone else."

Matt looks genuinely stricken. "I asked her if she wanted to use the honeymoon, and she said no way. I didn't want it to go to waste, either!"

"Well, good for you, Matt!" The anger in her voice is drawing looks from some of the other patrons, so Ivy tries to dial it down. "How could you do this to her?" she says, her voice now an angry shout-whisper. "She doesn't deserve it, and you know it."

"I know that, okay? You're right. I feel horrible about hurting her this way—but don't you think it would have hurt her more in the long run if we had gotten married when we weren't really in love? I know she thinks she wanted to marry me, but we were just ticking off boxes. It wasn't the real thing. What I have with Abby is—"

Ivy holds up her hand again. "Stop. I do not want to hear about what you have with Abby being the real thing. Holly is my *best friend*. I am on Team Holly always and forever. And you? You're just a . . ." She can't think of an insult that would be low enough. Calling him a rat or a snake would be an insult to both those animals. "Nothing," she says. "You're just a nothing."

He looks agonized, and she doesn't feel a shred of empathy. "Please don't tell Holly," he says. "I'm begging you. Not yet. Not now. I know I hurt her, and it's Christmas, and she's alone." He shakes his head. "Where is she, by the way? With her parents?"

"No, she is not with her parents, and if you actually cared about her, you would know that is the last place where she would get emotional support. She's in the Hudson Valley. We swapped holidays. She's in an eco-cabin, having some alone time and trying to regroup."

"Holly . . . is in an eco-cabin? Like, one of those off-grid ones?"

Ivy nods.

"And you're *sure* she's okay? Like, she's figured out the power and the water and . . . all that?"

"Of course I'm sure she's okay! Because we talk and text every day."

"Please don't tell her." Matt has now doubled down on his begging, and Ivy feels a wave of disgust. "Let me do something for you. Where are you staying? Can I pay for you to have a room here? What can I do?"

"I want nothing from you," Ivy says, keeping her voice as level as possible even though the rage is bubbling back up. "Please, could you just get away from me? Go back to Abby. Go have your *honeymoon*."

"But you won't tell Holly, right? You know this would destroy her."

"And yet you still did it." Ivy crumples up a cocktail napkin in front of her. "Yes," she finally says. "I promise I won't tell her."

Matt's face floods with relief, and Ivy feels a stab of revulsion. He doesn't deserve to feel anything but guilty. "I'm not telling her *yet*," she clarifies. "Not until I get back and can tell her in person. But I *am* telling her." It feels like making a deal with the devil, and she hates it, but she knows that Matt is not wrong about this, at least. The news that the fiancé who left you is now on your honeymoon with his new girlfriend is not something that should be received by telephone.

But she can still find a way to ruin Matt's night, can't she?

Abruptly, Ivy turns and walks toward the dance floor.

She approaches a woman who is swaying to the music happily, watching the fire dancers.

"Excuse me?"

Abby turns. "Yes, can I help you?"

"My name is Ivy Casey. I'm Holly Beech's best friend. As in Matt's up-until-very-recently fiancée? The one he dumped for you, the night before their wedding?"

Abby tucks a lock of her short, blond hair behind one ear and tilts her head. She doesn't look as shocked as Ivy feels she should. "Okay. Nice to meet you, Ivy. What are you doing here in Hawaii?"

"The question should be, what is Matt doing here, on his honeymoon?" She waits for Abby to have a reaction, but her face stays blank. Ivy tries again. "Did you know it was his honeymoon, Abby, or did he convince you he was taking you on a romantic holiday trip?"

Abby is still unfazed. "Of course I knew," she says. "We discussed it. Didn't we, Matt?" He has now reached his new girlfriend's side. "Matt explained that he had asked Holly if she wanted to take the trip, and she said absolutely not. Which meant a very expensive, nonrefundable trip was going to go to waste. We both agreed it just made good financial sense to go on the trip ourselves."

Ivy can see out of the corner of her eye that Oliver has approached to make sure she's okay, and is now standing behind Abby and Matt, trying to wipe a surprised smile off his face. *What the actual fuck?* he mouths.

Suddenly, Ivy can't sustain her anger. She starts to laugh and she can't stop. "Okay, wow," she says, pointing a finger from Matt to Abby. "I never thought you were good with Holly, but Matt, this woman is *perfect* for you."

"Thank you," Matt says. "I think so, too. Now do you see why I—"

"No way. I don't want to hear it. I told you before, Team Holly, all the way." She lets out another snort of laughter, while Matt leads Abby away, both of them casting concerned glances over their shoulder.

"Come on, *no*," Shira says moments later, when Ivy and Oliver have explained what happened. "We were all totally ready for this huge confrontation with you and Abby, and she knew the entire time."

"Said going on Matt and Holly's honeymoon *just made good financial sense*," Larry adds, and Ivy nearly doubles over with uncontrolled laughter again. "What a *jerk*."

"Holly is beyond better off without him," Oliver says. "And I'm glad to see you laughing, Ivy, because normally when you see him, I feel like I'm going to have to stop you from committing a murder."

"I was very close." Ivy grows serious again. "But confronting him felt good. And learning that he and Abby are a match made in hell? Kind of awesome, too."

They're dancing again, the moonlight and torchlight casting shadows across their faces. "I'm relieved for Holly," Ivy says to Oliver as their bodies move together. "I know she's going to be okay, even if it takes time." She pauses, looks up at him, tests out again how it feels not to have walls up around her emotions. "I'm happy, too. About us. About this . . ."

He pulls her close. "Me, too. But I have something I need to tell you."

"What is it?"

"I know it's Christmas tomorrow, and I hate to do this—but I managed to secure a camping permit at Nā Pali again, earlier today."

"You're going to take on the waterfall one more time?"

"I feel like I need to. And you're more than welcome to come with me . . ."

She shakes her head. "Of course not. You need to go on your own so you can focus. It's so important."

"I'll leave first thing and be gone twenty-four hours, tops. I really don't want to leave, not right now, but—"

"Oliver, I completely understand. You have to do this. If we go out into the wilderness alone together again, I'm sure working is the last thing you'll do. I'll miss you. A lot. But it's only one day."

"You're sure you don't mind that I'm leaving you alone on Christmas?"

"I won't be alone. I have Larry and Shira."

"And knowing Larry, she'll make a Christmas dinner for a hundred people, but it will only be you three."

"Exactly." She runs her hand down his chest and toys with one of the buttons of his shirt. "I'll survive. But . . . Oliver?"

"Yes?"

"If you're leaving at dawn tomorrow, that only gives us about eight hours."

"Eight hours for what?"

She stands on her tiptoes and kisses him deeply, then snakes her hand under his shirt and lets it run over his smooth, muscled back. The waves of desire she has been holding at bay nearly knock her off her feet, and she knows he feels it, too. "For a lot more than kissing," she whispers.

"Let's get out of here," he says. He grabs tight hold of her hand. In her haste, she's left her sandals on the beach, but she doesn't care. She feels the cool smoothness of the sand against the soles of her feet as they run. All she wants is to get back to the villa and be with him, but as they race through the night and she sees the sparkle of the moon on the ocean, hears the sound of crashing waves, she also wants time to slow down, to stretch. She's never felt this way before—not just filled with desire for someone, but also replete with a sense of rightness and connection.

Soon they're stumbling up the stairs into Ivy's apartment—and she forgets all about wanting to slow down. She tugs at Oliver's T-shirt, pulls it over his head, and tosses it away, then does the same with her sundress. "Ivy . . ." he murmurs.

"No. No words," she instructs. "We've waited too long for this already."

Together, they spiral into a place where time doesn't exist. His hands on her body, her hands on his, her legs around his waist as she tilts her body back on the bed and tells him—without words—what she wants him to do.

She runs her fingers through his hair as he kisses her, takes the condom from him when he pulls it from his wallet, puts it on him herself while she feels his body under her touch, so hot with want and desire.

He's above her on the bed, and then she pulls him inside her, presses her hips up, against him, feels the inside of her body ripple, squeeze, hold tight. *Harder, faster,* she hears herself say. Or maybe she doesn't. Maybe he simply knows what she wants and needs, because he is hers in this moment, and he knows her, mind and soul.

The pleasure is sudden, too much and just enough, coming in waves, inevitable. No more words inside her head, only the sounds their bodies and mouths make. Her eyes lock with his at the last moment. It's perfect.

After, they breathe hard, chest to chest. Ivy knows she has never felt this way before, not with anyone.

And suddenly, words pop into Ivy's head.

A bird may love a fish, but where would they live?

This, Ivy decides as she snuggles into Oliver's arms, is a problem for another day. And all at once, it doesn't really feel like a problem at all.

18

HOLLY
December 25
Hudson Valley, New York

Holly happily hums the tune of "Silver Bells" as she puts the finishing touches on wrapping the presents she managed to get last minute for Aiden's family just before the shops in Krimbo closed on Christmas Eve. She has used newspaper from the bin beside the cabin's woodstove to wrap everything, which she knows Aiden will appreciate. She finds a reusable bag for the Finger Lakes wine she bought, and then checks her watch. She feels a tingle of nerves. She's excited to see Aiden, and is looking forward to meeting his family—but it's also a big step. She hopes it goes well.

She gets in her car and follows the directions to Aiden's family home, a redbrick colonial on Main. The wraparound porch is lit up with multicolored holiday lights, and the driveway is already full of cars, so Holly parks on the street. She takes her gifts and the bottle of wine from the trunk and rings the doorbell—which promptly plays a lightning-fast version of the chorus of "Winter Wonderland" before a woman with short dark hair and eyes the same bright blue as Aiden's answers.

"You must be Holly," she says warmly, opening the door wide. "I'm Charlotte, Aiden's mother."

Another woman has joined Charlotte in the entryway, and she greets Holly in an equally welcoming manner. She has short hair, too, but it's pure white. Her eyes are just as blue and sparkly as Aiden's mother's. "I'm Grandma Hazel. Come in, come in! Merry Christmas!" she calls out. "We've been banned from the kitchen. The men are making a mess in there. But it's almost parade time, and Sidra has made some amazing sandwiches to tide us over until dinner. Come join us ladies in the living room. Just throw your coat on top of all the others. You can put your parcels under the tree there."

The living room leads to a dining room, and several of Aiden's family members are in there, everyone talking at once. Holly can see Aiden in the center of the group. Meanwhile, Alexa is holding a platter of sandwiches, and people appear to be fighting over them. Grandma Hazel throws herself into the fray. "I'm oidest!" she says. "I get first pick."

"Actually," says a man with a gruff voice and a kind smile, just like Aiden's, "technically *I* am, but ladies first."

"Ladies first, Gramps?" Alexa says. "What is this, the fifties? There are enough sandwiches to go around and then some, so everyone just calm down. No need to infantilize Grandma."

Holly feels suddenly shy and hangs back, but Aiden spots her and breaks off from the group.

"Hey! You made it."

His welcoming smile makes her feel sure of herself again. "Thanks for inviting me."

"Things have been a little hectic around here. There was yet another emergency—the mixer blew a gasket, which almost meant no dinner rolls, a key part of the Coleman family holiday tradition, so Alexa and Sidra needed to enlist some manual bread-kneading muscle. My arms may never recover, but everything's back on track. My dad's in the garage, and I think he almost has it fixed."

Just then, a man who looks like Aiden, only two or three decades older, opens the back door, holding a wrench up in the air. He calls out, "Victory! In the battle against machine, man has come out victorious yet again!" Holly finds herself smiling; she can now see where Aiden gets his charming geekiness from.

The hubbub around the sandwich tray simmers down slightly as Aiden approaches with Holly to introduce her to his father, Murray.

"And hey, everyone, may I remind you all that this is Holly. Our *guest*—who, by the way, should maybe get the first sandwich since she's never tried them before?"

Holly protests, embarrassed. Then Alexa says, "Well, she already got four free cookies this week, so it's not like we aren't giving her special treatment already."

"Wait," Holly says, determined not to let Alexa's prickly edges get to her. "We're having a full turkey dinner?"

"Yes," says Murray.

"And now we're eating sandwiches?"

"Well, we need something to eat during the parade," Grandma Hazel says. "It's Christmas Day. You're supposed to be full to the point of bursting all day long. And besides, we're not eating that turkey for hours."

Charlotte smiles at Holly. "If there's one thing this family likes to do, it's eat."

"Yeah," says Alexa. "You need to keep up."

"Oh, Holly can keep up," Aiden says. "You already know she's a huge Seventh Heaven sandwich and cookie fan."

Holly turns to Alexa. "I actually have a little gift as a thank-you for the cookies the other day," she says. "I have Christmas gifts for everyone, but this is more of a gratitude gift."

She reaches inside her purse and holds up a small paper bag. She had brought an unopened jar of Momofuku's coveted Chili Crunch Hot Honey to use on her ramen, but the night she made it for Aiden, she'd used the hot sauce he brought instead. "It's delicious on anything, but I bet it would be great on one of your sandwiches."

"That's so thoughtful of you," Sidra chimes in, but Alexa is looking over the jar doubtfully, and soon discards it on a chair.

"Quick, everyone, grab a hoagie and then let's get outside, it's about to start," says Grandma Hazel, her eyes sparkling even brighter with excitement.

When Sidra offers to get Holly some cider, Holly insists she can get it herself.

"Here, let me help you find the mugs," Aiden says. "Anyone else need anything? We'll meet you outside."

"Oh, I get it," says Grandma Hazel, winking at Aiden as Holly blushes. "You two lovebirds want to *smooch*."

Indeed, as soon as they're alone in the kitchen, Aiden reaches for her and pulls her in for a long kiss.

"Merry Christmas, Holly."

"Merry Christmas, Aiden."

He kisses her again, and eventually, she has to pull back and catch her breath. "You're kissing me like it might be the last time."

"It might be the last time for a few hours—Sidra's holiday-parade hoagies are amazing, but pretty soon we're both going to have fish breath."

Holly laughs and gives him another long kiss. "Aiden Coleman, I'd kiss you even with fish breath."

Alexa has poked her head through the kitchen doorway. "You two slowpokes coming? The first float is in view."

Outside, Holly and Aiden take their seats in a pair of camping chairs. Once Holly is settled, Aiden covers her knees and his own with a plaid flannel blanket, and Sidra hands them each a plate.

"It smells incredible. What exactly is this?"

"You can't go into this with any preconceived notions in your mind," Aiden says.

"Okay, so I've had the sweet French roll before. Fish with the crispiest breading I've ever had—and it's been marinated in something amazing—"

"A secret blend Sidra's dad passed down that she says she's never telling anyone, not even Alexa—"

"Is that Thousand Island dressing?"

"Close!" Sidra calls out, leaning forward from down the row of chairs. "Another secret recipe. *Like* Thousand Island, yes, but with a smoky, spicy kick. I learned to make it from my dadu. You'll never have anything else like it."

"There's something else." She takes another bite. "It reminds me of sandwiches from my childhood. Is it . . ." She closes her eyes. "Melted American cheese?"

Sidra smiles. "You guessed it! I've tried other fancier cheeses, but nothing works quite as well. My aunt and uncle had a sandwich shop in Philly, and even they could never find a better cheese topping for this sandwich than that."

At that moment, a hush falls over the street, and church bells begin to ring all through town.

"It's starting!" Grandma Hazel says excitedly. All at once, the streetlights are extinguished, and everyone falls quiet, waiting expectantly in the soft glow of dusk.

In the distance, Holly can see what looks like a crowd of bobbing stars coming toward them. As the stars grow closer, she realizes the lights are coming from paper cutouts held aloft on long staffs carried by children. The walking choir begins to sing "Song for a Winter's Night" in their earnest little voices, and Holly finds herself clasping her hands to her heart as they walk solemnly by. One little star carrier turns and, adorably, waves and shouts "Hi, Mom!" to a woman standing on the sidewalk—but most of the other children keep their faces turned forward as they walk through the town singing the old Gordon Lightfoot standard, their voices ringing out in the crisp night air as real stars begin to light up above them in the sky.

Just as the children's voices rise to their highest, singing about how happy they would be to hold the hand they love on a winter's night, Holly turns her head and locks eyes with Aiden. He seems to be watching her rather than the parade, too. "I'm glad you like it," he whispers.

"I love it. Every second." She turns her attention back to the street as a marching band playing a rousing rendition of "Jingle Bells" starts to approach, drowning out the children's choir. Many of the townspeople clap and dance as the music picks up—including Aiden's grandparents. Hazel laughs delightedly as her husband spins her.

The parade floats follow the marching band, on flatbeds pulled by pickup trucks. The surfaces of all the vehicles are strung with lights and decorations. Many of them feature vignettes reenacting various scenes from famous Christmas stories, including a Nativity scene, a Rudolph float, an Island of Misfit Toys–themed float sponsored by the antique shop, and a Dickensian Christmas-themed float sponsored by the town's bookshop. The townspeople on the floats ring sleigh bells and call out greetings, or throw candy or festive colored beads.

Aiden has moved his camping chair closer to her, and their bodies are now touching—shoulder to shoulder, arm to arm. The warmth of touching him moves all the way through Holly's body.

Holly finds herself *oohing* and *aahing* over a gaggle of donkeys wearing reindeer antlers, led past by a local farmer who Aiden says houses rescue donkeys at a picturesque acreage not too far from the eco-cabin. Then a huge float sponsored by the local dance school sails by, crowded with little sugarplum fairies and tin soldiers, dancing shyly as their parents cheer them on and crowd onto the street to take photos and videos of their adorable offspring.

Once the last float, a life-sized gingerbread house created as a collaboration between Seventh Heaven and another local bakery, has disappeared into the gloaming, an expectant hush falls over the town again.

"Oh, this is the best part," Grandma Hazel calls out as, in the distance, a white horse appears. The horse prances toward the townspeople, snorting clouds of snow-white air, sleigh bells jingling from an elaborate bridle and saddle. The stallion's rider is costumed majestically in a red-and-gold cape, a wooly white beard, and a red crown with a golden cross on the front.

"That's Angela Jenkins," Aiden whispers. "She was on the Olympic equestrian team back in the eighties and won the gold medal for dressage."

Holly shakes her head in wonder as "St. Nick" manages her fiery steed, all while throwing candies and calling out greetings to delighted children.

The prancing white horse eventually disappears over the horizon, the church bells ring again, and the parade is over. Holly's surprised to realize a whole hour has flown by.

"I can't believe how much I loved that," Holly says. "Thanks for inviting me today."

"I couldn't imagine spending Christmas without you," Aiden replies.

"I think it was the best one ever," Grandma Hazel adds.

"You say that every year," says Aiden's mom with a laugh.

"Well, it's true. It just gets better every year!"

"So, Holly," says Murray, leaning forward, "how long will you be with us in Krimbo?"

"I'm staying until just before New Year's," Holly says.

Alexa purses her lips. "You came here all by yourself? For Christmas?"

"Oh—well." Holly feels suddenly self-conscious.

"Not everyone's family goes as wild over Christmas as ours does," Aiden says. "And Holly has a high-pressure lawyer job in the city. She needs a break. You know how that is, Alexa."

Their conversation is interrupted by a group of neighbors crossing the street to wish them a happy Christmas. The friends and family all stand outside chatting and finishing their mulled wine, and then it's time to troop inside to check on the turkey and the rest of the dinner fixings.

"Another half an hour and then it needs to rest for a bit," Aiden's father announces. "Why don't we open presents?"

Everyone rushes into the living room, where Grandma Hazel is appointed "Santa." Aiden and Holly sit close together on a love seat.

Aiden glances over at Holly and smiles.

"What?"

"You just look happy," he murmurs.

"I *am* happy. This is the kind of Christmas I always dreamed of as a kid. I can't believe I'm lucky enough to be here."

He reaches down and squeezes her hand. "And I can't believe I'm lucky enough to have you here." He kisses her cheek.

"This one's for Holly, from Charlotte and Murray," Hazel announces—and soon, Holly realizes that even though they would have only found out she was coming the day before, everyone in Aiden's family bought her a gift: a cedar-scented candle from his parents that reminds her of Aiden, an ornament in the shape of a Christmas cookie from Sidra and Alexa, and a hand-knit scarf from Grandma Hazel and Grandpa Sam that perfectly matches the blue of Holly's coat.

"Can't say I can take any credit for that one," Sam says when Holly thanks them both. "But you're more than welcome, dear. We just like to see our Aiden looking so happy—and if someone decides to stay up until all hours knitting because of that"—he winks at Hazel—"so be it."

"Worth it," says Grandma Hazel. "I can hardly sleep on Christmas Eve anyway. Too excited. It was good to have something to keep myself occupied."

Aiden leans his head down to murmur in Holly's ear again. "Hey, I thought maybe we'd do our gifts later, alone? Back at your place or mine?"

Holly smiles and whispers back that, yes, she'd love that, and tucks the small gift she has for him away for later. She feels a glowing warmth inside at the idea that she gets to spend a magical night with his family—and then look forward to some time alone with Aiden, too.

Once the presents are opened and the living room is littered with the fabric ribbons and reusable bags, Grandpa

Sam announces he's going to carve the turkey. Soon, they're all gathered around the dining room table. The dining room is an old-fashioned one, with a fireplace on one end. It crackles and pops as they dig into the feast, which, surprisingly, Holly still has room for even after the enormous sandwich she ate earlier.

After the meal, the family decides to take a breather before dessert—Alexa and Sidra's legendary sticky toffee pudding, apparently—and the women all go into the kitchen to start the dishes while the men go to the living room to play Rummoli.

Between the five of them, surprisingly short work is made of the many pots and pans, and Sidra and Alexa eventually send Grandma Hazel and Charlotte to relax in the living room. "Why don't you both go relax, too?" Holly suggests to Alexa and Sidra. "I can finish these last few pots."

"I'll dry them," says Alexa. "Sid, you go. Put your feet up for a while until it's time to flambé the dessert."

Once Sidra is gone, the silence in the kitchen between Alexa and Holly suddenly hangs heavy.

"So, flambéed Christmas pudding, huh?" Holly says. "I've never had that before. Sounds great. I'm a big fan of your desserts."

"You've made that clear," Alexa says wryly, taking the clean chafing dish Holly hands her and drying it briskly. Then, "Can I ask you a question?"

"Of course. Anything."

Alexa puts down the dish. "Why did you come here, seeking out Aiden?"

Holly frowns. "Excuse me?"

"Why did you come looking for him? Is it because you found out how rich he is?"

"*What?* No, of course not. He only told me about his company yesterday."

"He said that when I asked him, but honestly, it just seems like way too much of a coincidence. He sold his company and suddenly, he had the right status for you so you came knocking. Aiden's such a great guy—he doesn't deserve that kind of treatment."

Holly struggles to get her bearings in the conversation, reminds herself that Alexa is just prickly, and a protective older sister. But still, her abrupt accusations are jarring. "I know he's a great guy. I think so, too."

"One more thing." Alexa tilts her head. "You two have become really close this week. But . . . apparently not close enough for you to tell him about this?"

She takes out her phone, taps twice, and turns the screen toward Holly. Holly's heart plummets when she sees what it is: the *New York Times* wedding announcement from a few months before, heralding her holiday nuptials to Matthew Carter.

"That . . . wedding didn't happen," Holly manages.

"Clearly. I made a few calls to some friends in the city. It was supposed to be last week."

"We broke things off."

"And then you just conveniently came here to seek out an old high school friend so you could switch out one rich husband for another?"

"I—I—" Holly stammers. "That's not it at all. I had no idea Aiden would be here in Krimbo!"

"Your best friend just coincidentally rented a place from him and gave it to you?"

Holly is blinking back tears now. "Yes," she says. "It was a coincidence. I swear. I wouldn't do that." But she can see how bad it looks—and it looks even worse when Aiden comes into the kitchen to see her squared off against his sister.

"What's going on in here?" he says. "Alexa, seriously, you made Holly cry? On Christmas? You really need to cool it."

Alexa has her hands on her hips, staring Holly down, daring her to tell the truth. Holly knows she has no other choice, that if she doesn't try to explain things, Alexa will just give her version anyway.

"It wasn't her fault. There's something I should tell you, Aiden."

He looks even more alarmed now. "What is it? Are you okay?"

"I'm fine. I just . . . haven't been totally honest with you about why I came here alone for Christmas. I was engaged to be married. My wedding was supposed to be"—she closes her eyes briefly—"just over a week ago. But my fiancé broke things off the night before our wedding, and I came here because I was in shock. Because I needed to take some time on my own."

"You were supposed to get married last week?"

She can't blame him for looking so surprised, so horrified. It feels like they've talked about so much over the past few days—but she realizes as she spills out the truth how inaccurate that is. She kept so much from him.

"I'm sorry to do this on Christmas," Alexa says. "But Aiden, I'm just trying to protect you. You know that."

Aiden doesn't look at Alexa, just keeps staring at Holly, his face the picture of shocked dismay.

"I'm sorry, Aiden," Holly says. "Everything with us—" She glances at Alexa, who does not make a move to leave the kitchen and give them any privacy. "It happened fast, and it feels so right, and I didn't want to ruin it. But I have. By not telling you, I have ruined everything."

Aiden presses his palms to his eyes. "I don't know what to say. I think I just need a minute." He looks dazed as he heads for the back door without even bothering to get a jacket. The door slams and he's gone.

Holly stands in the silent kitchen, staring at the closed door. Then she turns to Alexa.

"I'm going to go," Holly says. Alexa says nothing in response. Holly turns and rushes out of the kitchen, barely stopping to get her coat and handbag as Aiden's family looks on, stunned.

19

IVY
December 25
Kauai, Hawaii

Ivy wakes at dawn and hears Oliver in the shower. Her body is pleasantly sore from the night before with him—and, knowing he's leaving soon for his camping trip, she goes to join him in the shower. "Merry Christmas," she says, stepping into the hot water's stream.

He groans at the sight of her. "Best Christmas present ever," he says, reaching for her right away. "But honestly, I can't believe I, Mr. Crazy About Christmas, am leaving on today of all days. What was I thinking?"

She kisses him as the water sluices between their bodies. "You were thinking your work is important to you. Your art." She presses herself closer. "And that's sexy to me, too . . ."

After their shower, they sit on her deck and have breakfast.

"So, what do you think you'll do while I'm gone, other than pine for me?" Oliver asks with a wink as he bites into a wedge of pineapple.

"Well," she says with a laugh, "once I'm done pining, I'm going to draw all morning, as much as possible—make the best use of my time without you."

Her portfolio is sitting nearby, and he glances over at it and says, "Mind if I look, before I go?"

"Sure," she says, and tries not to feel shy about it. He's seen her naked; surely she can show him her artwork.

He flips through the plastic-clad pages, doling out appreciative compliments. "So, really?" He looks up at her when he's done. "These are just for you, and for friends, family? You never show them at galleries?"

Ivy shakes her head. "Not anymore."

"They're so good, Ivy. You really should be showing them somewhere. I don't get it."

Suddenly, Ivy feels defensive. The afterglow of the night before and that morning in the shower dissipates. "I'm fine," she says. "I like my life this way."

He puts down the portfolio and looks at her thoughtfully. "So your art—it's just two weeks a year, that's it?"

"I've already explained to you how my art holidays work."

A long pause. "And me?"

She looks up, surprised. "What about you?"

"I mean, where would I fit into all that? Because I don't want this, us, to be just a two-week thing. I want to see you again after this."

"I want to see you again, too."

"In New York City, though. That's where we'd see each other?"

"I don't know. I guess I haven't thought that far ahead. But yes, I'll be in New York."

"Right. We can talk about this later, I guess. I should go pack up."

She sits alone on the deck after he's gone inside, but then gets up and follows him in, the defensiveness still flowing through her.

"What am I supposed to do, tell you that now that we've met, I'm going to change everything about my life?"

He zips shut his pack and turns to her again. "That's not what I'm saying." He runs a hand through his hair, messing it up in that familiar way. "Look, I'm sorry. I shouldn't have said any of this. Not this morning. I'm getting ahead of myself." His expression softens as he looks down at her. "I really like you, Ivy."

She reaches for him. "I really like you, too," she says. "We can figure it out."

He wraps his arms around her and pulls her close, speaks into her hair. "You're right."

"And thank you for saying such nice things about my artwork."

"It's incredible," he says. "I mean that."

"So is yours." She pulls away and looks up at him again. "And you need to get to that waterfall. Meanwhile, I need to work on your Christmas present, which, I'm sorry, is going to be a day late."

He raises an eyebrow, flashes his dimple at her. "I thought I got my Christmas present in the shower?"

She laughs. "That was just part one. Okay, go. I'll see you tomorrow, okay?"

He kisses her deeply. "Merry Christmas, Ivy," he says, his voice soft. "I'll make this up to you, I promise."

One more parting kiss, and he's gone.

Later, back in her bedroom, Ivy sees the gifts and card on her pillow.

"Open the presents first" is scrawled across it.

Inside the box is a pendant on a delicate gold chain. The pendant is aqua blue, a similar color to his eyes, she notes, but studded with golden flecks. It reminds her of the way the sun dapples the ocean as it rises. She puts it on and misses him even more.

The second package is a framed photograph. One of Oliver's waves, stunning in its powerful simplicity. She smiles at his signature in the corner and knows this is a photo she will always treasure.

Then she opens the card.

Dear Ivy,

The pendant on the necklace is a Kauai Ocean Opal. The color reminds me of the ocean, and specifically the way you draw the ocean with your pastels—the perfection with which you capture sunlight on waves.

The print is of one of the first wave photographs I ever took. I think it might have been the moment I realized I wanted to be a photographer. I think—I hope—you might find that inspiring.

I can't wait to see you first thing tomorrow morning. Twenty-four hours feels like forever.

Merry Christmas.

Yours, Oliver

Suddenly, Ivy is blinking back tears.

I think—I hope—you might find that inspiring.

But he doesn't understand, does he? Just because she feels inspired, just because she loves making her art more than anything else, does not mean she can upend her life. Only, was that what he was even asking her to do, earlier? Her inner voice tries to get her attention with that. He was just trying to suggest there were other lifestyles out there—and that maybe they had a future, one he was wondering about.

Ivy gets out her art supplies and sets up her easel, but she can't concentrate. Every time she lifts her hand to draw, all she can think of is the color of Oliver's eyes, the texture of his hair. What is she so afraid of? Why can't she truly give in to her feelings for him?

"Merry Christmas!"

Larry is standing at the top of the stairs wearing a Santa hat over her tumbling dark curls.

Ivy smiles. "Good morning."

"I see Oliver is off on his camping trip. But I hope you two had a great night last night?" She raises her eyebrows.

"We did," Ivy says, trying to keep her tone lighter than she feels.

"You'll join us later? We're going to have a big dinner, and I'll be cooking all day, and making festive cocktails."

"Sounds perfect," Ivy says. "I'm going to finish this and then I'll come down."

Ivy sets back to work, struck by a sudden idea. She draws the beach, and then Oliver and Larry walking on it with their surfboards, the way they looked the first morning she saw them out there. Two soulmate best friends. She feels a twinge—she misses Holly—and pours that emotion into finishing the drawing.

Oliver will be back the next day, she tells herself as she

sets the pastel drawing out to dry. They can talk. They'll figure this out, what their future could look like. Everything is going to be fine.

"Cheers!" Larry says. "To new friends, and to love." She looks to Shira, her face aglow with happiness in the candlelight. "Enduring love. Merry Christmas, everyone!"

"Merry Christmas!" Ivy repeats, feeling a dull ache in her heart at how much she still misses Oliver, especially after their argument. She clinks glasses with her new friends, sips her wine, then puts her glass down and leans back in her chair. "That was an amazing dinner."

"I know, I'm sorry Oliver missed it."

"But because it's Larry, there will be leftovers for days," Shira says with a smile at her fiancée.

"You can never, ever have enough leftover pineapple-ham sandwiches," Larry says. Then she glances at Ivy. "Or vegan Manapua Man dumplings."

Ivy laughs. "This is true. Those are so amazing, I might need to find a way to smuggle some home in my suitcase." She takes another sip of wine, but the mention of a suitcase has sobered her. She looks across the table, at Larry and Shira snuggled close in the candlelight.

"I hope you don't mind my asking, but is it hard to make a long-distance relationship work?"

Larry laughs. "Gee, I wonder why you want to know that."

Ivy blushes and ducks her head. "But seriously . . ."

Shira glances at Larry. "I think it was harder at the beginning. I won't lie and say being apart wasn't agonizing sometimes."

"Almost all the time," Larry says. "I missed Shira like crazy. We went months without seeing each other when she was working on a movie. But it also made it kind of exciting, right?"

Shira nods. "Every time we saw each other again, it felt as exciting as the first time. And we had to be really conscious about our relationship. We had to plan phone calls, Face-Times, visits. We could never take each other for granted—and I think that has trickled down into the rest of our relationship. We're stronger because of it. I think we always will be."

"So, there's hope for you and Ollie," Larry says. "I promise."

Ivy sighs, and Larry clocks her somber expression. "Hey, you okay?"

"I'm fine," Ivy lies. "I guess I do just wish he were here."

"You two are so cute. I love it." She lifts up the wine bottle. "Uh-oh, empty." Shira gets up to find another bottle and change the record, and in the silence, Ivy hears her phone ringing.

She looks at the call display: Holly. "Hello?"

A gasping, wrenching sob. "Ivy?" She hears her friend take what sounds like a deep, painful breath.

"Holly! Are you hurt?"

"I'm fine. But . . . I'm not really okay, no. I need you. I can't be alone right now, Ivy. I'm so sorry. Please, come."

20

HOLLY
December 25
Hudson Valley, New York

Holly turns left on the North Service Road and drives slowly and carefully, because her vision is blurred by the tears that have not stopped falling since she left Aiden's family's home, then pulls over at the side of the road to call her best friend.

"I'm coming," Ivy had told her. "I'll be on the next flight out. I'll be with you as soon as I can." And while Holly feels terrible for begging her friend to leave her Hawaiian art retreat and come be with her, as she takes another gulping sob, she knows she had no choice. She really can't be alone right now. The tears she never shed when Matt broke off the wedding have arrived, and they're a deluge. Her heart is broken. But she knows she's not crying over Matt—or at least, not directly. And she's not just crying over Aiden, either. All the emotions that have been pent up inside her have rushed to the surface. She's crying over ten lost years. She's crying over fooling herself into thinking Matt could ever be the one. And yes, she's crying because she ruined things with Aiden—and she really, really likes him.

Out of the corner of a tear-blurred eye, she sees a light swinging around at the side of the road. She slows her car even more and looks into the darkness. Among the trees there's definitely a light, its beam going back and forth, up and down.

Holly stops and rolls down her window, listens. Eventually, she hears a voice, faint but audible. "Mrs. Claws! Mrs. Claws! Where are you, Mrs. Claws?"

She turns off the car and steps out, her tears abruptly forgotten. "George! Mr. Plaskett? Is that you?"

"Hello?" The light is still swinging in the trees, but then George steps out onto the soft shoulder at the side of the road and Holly gasps.

"George! What are you doing out here at night with no coat on?!"

"Oh, dear, I'm just frantic. The latch on my front door has been finicky lately, and I suppose when I said goodbye to my Christmas visitors tonight, and sent Drew off to spend Christmas with his family, it didn't close properly. I was heading up to bed, and Mrs. Claws normally follows me—but I felt a terrible draft and then saw the door swinging open. And Mrs. Claws was nowhere to be found! She only goes outside with my direct supervision, and never at night. There are wolves, coyotes about. Oh, dear."

"How long ago was this, George?"

"I'm not sure . . . half an hour, maybe more?"

"Come. Get in my car."

"But please, I can't, I have to find her—"

"I'll help you, George. I'll look for her. But you can't be outside in the middle of winter like this. We need to get you inside, get you warm."

"I suppose you're right," George says as he reluctantly gets in the car. "But you'll help me find her?"

"I promise," Holly says, wishing with all her heart this will be a promise she can keep. She turns her car back on and puts the heat on full blast as she drives toward the old Christmas tree farm and George's house. They soon pull up out front of the charming old manor. "Why don't we check and see if she's come back while you were gone?" Holly says, and follows him inside. George calls out the cat's name hopefully, but there's no *mew* in response, no sound of a bell on a collar as the cat runs to greet him.

"George, does Mrs. Claws have a favorite treat, perhaps?"

"She certainly does. She just loves freeze-dried minnows, and I have a bag in the cupboard. Always makes me think

I'm feeding her fishing bait, but she can't seem to get enough of them."

"Could I get that bag, please? I'll take it out with me and start looking around the property. May I use your flashlight? Thank you. And here." There's a pad and pen on the kitchen counter; Holly writes down her cell phone number. "Put on an extra sweater, light the fire, and leave the door open for her. We'll put a few of her treats in the doorway, and perhaps she'll smell them and come back in while I'm out looking for her. And if she does, you call me right away."

He takes the piece of paper from her hand and nods, his expression still distraught. "Thank you, Holly, for coming to my rescue."

"Of course, George. I completely understand—Mrs. Claws is important to you. And I'm going to find her, okay? Cats rarely go far—she's probably just out exploring a little, maybe chased after a mouse."

"She used to love to do that, when she was younger," George says. "But she's too old to be out at night on her own."

"I'll find her," Holly says firmly. "You wait here."

Holly turns on the flashlight and holds it in one hand while shaking the bag of treats with the other. *Shake, shake.* "Mrs. Claws, where are you?"

She shines the flashlight's beam over the snow and eventually sees tiny paw prints leading around the back of the house. She follows them toward the rows and rows of

Christmas trees, but the snow has blown around a bit, and she loses the cat's tracks. She keeps on walking in the same direction, shining her light in the darkness, shaking the treat bag, calling out in a gentle voice so she doesn't scare the cat.

After several minutes of fruitless searching, Holly decides to be systematic. She'll head down one row of trees at a time, checking under some of the bigger ones, with their weighty pine skirts. Mrs. Claws might be hiding there.

An hour passes. Even in her warm winter boots, Holly's feet are growing numb—but she keeps on searching, row after row. "Mrs. Claws, hello?" *Shake, shake.* "I have something for you. Come out, pretty girl!"

Holly stops. Was that a faint *mew*, or was it the wind in the trees? She stands perfectly still, listening, shakes the treat bag again.

Mew.

Shake, shake.

Mew.

Holly checks under one tree, then another, but Mrs. Claws isn't under any of them. Then she approaches a particularly large tree with heavy branches hanging down to the ground, and as she lifts one up, she catches a glimpse of the little cat, her eyes shining bright blue in the snow her pale coat almost blends into.

"There you are," Holly says softly. She knows she has to be

careful not to scare the cat into running off, especially since Holly is unfamiliar to her. She makes no sudden moves, slowly takes a dried minnow out of the treat bag, kneels down, and holds it out. Mrs. Claws doesn't hesitate, and steps forward for the treat immediately, then flops down in the snow for a belly rub. Holly laughs softly and gives her one more minnow before gently picking her up and holding her close. Mrs. Claws purrs, pressing herself into the softness of Holly's parka. "You didn't mean to run so far, did you? It's okay, you poor thing. We'll get you back to George." Mrs. Claws seems to purr even louder at the mention of her dear owner's name.

As the house comes into view, Holly can see that the lights inside are all ablaze, and there are cars in the driveway.

"Holly?"

She slows.

"Holly, are you out there? Are you all right?"

It's Aiden, and when he sees her step out of the Christmas tree forest with the cat in her arms, he gasps with relief. "Oh, thank goodness. You're okay. And you found Mrs. Claws."

The rest of Aiden's family comes tumbling out of the house, all talking at once as usual, calling out to George that Mrs. Claws has been found. There are cries of "Holly found her, Holly found her"—and then Holly is in the warm house again, and Mrs. Claws is rolling happily in front of the fireplace.

"Aiden, my boy, could you check her over and make sure she isn't hurt in any way? I'm a bit too shaken to stand," George says, smiling gratefully at Holly, as he has been since she came inside with the cat.

Aiden kneels down and runs his hands over the cat's body. "Just a little cold, and that's nothing a few minutes in front of the fire won't cure. She's perfectly fine. Thanks to Holly." He looks at her from across the room, but Holly can't tell what he's thinking—the urgency of her sadness is suddenly back, full force.

"Excuse me," Holly says, and slips from the room to find somewhere she can be alone and collect her thoughts.

"Holly?" She turns. Alexa has followed her out into the hallway. Holly takes a deep breath, willing her tears to stay at bay.

"Please, Alexa. I can't take any more, okay? I'm a little shaken up. I just need a minute."

But there's something different about Alexa's expression. Her eyes are wide, and she's clasping her hands together. "I came out here to say I'm sorry. I wasn't fair to you. Aiden was so upset to find you'd left—and he was going to go out and find you, but then George called to tell him Mrs. Claws was missing, so we all rushed out here to help find her. But *you* had gotten here first, and were out in the snow, on Christmas night, looking for an old man's cat."

"Of course I was. George adores Mrs. Claws."

"It was really kind of you to go out looking for her. I'm

sorry for what I accused you of—finding Aiden on purpose because you knew he was rich and successful now, and therefore more up to your standards. I don't know what's been getting into me lately." She sighs. "Well, actually I do know. But just because some anxiety I thought I had kicked is getting the better of me, it's no reason for me to treat people the way I have been. People like you. I hope you can forgive me."

"Of course," Holly says, then offers a tentative smile. "No grudges allowed at Christmas, right? It's really okay. And what you're going through—that's hard. I'm sorry. But I know everyone in your family loves you a lot." She can feel the tears rising up again. "Alexa, I think I need to go," she says.

"Holly, wait, no—"

"I have to, Alexa. I really do." Alexa looks stricken as Holly turns for the door. "Could you say good night to everyone from me? Thank them for everything? I'm sorry. I really am."

She fumbles with her boots and coat and is barely out the door before the tears start again almost at once, flowing hot down her cheeks in the cold night air. She breaks into a jog, heading for her car.

"Holly!" In just a few steps, Aiden has caught up to her. "Holly." He says her name again, gently—the same way she said Mrs. Claws's name earlier, being careful not to startle her into running away.

"Please, don't cry," he says.

"I can't stop myself. And this isn't something that you should have to deal with."

He steps closer. "But why not? I care about you, Holly. A lot."

"Even after everything? Even after the fact that I was engaged to someone and I didn't even tell you?"

"I think I understand," he says. "You came here to heal, and you didn't want to talk about it. And I promise, I never thought it was what Alexa said—that you had come out here looking for me because you'd heard I was successful, and you never would have given me the time of day before. I know we haven't seen each other in years, but I just know you would never do that. Back at my parents' place, I went outside because . . ." He trails off.

And all at once, Holly finds herself smiling, even through her tears. "Because you needed a minute," she says. "Because it takes you time to think, and you just wanted to do that, to think. So you went out to the yard."

He smiles, too, and reaches for her. "Exactly." They stand like that, holding each other's hands, but not embracing, not yet. "And then I came back in ten minutes later, and you had gone. I was so upset with Alexa for being that hard on you."

"It's okay, really. We talked in the hallway."

He shakes his head. "It's nice of you to be understanding, but she and I need to have a big talk, too. Meanwhile, I'm worried about you. It was so great of you to help George. Please, don't run off."

"Of course. I'm so glad I found her."

"I'm so glad I found *you*," he says, his voice hoarse now, full of emotion. "But Holly, I also don't want to be a rebound for you. I care about you way too much for that. So, as hard as it would be for me, take all the time you need."

Holly swallows hard over the lump in her throat. "I know. And I don't want you to be a rebound, either. I like you so much, Aiden. I was with my fiancé for a long time, I thought I was going to spend the rest of my life with him—and yet I know already that the way I feel for you is different. Stronger. It's what I think I've always wanted, even though I half convinced myself it didn't exist." She pauses. "After tonight, though, I've realized that I want to do it right. I can't rush into anything with you because I'm afraid I'll ruin it. And the idea that I might have ruined it was completely devastating for me. I think that means we have to slow down a little." As she says this, she finds herself drawn toward his lips, as if they're twin magnets, pulling her closer. He seems to feel the same, lowering his head until their lips touch, softly, barely.

"I understand," he whispers. "I don't want anything to ruin this, ever."

They kiss gently in the snowy Christmas night, and then pull away from each other. Every single part of her wants to ask him to come back to the cabin with her, but instead she says, "I'm going to head back alone. But I'll call you in the morning?"

"Okay," he says, kissing her one last time. Then he stands and watches as she drives away into the darkness—but when she reaches the end of the driveway, she hits the brakes. She can see the words on his long-ago card in her mind: "Dear Holly, I'm writing to wish you a very Merry Christmas—and to profess my deep affection for you. I think you're the best girl in the school. You're pretty, you're smart, you're kind, you're funny, you're entirely you, and I've never met anyone I liked more. I hope we always know each other."

She held these words in her memory for twelve years. Never forgetting a single one. And the person who wrote them was Aiden.

She puts on the emergency brake and gets out of the car, runs back toward him in the gently falling snow, her steps growing lighter with every one that takes her back to the place where he is standing, waiting. The tears are streaming down her face again, but she knows they aren't tears of sadness. And when she gets close enough to him, they stop falling.

He looks confused, but cautiously happy. "Did you forget something?"

"Yes!" she says, and now she feels like laughing instead of crying. "I forgot that I actually don't want to take things slow. I've been waiting forever for you. I was with the wrong person—but that has nothing to do with us. I want to be with *you*, Aiden. I don't need to think it over, or take my time, or take things slow. I know what I want. And it's you. Somehow, it's always been you. And I don't want to waste another moment."

The smile on his face lights her up from the inside, causes joy and love to flow through every part of her body. She's made the right decision, knows it with every fiber of her being. Aiden picks her up by the waist, swings her around, and kisses her like it could be the last time—but she's certain it won't be.

21

IVY
December 26
LaGuardia Airport, New York City

Ivy is so fatigued she can hardly see straight when she lands at LaGuardia, after flying out of Lihue Airport the night before, stopping over in Denver, and continuing on to New York City. When she turns her phone from airplane mode, she notices with a pang that Oliver has not sent her any texts, and she doesn't have any voicemails, either. She can't imagine how he must have felt to come back from his camping trip and find her gone. She left him the drawing of the beach, of him and Larry going surfing in the early morning, and, while she waited for her airport taxi, drew a card with a sketch of them at the waterfall in Nā Pali, the two of them tiny figures, kissing in the water. She wrote him a letter, too, telling him how she felt.

Dear Oliver,

I can't believe I have to leave, but I hope you understand. I told Holly to call if she needed me and promised her I'd be there day or night—and she needs me. I have to go.

This time with you has been some of the most memorable of my life. The first moment I saw you, I was feeling terrible—and you made it all right, just by being you. I tried to resist my feelings, but I thought of almost nothing but you from that moment on. You know that. Every time I sat down to draw, even while surrounded by the most staggeringly beautiful scenery I've ever witnessed—I just wanted to draw you. Get your hair just right. Your beautiful sea green eyes.

I don't know what the future holds for us. Maybe we'll never see each other again. I know things weren't great when we saw each other last, and I hate that. But I swear, I won't forget you.

Merry Christmas.

Ivy

With every mile away from Oliver, her heart has increased its ache, and she almost can't stand it. She thinks about texting Larry, to see if he got back from his camping trip safely—but she knows she needs to wait, to give Oliver the chance to contact her when he feels ready. *If* he feels ready. He might not.

Maybe he won't call. Ever.

The ache intensifies.

But what if it's for the best? Ivy asks herself. Maybe it was a fantasy, it was just for fun, it was some of the best sex of her life, and she won't forget it. But she and Oliver didn't have a future—so maybe the abrupt ending is what's best.

She glances at her phone and notices with a pang that Oliver did not send her any texts while she was in-flight, and she doesn't have any voicemails either. A few texts come in from Holly, sent the night before, when she was on the plane. **Have you already left Hawaii? Call me.** But Ivy doesn't have time to call her now. It's the holiday season, and she knows rental cars will be at a premium. She texts back, **I'm here. Just landed at LaGuardia. I'll be in Krimbo within two hours.** Then she slides her phone back in her bag and takes off, fast, toward the car-rental line.

A small SUV rental secured, Ivy leaves the airport behind and stops at a Starbucks for a venti with an extra shot of espresso—then turns her phone on "do not disturb" for the snowy drive upstate. She hasn't slept in almost a full day, her heart is achy, and her body is still longing for a man she might never see again. She knows any sort of distraction while driving could be risky. She and Holly will have plenty of time to talk when she arrives at the cabin—and if Oliver is trying to reach her, she thinks with a pang, that will just have to wait.

Despite the extra-strong coffee, Ivy still feels bleary-eyed as she drives north. She opens the windows, blasts the music, and finally, she sees the signs leading her toward Krimbo and the tiny, snowy cabin where her poor, brokenhearted friend is waiting for her. This lightens her heart, at least, knowing that she'll be here with Holly when she needs her, just like she promised she would. In their entire relationship, Ivy has never heard Holly cry like that. As if her heart had been cracked right in two. Ivy feels relief as she sees the North Service Road and then, finally, turns onto the driveway leading her to the little cabin. It looks just as it did in the photos she saw online: cozy, small, and very remote.

Ivy sees Holly's car but is also surprised to see a white pickup truck parked beside her friend's vintage baby blue BMW. She pulls up beside the BMW, takes out her bags, and carries them up the path toward the cabin. She taps at the door, and Holly answers—and she does not look at all sad. In fact, her hair is bed-mussed, her skin is glowing, and she looks downright happy.

"Ivy! You came!" Holly throws her arms around Ivy and gives her a big hug, whispers in her ear, "You're the best friend in the world." Then she pulls away and glances behind her. "But . . ."

It dawns on Ivy. The pickup truck. The bed-mussed hair. The happy, glowing expression on her best friend's face. In fact, she's never seen her look so happy. "You made up," she says in a low voice. Holly nods. "You made up, and you've spent all of today having makeup sex." Holly nods again, and Ivy is happy for her friend—but she also feels a tug at her heart. Oliver. She left Oliver to come be with Holly—and Holly is perfectly fine. She almost cries then and there, but forces herself to smile. She did what she had to do. She thought Holly needed her. Of course she came.

Holly pulls her into the cabin. "He's sleeping upstairs, but I'm going to kick him out as soon as he wakes up."

"Oh, no, that's okay . . ."

"He'll understand. We have a lot of catching up to do. Ivy, honestly, you are the absolute best person for jumping on a plane and flying back to be with me. I'm sorry I was so dramatic. I tried to call you, but I guess you were on airplane mode. I texted, but I didn't hear back."

"It's fine," Ivy says, dropping her exhausted body down on the couch. "Really. I'm so glad you're okay. You deserve so much happiness, Holly."

There's a sound from the loft above, and a very handsome man pokes his head over the railing. "You must be the famous Ivy."

Ivy grins up at him. "And you must be the famous Eco Superman. Oops, I mean, Aiden Coleman."

He climbs down the ladder, dressed in jeans and a flannel shirt—with hair just as messy as Holly's—and shakes her hand. "I've heard so much about you," he says, and Ivy notes that what Holly said was true: He smells *great*. And he does look a lot like Henry Cavill. When his beautiful blue eyes wander across the room to land on Holly, which happens about every three seconds, Ivy can tell he's completely besotted. Whatever went wrong between them, it didn't last long.

Ivy finds herself glancing at her phone, which she left beside her on the couch, but the screen is blank and it has been totally silent since she arrived. Nothing from Oliver.

"I'm going to get out of your hair," Aiden is saying.

"Good, because we need to talk about you," Ivy says with a laugh, trying hard to keep her happiness for her friend at the top of her emotions.

"That's my Ivy, honest to a fault," Holly says from across the room, where she's boiling the kettle to make them a pot of coffee. At this, Ivy feels a pang. There's so much she hasn't told her best friend. But as soon as Aiden is gone, she promises herself, she's going to tell her everything.

Ivy looks away as Holly and Aiden share a long, lingering kiss at the door. It closes behind him, and Holly lets out a happy sigh. "He's so great," she says, flopping down onto the couch. Ivy's phone falls to the floor, and she picks it up and sets it on the coffee table, then sits down beside her friend, cross-legged on the end of the couch, holding a steaming mug of coffee. "Tell me everything," she says. "I think this coffee will buy me about one hour before I fall asleep with my eyes open, so *go*."

She listens as Holly explains about Christmas with Aiden's

family, and his sister finding out about her canceled wedding, their misunderstanding—and then a heroic scene with a missing cat. "When I came out of the woods with Mrs. Claws, Aiden was calling out my name," Holly says, her expression rapt as she continues the story, eventually getting to the part where she realized she couldn't live without Aiden.

"Am I being illogical? Should I be taking my time?"

"I think you're being amazing, Holly. What does logic have to do with any of this? You're literally levitating!"

"Dancing like a dervish."

"Screwing like a horny titmouse."

Holly laughs and brings the French press coffee carafe over to refill Ivy's cup. "Okay, a little more coffee and you tell me about your trip. Did you spend the week making amazing art?"

"Yes," Ivy says, taking a sip of coffee. "And . . ."

"And?"

Ivy puts her coffee down and looks her best friend in the eye—and feels her own eyes growing wet with tears. She blinks them away, but it's no use. One leaks out the corner of her eye and falls down her cheek.

"Ivy, what happened?"

Ivy puts her face in her hands. She needs to tell Holly everything, but where to begin? And what will it do to that happiness to tell her about Matt and Abby?

"Ivy, come on. Why are you crying? What happened? I'm your best friend. Tell me."

So Ivy begins. "I didn't stay at the hotel," she says. "I met someone." She starts to tell her about Oliver, but knows she is still leaving out important details, leaving Matt totally out of it. She just can't do it. Not yet. She needs to talk about Oliver first. "And I'm so scared, Hol. I've never felt this way. I've never made myself so vulnerable with a man. Only you. And now that he's five thousand miles away, I realize how completely unrealistic the whole thing is. But it still hurts so damn bad. And he hasn't called or texted, probably because I was awful to him." The tears start falling again, and Holly looks agonized.

"I had no idea," she says. "I'm so sorry I called you. I'm so sorry I made you come here. I messed up everything for you."

"No! Please don't feel bad. You needed me in that moment, and of course you're supposed to call me when you need me! Always. I'd do the same with you. I'm glad you two made up. I'm happy for you. I'm just . . ." She sniffles. "A little sad for myself, I guess."

"Why don't you call him?"

Ivy checks her phone again. No missed calls, no texts. "I wrote him a letter," she says. "And I left him a drawing. I know I left—but I also left the ball in his court. I can't call him. Not yet."

"He's *going* to call you, Ivy. I know it. There's no way you fell for someone this hard who didn't fall for you twenty times harder in return."

"I guess I could text Larry and see if he's okay, but I don't really want to do that. She's his friend, not mine."

"She? Larry isn't a guy?"

"No, Larry is a beautiful woman, actually. His bestie—and she's engaged to a woman named Shira."

Holly considers this. "Wow, it's like you've led this whole existence I know nothing about. Can I see photos? Of Oliver, of Larry? Of some of the places you went to?"

"Of course." Ivy unlocks her phone and scrolls through the photos with Holly at her side, feeling sharp pangs of nostalgia as she looks at images of the tree by the bar where she first met Oliver, the view from the villa right after he showed her around, the tree-lighting ceremony in Hanalei, Larry's bar, their camping trip, the waterfall, and, finally, the Christmas Eve beach lūʻau. "Aw, look at you two, slow dancing," Holly sighs, taking Ivy's phone and peering closer. "That's adorable."

"Yeah. Larry took that one."

"The way he's looking at you," Holly says, zooming in on the photo. "He's smitten, Ivy. He's going to call. He's probably just trying to figure out what to say." But then, abruptly, her expression changes. She zooms in on another segment of the photo—just as Ivy realizes with a plummeting heart what she has seen in the background.

Matt. And Abby. Dancing right behind Ivy and Oliver.

"What the . . ."

Ivy puts her hand on her friend's wrist. "Holly. I'm so sorry. I was going to tell you."

Holly is peering at the phone. "Matt went on our honeymoon?"

Ivy nods and finds she can't speak. It's just too awful.

"Who is he dancing with?"

Ivy swallows hard and manages to get the name out. "That's Abby," she says.

"He went on our honeymoon with Abby." Holly puts down the phone and looks up at Ivy. "And you kept it from me."

"I'm sorry. I didn't know how to tell you. I was so afraid it would crush you. And then, when you started to sound so happy, I didn't want to bring you down."

"So, that's why you didn't stay at the hotel," Holly says. "It isn't because it didn't feel right to you—it's because Matt was already there. You lied to me. You've never lied to me."

"I know. I did. I'm so sorry. It felt horrible. But I thought I was doing what I had to do. I'm sorry."

Holly picks up the phone again to look at the photo. "I don't know," she says. "This is hard to wrap my head around. You didn't tell me about Matt and Abby—but you also didn't tell me you were falling for someone. You didn't tell me anything about Oliver, any time we spoke. We tell each other everything, Ivy. Always. I don't understand."

"I'm so sorry," Ivy says again, because she doesn't know what else to say. But she can tell from Holly's expression that it isn't good enough. She's messed things up with her best friend—and combined with the pain she feels over Oliver, she's certain she has never felt worse in all her life.

22

HOLLY
December 27
Hudson Valley, New York

Early the next morning, Holly climbs the loft ladder to check on Ivy again, as she has several times in the night. Her friend is still breathing slowly and evenly, in a deep sleep that lasted all night. Holly climbs back down to her nest of blankets on the couch, where she slept to give her friend extra peace and quiet, and looks again at Ivy's phone, but no one has called or texted. "Darn you, Oliver."

She leans back on her pillow and thinks of the night before, when she reached for her best friend's hand and told her she didn't need to beg forgiveness for not telling her about Matt and Abby for one second longer. "I get it," she told Ivy. "And there's nothing to forgive. You were trying to be a good friend to me by shielding me from something that, you're right, would have been devastating a few days ago. But somehow, today, it's not. If anything, it makes me more certain than ever that I made the right decision about Aiden. Matt does not deserve even one more moment of my life, or my thoughts."

Ivy had breathed a sharp sigh of relief and wiped away another tear that had fallen. "And not telling you about Oliver and my feelings for him—I could hardly even admit it to myself, let alone to you. I was afraid telling you about it might jinx it somehow." At that point, she had looked down at her phone, still devoid of notifications. "But maybe he didn't feel it as strongly as I did. Maybe he's upset I left. I'll get in touch eventually, but right now, I'm just so tired."

"Of course you are. Why don't you go up and get in bed, and sleep for as long as you can? If your phone rings, or if he texts, I'll wake you up."

Ivy nodded wearily. "I'll just leave it down here," she said. "So I'm not tempted to check it every minute. I really need to get some rest."

Holly had watched as her friend climbed tiredly up the ladder before setting herself up for the night on the comfy couch.

Now she checks her friend's phone for the umpteenth time. "What is *with* you, Oliver?" Holly mutters through gritted teeth. She can only imagine how sad Ivy will be when she wakes to find out the guy she fell for harder than anyone else in her life has still not reached out.

But then, Holly notices something. A little crescent moon at the top of Ivy's phone—meaning it has been on "do not disturb" since Ivy arrived. She taps in the passcode without thinking twice—Ivy knows hers, too, and would do the same. Practically the moment she turns off the "do not disturb" function, the phone rings in her hand. Knowing she wouldn't be able to get up the ladder to alert Ivy fast enough, she hits answer.

"Hello?"

A deep, appealing male voice. "Ivy?"

"No, actually, it's Holly."

"The best friend. Hello. My name is Oliver Donohue. A friend of Ivy's from Hawaii."

"Oh, she told me about you, Oliver."

He sounds concerned. "Is Ivy okay? Larry gave me her flight info, but her phone has been going straight to voicemail since she landed, and she hasn't replied to any of my texts."

"She's fine. She's sleeping. It looks like she accidentally left her phone on 'do not disturb.' It must have been an accident."

She can hear him breathing a sigh of relief. "I thought maybe she had ghosted me," Oliver admits, and Holly likes him already, admires his candor.

"No way," Holly says. "Ivy wouldn't do that." She refrains

from adding *Especially not to you*, because she knows Ivy is very good at playing it cool, and would want Holly to do the same on her behalf—no matter how head over heels her friend is for this guy.

"Good," he says. "I was starting to wonder. Which was starting to make the fact that I flew to New York after I found out she was gone . . . well, a little awkward."

"Oliver!" Holly claps a delighted hand over her mouth. "You're in New York?"

"I just landed at LaGuardia about half an hour ago. You're her best friend, so you're going to find this out eventually, but I fell hard for her. And when I read her letter, I made a decision. I think Larry called it a grand gesture. I decided to get on a plane. I decided to chase after her."

"Levitate," Holly whispers, still in awe.

"Pardon me?"

"Oh, nothing. So you're in New York," she says again.

"I am. And I've been trying to call Ivy to get the address of your cabin. But she wasn't answering. Now I know why."

Holly's cheeks hurt, she's smiling so hard. She glances up at the loft, where her sad, sleeping friend is—and her heart feels like it's expanding in her chest. She gives Oliver the address. "I'm going to head out," she says. "So that you two can talk in private when you get here. But Oliver? I *really* look forward to meeting you later."

She hangs up and leaves Ivy a note, explaining how to use

the solar shower and telling her she'll be back later. *Text me when you want me to come back*, she says, hoping it's not too obvious that there'll be a reason Ivy might not want her friend around. Then Holly dresses, texts Aiden, and drives to his cabin, the smile never leaving her face.

23

IVY
December 27
Hudson Valley, New York

Ivy wakes and climbs down the ladder, but Holly is nowhere to be found. She sees the note left for her and feels a jolt of surprise. She knows Holly has completely forgiven her for not telling her about Matt and Abby, but she's still a bit rattled that she'd leave her alone in her heartbroken state.

She looks at her phone screen, but there are no text notifications or missed calls. She was wrong about him. It doesn't feel possible that she could have felt such a strong connection with someone, only for it not to be real—but it must not have been. She'll get over it, somehow. Maybe not today, and maybe not for a little while, but she's strong. She will.

She goes outside for a fast, bracing shower, then runs inside before her hair can freeze. She's dressing upstairs in the loft when there's a tap at the door. "Hang on!" she calls out. She throws on a T-shirt and pulls on track pants, then climbs down the ladder. She can see a tall shadow of someone standing at the door, but she can't tell who it is.

She opens the door.

Oliver.

It nearly takes her breath away.

"You're . . . really here?" she manages. "I'm not dreaming?"

He looks nervous. "Is that okay? That I'm here?"

"Yes," she breathes. "How did you find me?"

"I called while you were sleeping. I talked to Holly. Your phone had been on 'do not disturb.'"

"Oh! So it's not that you didn't call or text . . ."

"No. Not at all. I tried and tried, and I finally decided that I had to see you again. So, I flew to New York."

"Of course you did. Because you're you." She feels dizzy with happiness, breathlessly, perfectly thrilled to see him. "I'm so sorry," she says, stepping back and leading him inside. "I'm sorry I left. I'm sorry for the thing I said before you did."

"No," he says. "Don't be. I was pushing you. I was being judgmental. I don't know what I was doing, trying to make it seem like I wanted you to decide on something. You're twenty-nine. Your life can be what you want it to be. We can just take things easy."

She reaches up to touch his cheek, his hair. "You're here," she repeats. She steps closer. "Did you get your waterfall shot?"

He smiles down at her. "Yeah. I got the perfect one. I submitted it to *National Geographic* just before I left."

"I'm so glad." Her face is close to his, so close their lips are practically touching. "You came," she says again.

"Of course I did," he says. "I don't know what our future holds, Ivy, but I do know this: I couldn't let you walk out of my life. I want to see where this could go."

"Me, too," she says. "I haven't been able to think of anything but you since I left. I've missed you so much."

His lips brush against hers. "I was thinking, I can hang out in New York for a while. I was going to anyway—as much as I hate winter, I had planned to come for a few weeks because my agent wanted me to meet with a few galleries. I'll go back to Hawaii a few times. Maybe you can take some vacation from work and come with me?" He smiles, touches his lips to hers. "But no pressure. We'll figure it out."

"We will," Ivy says softly. "Now, please—can you just kiss me? And then I want to see your waterfall photo!"

He does, and it's like it was at the waterfall, the first time—perfect, all-encompassing, yet another best kiss of Ivy's life, to go with all the other kisses she has had with him.

"So," Oliver says when he pulls away to catch his breath. "I guess getting on a plane was the right move?"

Ivy laughs. "Absolutely the right move." It's as if the distance between them never happened. And she knows with sharp clarity that they are going to figure it out—that distance between them is never going to matter. That she has been swept away by her feelings for him—like the waves he finds so endlessly, beautifully fascinating. And that she has never felt more grounded, even though her future has suddenly opened up wide. "Now show me your perfect waterfall photo. And then, let's go to bed."

24

HOLLY
December 31
New York City

Holly opens Ivy's bedroom door and freezes at the sight of her wedding dress—at least the train of it—stuck between Ivy's closet door and the wall.

Ivy is behind her. "Oops. Should I have hidden that?"

"No. Not at all."

Holly walks to the closet door and opens it—and there is the dress that once felt like it came straight out of her dreams. Now it feels like it comes from another era, another lifetime. "It *is* a nice dress, though," she says, touching the impossibly soft silk.

"You looked like a Disney princess in it. In the best way possible."

Holly's smile is a little sad now. "I know." She turns to her friend. "Tell me again about how you said, 'Hold my mai tai,' and then tried to drop a bombshell on Abby about her being on my honeymoon and not knowing it—only she already knew and . . . what did she say?"

"'It just makes good financial sense,'" they both say at the same time, then fall back on Ivy's bed, laughing so hard tears leak out of the corners of their eyes.

"I'm really grateful," Holly says. "For everything that happened. Even the hard parts."

"Me, too," Ivy says. "Remember the last time we were here, in this apartment?"

"I do. I thought it was the worst night of my life. But it was leading me somewhere great. And you, too. That's the best part—that we're both so happy. Remember how I told you the guy for you was out there somewhere—"

"Maybe on a dude ranch in Montana, you said."

"And then, along came the Hot Bartender. He really *is* hot," Holly says, and Ivy rolls over, staring at her friend with wide eyes.

"Isn't he? I mean, oh my God. He is so hot. And I resisted having sex with him forever. How did I do that?"

Holly laughs. "Well, wasn't it just, like, a few days? But still. Very virtuous." She laughs again, then peeks over Ivy's shoulder at her bedside clock. "We'd better start getting ready. Our reservation is in an hour."

They hop from the bed and share space at Ivy's bathroom

mirror as they put on makeup, then get dressed, Holly in a low-cut champagne silk sheath, and Ivy in a tight black cocktail dress with a hint of glitter woven into the fabric.

"Think the guys will actually show up?" Ivy jokes as they wait downstairs for their Uber.

During the few days they spent together in the Hudson Valley, Aiden and Oliver bonded, fast—at first because Oliver had heard of Air Works and was in awe of Aiden, and then because it turned out Aiden was a huge fan of Oliver's work and even owned a few of his prints. Today they had spent the afternoon at MoMA together, checking out the Karl Blossfeldt exhibit, and were meeting Holly and Ivy at Alice, the restaurant where they've booked a table for their New Year's Eve get-together.

As they settle themselves in the back of the car, Holly turns to Ivy.

"It's okay, right?"

"What is?"

"That I'm showing up at our New Year's Eve party with a new guy, when I was with Matt not too long ago, about to get married."

"Does it feel right to you?"

"It feels like the rightest thing in the world."

Ivy smiles. "Then it is. And besides, it's just going to be us, and Ted and Ming—who already hated Matt, let's face it. And Larry and Shira, who you are going to love."

"I already do love that they have enough respect for our

obsession with New Year's Eve to have flown all the way in from Hawaii."

"Trust me, they are the best."

The car lets the best friends out in front of the restaurant, where Aiden and Oliver are already waiting for them, smiles on their faces when they see the women approaching as a gentle snowfall begins to blanket the city streets. Oliver gives a low whistle as he gathers Ivy into his arms for a kiss, and Holly feels yet another wave of happiness that, finally, her friend has found someone who makes her so happy. And who, yes, is very hot.

For Holly, the night is a blur of happiness. Food, drinks, friends—and Aiden by her side through all of it. Always just a glance, a smile, or a touch away.

Just before midnight, Holly taps on her glass. It reminds her of the night of her rehearsal dinner—but better, because she feels so much more relaxed tonight, so much more *herself*. "I'd like to make a toast," she calls out, holding up her champagne glass. "To love, and to friendship. The two most important things in the world."

"Hear, hear!" calls out everyone—including the man she suddenly and unexpectedly loves and already knows she couldn't live without. The man she knows without a whisper of a doubt is her match, her destiny. And that he always has been, since they were trying to keep pace with each other in high school, and since he wrote her the card she has always cherished, and will for the rest of her life.

Moments later, as the clock chimes midnight and cheers erupt around the terrace, Holly and Aiden share a kiss just as perfect as all the other kisses they've shared. She watches as Ivy and Oliver do the same. Then the two men each step back, and Holly and Ivy rush across the room to embrace each other, their hearts full of love, joy, hope, and the delicious anticipation for all that's to come, all that will be. The best friends agree in happy whispers that this is what makes New Year's Eve the most special night of the year—but that Christmas is magical, too.

EPILOGUE
One year later...

Holly closes her eyes as Ivy applies her mascara and the finishing touch on her makeup, then opens them and takes in the effect. "Love it," she says.

"Perfect," Ivy agrees. "As usual, Holly, you look like a Disney princess—in the best way possible." She picks up her own makeup kit and sits down on the stool in front of the bathroom mirror. "Okay, do me now," she says.

"Your skin is so glowy. You hardly need anything," Holly says, swiping just a touch of bronzer and then blush across her friend's cheekbones.

"It's all the great sex." Ivy winks, and Holly turns and examines herself in the mirror.

"Yeah," she says thoughtfully. "That *is* good for the complexion, isn't it?"

"Tell me, how often does Paul Bunyan carry you across the room like he's a lumberjack and throw you on his bed?"

Holly laughs, then blushes. "We do that all the time," she admits. Then she turns back to her friend to finish her makeup. "I can't believe the wedding is *today*," she says.

Ivy sighs, her eyes bright with joy and anticipation. "I know. Me neither."

She turns and pulls a bottle of good tequila out of her bag. "I brought this. A little shot, for good luck? Not that it's needed, really. But just for fun." She pulls out two plastic shot glasses while Holly examines herself in the mirror again, then looks back at her friend.

"I've never seen two people more in love, you know, or more perfect for each other."

"Other than you and Aiden, of course."

"Well, that goes without saying," Holly laughs.

They touch their glasses, toast to their futures. Then Holly looks down at her glass. "The last time I drank this kind of tequila with you, almost exactly one year ago, I thought my world was ending."

"I know. And I never imagined any of this could happen."

"Really, our worlds were about to change. Things fell apart, but only so we could rebuild them the way they needed to be." She smiles. "You know, I think one of the best parts of this year was seeing your work in galleries again."

Ivy smiles back at her. "I can't believe how lucky I am. That I fought it for so long, yet it's all working out."

"The art you did here in Kauai last year was some of your best—and you just keep getting better." Holly taps her glass against Ivy's again. "Plus all those commissions for the restaurant chain meant you could quit your job. And travel with Oliver."

"The only drawback is not being able to see you as much," Ivy says, meeting Holly's eyes in the mirror as she swipes gloss over her lips. She turns to Holly, her expression warm. "But we make it work, don't we?"

"And we always will. We have our rule: once per season, bare minimum. Plus, I love spending every weekend in Krimbo with Aiden, but it's nice that when the four of us go on vacations, it's always somewhere exotic and fabulous with you two."

"And *I* love that when we come to stay in Krimbo, we get to be at that magical Christmas tree farm Aiden bought, after George Plaskett decided he and Mrs. Claws needed to downsize to an apartment above . . . where is it?"

"Above Viola's Dress Barn," Holly says. "He's very happy— and Mrs. Claws never gets outside by accident anymore."

"So, how much vacation do you think your new firm is going to give you this year? Oliver and I were thinking late-winter vacation in Thailand, beach huts, weeks of relaxation?"

"Oh, that sounds heavenly. And they're pretty easygoing— I really love working at a start-up environmental justice firm. We're in."

Ivy turns and takes a mermaid-style slip dress from a hanger on the back of the bathroom door, then says, "Help me so I don't get makeup on it?" The dress is silk, its color subtle, just the barest hint of blue.

Holly helps her friend with the dress, zips it for her, then says, "You look *perfect*. Just like I knew you would. Okay, now help me."

Holly's dress is the color of the Hawaiian sky at dusk, and shorter than Ivy's, simpler in style. Once her dress is on, Holly sets a flower crown on her friend's head and sighs happily as she looks at her. "The most beautiful bride in the world."

"Will you be next, do you think?" Ivy says, adjusting the flowers, releasing their gentle frangipani scent into the room.

"Oh, sure," Holly says. "I know I'll always be with Aiden—we just work, you know?"

"Oh, I know. I've seen you two together," Ivy says, her smile growing.

"But we're in no rush. It's nice to just . . . see where life takes us. Focus on this new job, on our time in the city and Krimbo, on how much I love Aiden and how glad I am he's in my life. On planning our next epic vacation."

"I love that Oliver and Aiden have become such good friends," Ivy says.

Holly laughs. "Very convenient," she says. "I'm not sure

we could have had it any other way. Okay, I can hear the music starting. Are you ready?"

"*So* ready," Ivy says.

They leave the villa and walk out to the deck, where they see a small group of friends and family gathered on the sand below. A musical trio plays a slow, romantic version of "Sea of Love" on lutes and ukulele. Aiden is waiting at the base of the stairs and takes Holly's arm, but not before smiling down at her lovingly, whispering "You look gorgeous," and giving her a kiss. The maid of honor and groomsman walk down an aisle in the sand strewn with hibiscus petals, followed by Larry—whom Oliver christened his "best mate" for the ceremony—and Shira. They all head toward the arc of flowers set up just out of reach of the ocean waves.

Ivy steps forward and walks barefoot toward Oliver, who is standing with Ivy's father—who got himself ordained as an ecumenical minister so he could perform the wedding ceremony. Ivy's mother sits in the front row beside Oliver's sister. Ivy blows her mom a kiss, then turns her attention to Oliver, standing waiting for her by the sea. He mouths *Wow* as she walks toward him, surer this is what she wants than she has ever been of anything. When she reaches Oliver's side, she turns to Holly, and the best friends hold each other's gazes for a long, perfect moment.

Just as the sun begins to set over the Kauai beach and the shadows start to lengthen, the small holiday wedding party witnesses a happy ending to a story about true love—not just between romantic partners but also between true friends forever.

"I do," Ivy whispers.

"I do," Oliver whispers back.

Then she turns and tosses her orchid bouquet in the air, and Holly catches it before tumbling backward into Aiden's arms. He is only too happy to catch her.

Acknowledgments

This book is a holiday romance, but it's also a love letter to friendship—and I would never have been able to write it so authentically without learning about friendship from some of the best.

To my colleagues who feel like friends: editors Tara Singh Carlson at Putnam and Deborah Sun de la Cruz at Penguin Random House Canada, you are the most delightful names in my inbox. This was a true collaboration and I enjoyed every minute I spent with you and this novel. At Putnam, special thanks to Sally Kim, Aranya Jain, Katie McKee, Molly Pieper, cover designer Tal Goretsky, and copy editor extraordinaire Mary Beth Constant. At Penguin Random House Canada, my gratitude goes to Dan French, Beth Cockeram, Sabrina Papas, and Jasmin Shin; and to Nicole Winstanley and Kristin Cochrane for always making me feel so welcome.

My more-than-an-agent, Samantha Haywood, thank you for standing by my side and sharing my biggest dreams.

Somehow it feels like we're just getting started. At Transatlantic Agency, thank you also to Laura Cameron, Megan Phillip, and Barbara Miller.

Sophie Chouinard, Alison Gadsby, Kate Henderson, Sherri Vanderveen—our laughter is my favorite. Asha Frost, Nan Row, Beatrix Nagy—I'm so lucky to have you in my circle.

I'd be lost without my coven of writing world confidantes: Kerry Clare, Chantel Guertin, Kate Hilton, and Liz Renzetti. Also, Lauren Fox, Laurie Petrou, Kelly Thompson, and Uzma Jalaluddin.

Bruce Stapley, dad and friend, greatest hype man alive; Jim Clubine, for such steadfast support; my brothers, Shane, Drew, and Griffin; Joe and Joyce Ponikowski, and the rest of the Ponikowski family.

My mother, Valerie Clubine, who sang me Dionne Warwick songs and taught me exactly what friends, and moms, are for. (In a word, everything.) I miss you every day, dear Mumma, but you're with me and I know it.

My children, Maia and Joseph. I can only paraphrase Dionne here: in good times and bad times, I'll be on your side forevermore—that's what [moms] are for.

Last, but definitely not least, my Joe. You're a good friend to so many but especially to me. Also, you can carry an entire tree on your shoulders, which is quite sexy. Please keep lifting weights so you can do that every Christmas. Love you forever.

About the Author

Julia McKay is the pen name of Marissa Stapley, a former magazine editor and *New York Times* bestselling author of the Reese's Book Club pick *Lucky*, as well as international bestsellers *Mating for Life*, *Things to Do When It's Raining*, and *The Last Resort*. She is also one half of the writing duo behind *The Holiday Swap* and *All I Want for Christmas* by Maggie Knox, and coauthor of *Three Holidays and a Wedding*. Many of her novels have been optioned for television, and her journalism has appeared in *The Globe and Mail*, the *Toronto Star*, *Elle*, *Today's Parent*, and *Reader's Digest*. She lives in Toronto with her family and a precocious black cat named Oscar.

Connect Online

MarissaStapley.com

 MarissaStapleyAuthor

 MarissaStapley